They were going to celebrate the engagement now—they must be!

Oriole took her place at the banquet table beside her brother, Di-di—across from Jun-rui, the man who had earned her love. She imagined an invisible thread running between the two of them, binding them together. She heard the conversation and laughter echoing around her, as though from a long way off.

Then her mother's stiff, rasping voice silenced the pleasant hum of voices.

"As you all know," Lady Cui began austerely, "the Cui family owes an enormous debt of gratitude to my guest of honor, Mr. Zhang." A murmur of appreciation passed around the table. "It is for this reason," she continued, "that I am now honored to welcome Mr. Zhang into my family...as a son."

A look of warm excitement flashed between Oriole and Jun-rui. The suspense was almost too much to bear. Finally, after everything that had happened—after he'd saved them all from Flying Tiger and his rebels—she and Jun-rui were going to be officially engaged!

"Oriole and Di-di," Lady Cui said, glancing sharply at her daughter, "I want you both to lift your wine cups and drink to the good health of Mr. Zhang. From now on you will look on him as a *brother*."

Oriole felt anger rising in her, felt a tightness in her chest. A "brother"? Lady Cui had broken her promise!

About the Author

Rachel May, who currently lives in Hong Kong, was brought up in the south of England. After a college education in London, she embarked on a wide variety of jobs—ranging over the years from teaching, writing and editing, on the one hand, to excavating a Saxon graveyard, picking grapes in the foothills of the Pyrenees and working with mentally handicapped children, on the other. For the past twenty years—her entire married life—she has lived outside England: in Australia, China, Hong Kong, New Zealand and France. A good deal of this time, she has been busy with her family of four children, three of whom are now grown up.

In 1986 Rachel co-translated *A Chinese Winter's Tale*, a pioneering feminist novel by the mainland Chinese writer Yu Luojin and the prizewinning short story, *A Girl Like Me*, by the Hong Kong writer Sai Sai. She is in the midst of working on the translation of a sixteenth-century Chinese novel and has also written book reviews for the *Far Eastern Economic Review*.

Rachel and her husband are looking forward to moving to their rural home in the south of France with their daughter and two dogs. There she plans to lead a quiet life tending a vineyard...and perhaps working on another romance!

LOVE IN A CHINESE GARDEN

Rachel May

Harlequin Books

TORONTO • NEW YORK • LONDON
AMSTERDAM • PARIS • SYDNEY • HAMBURG
STOCKHOLM • ATHENS • TOKYO • MILAN
MADRID • WARSAW • BUDAPEST • AUCKLAND

HARLEQUIN BOOKS
225 Duncan Mill Road, Don Mills,
Ontario, Canada M3B 3K9

ISBN 0-373-83348-2

LOVE IN A CHINESE GARDEN

CAST OF CHARACTERS

Oriole Cui	daughter of a deceased government minister, a cultivated young lady still in mourning
Scarlet	Oriole's maid
Lady Cui	Oriole's mother, recently widowed
Di-di	Oriole's ten-year-old brother
Pug	Oriole's dog, similar to a Pekinese
Zhang Jun-rui	an orphaned young scholar studying for the civil service examinations
Lucky	Zhang Jun-rui's manservant
General Du	Zhang Jun-rui's close friend
Abbot	connected with the Cui family, abbot of the Buddhist Monastery of Universal Salvation
Heng	Oriole's cousin and fiancé
Flying Tiger	an Imperial soldier, turned rebel leader
Constance	one of Lady Cui's maids
Lily	Heng's maternal cousin and sweetheart

PLACE NAMES

Chang-an	the western capital in the Tang dynasty; present-day Xi'an, in Shaanxi Province (famous to tourists for the Buried Army)
Boling	500 miles northeast of Chang-an; close to present-day Baoding, a city in Hebei Province
Puzhou	a town between Chang-an and Boling, about 150 miles from Chang-an
Luoyang	the eastern capital in the Tang dynasty; about 200 miles from Chang-an; Zhang Jun-rui's birthplace

A NOTE ON NAMES

Chinese names often seem difficult to Westerners.
To Chinese speakers, Chinese names are easily memorable: this is because they are not so much sounds as written characters. Furthermore, the written characters have meanings, and the characters chosen for names often have a special resonance. Both meaning and resonance get lost in any other language.

I have basically followed the system of spelling known as *Hanyu pinyin,* not the older Wade-Giles system which is now becoming obsolete. *Hanyu pinyin* is used today in the People's Republic of China.

Some of the names have been translated—Ying-ying is Oriole, Hong-niang is Scarlet. Some of the names have been given in romanized form—Jun-rui and Di-di.

Note that in Chinese names, the surname precedes the personal name.

PRONUNCIATION GUIDE
—in alphabetical order

Boling	pronounced *Baw-ling*
Chang-an	pronounced *Chung un*
Cui	pronounced *Tsway*
Di-di	pronounced *Dee-dee*
Du	pronounced *Doo*
Heng	pronounced *Hung*
Jun-rui	pronounced *June-ray*
Luoyang	pronounced *Lore-young*
Puzhou	pronounced *Pooh-joe*
Zhang	pronounced *Jung*

FOREWORD

Once upon a time in China, during the early years of the ninth century—in the golden age of the Tang dynasty—a famous poet by the name of Yuan Zhen wrote a tale called *The Story of Oriole*. It was written in the most elegant classical prose. It told the touching story of his own passionate encounter as a young man with a beautiful maiden in the grounds of a Buddhist monastery, some hundred and fifty miles east of the fabled capital of Chang-an. His autobiographical tale ended unhappily, with the young scholar choosing to renounce his love to pursue a conventional career as a mandarin. The beautiful Oriole was left abandoned and heartbroken.

Ever since that time, this has been the most famous of all Chinese love stories. It is the *Romeo and Juliet* of Chinese literature. And it has been retold countless times, as story, ballad and drama. But where the original story ended in separation, the retellings— from the twelfth century till the present day—have almost without exception brought the lovers together to live happily ever after.

The most famous retelling of Yuan's story was the play known as *The Western Chamber*, written some four hundred years later during the Mongol dynasty. The power of this long play lies almost entirely in its magical poetry, and its highly sensual and evocative atmosphere.

Generation after generation of young lovers has since found inspiration in the story's depiction of true love. Oriole and the scholar Jun-rui have become role models for young people through the ages wishing to throw off the shackles of convention. The strict and oppressive prohibitions of the Confucian family code, or the tolling of the bell of renunciation ringing out across the other-wordly setting of the Buddhist monastery—neither were able to deter the young couple. Oriole and Jun-rui are driven by the sheer force of their mutual attraction to defy convention and to recognize their own sensuality. Together, in the magical moonlit environment of the monastery garden and the west wing where the scholar is lodging, they explore the forbidden world of erotic love, known to the Chinese through the centuries as "The Clouds and the Rain." Aided by Oriole's resourceful maid—the talkative and irrepressible Scarlet—the two lovers find a way of coming together, and once together, they persist down the irrevocable road of love.

Love in a Chinese Garden is a contemporary retelling (or adaptation) of this ancient tale of love. It invites the English-speaking reader of today to enter the heady world of Chinese romance. It takes the reader into the very heart of the Chinese traditional world. And it brings a faraway time and place a little nearer for the reader of today. These, at least, are its aims.

Time and again, Chinese storytellers and opera performers have moved audiences to tears with their reenactments of this universal theme. Readers of this new English version—the first of its kind in the form of a novel—are not intended to cry! Instead, they are invited to share in the celebration of the power of love, and to enjoy the timeless poetry, humor and drama of this classic Chinese romance.

Rachel May
Hong Kong, 1997

CHAPTER ONE

IT WAS MIDAFTERNOON, a glorious early-spring day—a day for contentment, whether indoors in the monastery's west wing or outside in one of its many gardens. Nevertheless, Oriole found herself in a strangely restless mood. With a long sigh, she sank down at her dressing table and reached languidly for her silver mirror. She held it up to her face, looking closely at her reflection, then gave a little nod. Her makeup was still intact; she'd obviously done a competent job that morning.

Every day her makeup routine was the same. First she would check her eyebrows for any little hairs that had dared to grow; these must be plucked out at once. Then she would apply powder liberally to her face, neck and shoulders, and brush rouge onto her cheeks, from just below the eyes. Next she would paint artificial eyebrows, in a deep blue cobalt, which slanted upward from where her natural eyebrows had been. It was the fashion among women of her status and background in ninth-century China. Between her eyebrows she would paint a beauty spot in red or black, sometimes two or three if she felt like it. Finally she would apply a dark red lip salve. This ritual, together with styling her hair into an elaborate coiffure—which her maid, Scarlet, always did for her—usually took at least an hour.

Although she was pleased that her makeup was still in good shape, Oriole continued to feel troubled. Studying her reflection in the mirror more closely, she could detect a definite flush beneath the rouge on her cheeks. Her dark eyes had a shine, almost a glitter, she'd never noticed before. She touched one hand to her forehead, but her skin didn't feel warm or feverish. If anything, it was rather cool. She sighed again and put the mirror down more noisily than her mother would have considered ladylike. Fortunately the clatter didn't wake her tiny dog, Pug, who lay curled up on a silk cushion on her bed, snoring wetly through his squashed-looking little nose.

She'd started a painting of Pug after lunch, but had been forced to stop because of this odd restless feeling inside her. What was it? Where did it come from? Surely today was no different from any other day, so why did she *feel* different? Such an unfamiliar sensation, too. A kind of…excitement. Now that she thought about it, she'd been feeling like this ever since yesterday. Ever since…

Yes! The man. The one she'd seen yesterday afternoon when she and Scarlet were on their way to the temple. It had been another glorious sunny day, and they'd wandered into the Flower Garden. She'd picked a small sprig of plum blossom, she remembered, and was twirling it between her fingers as they walked to the temple. They were laughing at something Scarlet had said. The next thing she knew, they'd rounded the corner and just about collided with the abbot and that young man, the two of them deep in conversation.

She'd caught a glimpse of the stranger's face. It was no more than a fleeting glance, but their eyes had met, and her heart had jumped a little. Just thinking about it now made her heart jump again. She'd seen at once that he was handsome, and his eyes had a kindness and warmth that had drawn her in. A sadness, too. It was an interesting face; she wanted to know more about him. He was obviously a gentleman-student type—she could tell that much from his black hat and the clothes he wore—but there was a strength in his physique that suggested he must be athletic as well as intellectual. Perhaps he practiced one of the manly sports or skills, like archery or boxing or swordplay. Or riding? She'd certainly noticed his riding boots.

Oriole smiled at her presumption. Was it really possible to know all this from one glance? No, two glances, if she was honest. After her initial embarrassment, when Scarlet had hurried her on, she'd impulsively turned around—and she'd found him standing there, watching her with an intense gaze.

Scarlet had given her quite a scolding when they got back to their quarters in the west wing. "You ought to be ashamed of yourself!" she'd said.

"And why's that?" Oriole had replied archly.

"Don't you use that high-and-mighty tone with me, young lady," Scarlet had snapped. "You know perfectly well why. That scruffy student we bumped into just now—you were positively ogling him!"

"No, I wasn't," Oriole protested.

"Of course you were! And right under the abbot's nose, too. What if—"

"Well, suppose I *was* looking at him." Oriole blushed, turning her back and moving to the tea table so Scarlet couldn't see the guilt and confusion on her face. "It's hardly surprising, is it! I mean, I don't see a member of the opposite sex from one week to the next, unless of course you count that sniveling little brother of mine or that bald-headed ape of an abbot! Not to mention the dirty old monks' brigade!"

"Now, now," Scarlet cautioned. "You watch your tongue!"

"Well, what do you expect?" Oriole continued, pulling a tortoiseshell comb from her hair and fidgeting with it. "I'm cooped up in this room day after day with nothing to do, nowhere to go and nobody to talk to. I feel like Di-di's stupid canary locked up in its stupid cage!''

''Don't exaggerate,'' Scarlet said, a little more kindly. ''You're free to go anywhere you like in the women's quarters. Plus, there's the temple and the Flower Garden. And you've got me to talk to and the other maids. And your mother.''

''Don't even *mention* my mother,'' Oriole answered with a touch of bitterness. ''It's because of her that you always trail around after me! It's like having a…a watchdog!''

''You know it's not up to me. Watching over you as if you're a naughty child isn't *my* idea of fun! I just have to do what I'm told, that's all.'' Scarlet shrugged. She moved over to the tea table, took the comb from Oriole's hand and put it back in her hair. ''Let's be friends now,'' she cajoled, giving Oriole's fingers a squeeze. ''I'm just asking you to be careful. You're a very attractive young lady—a real beauty, in fact—and you know what they say about those student-types.…''

''No.'' Oriole looked at her innocently. ''What do they say?''

''Oh, you know.'' The maid's face reddened.

''Scarlet, I *don't* know. Tell me. Come on!''

This time it was Scarlet's turn to fidget. ''Well…young men like him, from all over the country, they go flocking to the capital to take the civil-service examinations. You know that, right?''

"Right," Oriole agreed.

"Before that, they've been locked away with their noses buried in their books for goodness knows how long...." Scarlet hesitated.

"And?" Oriole prompted.

"And to them the city's like one big playground," Scarlet said mysteriously.

Oriole frowned. "What do you mean?"

The maid took a deep breath. "Well, it's crawling with painted singsong girls, that's what I mean. And it's where these students go to learn the, uh, facts of life."

Oriole lowered her eyes, feeling distinctly uncomfortable.

"You can just imagine," Scarlet went on. "A man like him, traveling alone, his mind full of the pleasures ahead. He meets an attractive girl along the way. She's interested, he's raring to go. What's to stop him having a little fling? A quick roll in the hay and then off he goes!"

"Scarlet, that's vulgar!" Oriole was genuinely shocked. "Anyway, he didn't seem that type to me at all. I thought he seemed nice. A little down-at-the-heels perhaps, but quite refined."

"I shouldn't think he thought *you* were refined!" Scarlet laughed crudely. "You had your robe hanging halfway down your arms—not to mention all that cleavage on public display!"

"That's absolute nonsense," Oriole said primly, glancing away.

"All right, then. Let's be serious for a moment. What I'm saying is—refined or not—they're all the same. They're all after a quick—"

"Don't you dare say that word again!" Oriole exclaimed, jumping up to chase Scarlet, who was rushing toward the door.

"Roll, roll, roll. Roll in the hay!" Scarlet teased mercilessly, her plump little figure bobbing out the doorway and into the courtyard.

AH, WELL. Oriole sighed now as she looked in her mirror. It was foolish to dwell on the handsome student a moment longer. She'd certainly never see him again, so what had been the point of those sharp words between her and Scarlet yesterday? Scarlet was probably right, anyway; he'd turn out to be one of those countless young men traveling up to Chang-an, the western capital, to take the civil-service examinations, hoping to make a career for himself as a government official. She'd read plenty of stories about people like him.

Oriole could imagine it all quite clearly. He was passing through the region and had a bit of time on his hands, so he thought he'd visit the Monastery of Universal Salvation—everyone said it was a fine example of early Buddhist architecture—and the abbot had been showing him around when he'd chanced to bump into an unattached young woman, evidently of good family. He'd probably been staying at the inn in Puzhou and would have left early this morning. By now, traveling on horseback, he would have covered a good five miles. Oriole pictured his horse—a fine white stallion, she decided, with an embroidered saddle. She was sure the young man had a servant, who'd be riding behind. The horses were no doubt laden with bags of books, clothing, perhaps one of those seven-stringed musical instruments students were supposed to have. Zithers, like the one she played herself. And all the while, Oriole imagined, he was thinking about that beautiful young woman he'd seen at the monastery....

Stop it! Oriole told herself firmly. She couldn't allow her imagination to run away with her like this; she had to stop herself from indulging in these absurd fantasies about a man she'd only seen once. She realized that her hands were moist and her breathing was much too fast. She had to calm herself, put this chance encounter out of her mind.

Oriole opened her makeup box and took out her powder, dabbing it slowly on her neck, then working downward to her chest, making a conscious effort to breathe slowly and clear her mind. When she was confident that she'd regained her normal composure, she put the powder away and swiveled around on the wooden stool to survey the room she'd so crossly described as her "cage" the day before.

It was sparsely furnished and plain compared to the luxury and elegance she was accustomed to in her quarters at home in Chang-an, but it was the best the monastery could offer in the way of guest accommodation.

Next to the ornate rosewood dressing table and stool was an attractive round tea table and four stools in carved sandalwood; beside them stood a bronze brazier, which could be used to boil water for tea or medicine, or to heat the room in cold weather. The room was dominated, however, by a large antique ebony bedstead with a carved canopy, from which hung thick red brocade curtains. These were now open, so that she could keep an eye on Pug. He was still snoring quietly on his cushion.

To the left of the bed was a doorway leading to a small dressing room in which Oriole's silk robes, jackets, trousers and scarves were folded away in lacquer trunks or hanging on the wooden clothes rack. To the right of the bed was a low ebony side table, and opposite the bed, the high wooden double doors that led outside to the courtyard. A screen, made up of four painted panels, stood in one corner of the room; it concealed a large round porcelain bowl and a low table bearing a brass water basin and jug.

A scroll painting of lotus blossoms hung above

the dressing table. The wooden floor was covered with reed matting, and a thick blue woven rug lay in front of the bed. The walls were lined with carved and latticed wood paneling. A heavy rose-colored curtain, embroidered with two dragons chasing a pearl, hung over the dressing-room doorway. On the tea table Scarlet had arranged a vase of white plum blossoms and a little tea set on a tray.

Scattered around the room were a few of Oriole's personal effects. Her makeup and jewelry boxes lay on the dressing table, together with an assortment of hair ornaments and fans, as well as her mirror. A tall varnished bamboo basket with a lid and handle stood next to the dressing table; this contained her embroidery materials—and something else besides. Wrapped inside an unfinished embroidery at the bottom of the basket, Oriole had hidden a few slim volumes of poetry and stories. She wouldn't have bothered concealing them in this way, except that she knew how strongly her mother disapproved of girls being "bookish."

Her red-lacquered leather writing chest, which held scented notepaper, brushes, ink and inkstone, had been placed underneath the side table, next to her medicine box. On top of the table were two brass candlesticks and, in the center, her brass lion-shaped incense burner and a small tray of aromatic oils and pastes.

But of all her personal possessions, the one Oriole valued most was the miniature portrait of her father. It stood in a small silver frame directly in front of the incense burner. As soon as it caught her eye, she got up from the stool and went to squat down on the brocade cushion beside the table. She picked up the portrait and gazed mournfully at it. Tears soon welled up in her eyes and rolled down her cheeks, leaving little trails in her face powder.

"If you only knew how much I miss you," she whispered. "Oh, Father, why did you have to go and die? We're all on our own now, all alone...."

It had been more than a year since his death, shortly after Oriole's nineteenth birthday, but she felt his loss keenly. She and her mother and younger brother, Di-di, were still officially in mourning. Oriole was therefore expected to dress in white—most of the time, anyway. Fortunately her mother wasn't too strict about this and only insisted on white robes when Oriole left her quarters. In her room or in the enclosed courtyard, she could wear some of her favorite embroidered gowns and jackets.

"You don't mind, do you, Father?" she said fondly, putting the picture back on the table and dabbing her wet cheeks with a silk handkerchief. "White is such a cold color, and you know how much I love my clothes."

Strange, she thought; she could talk far more intimately to her father's picture now than to his face when he was alive. He'd been a busy man, an important minister who was often away on government business. Even when he was home, tradition demanded that she treat him with respect, speaking only when she was spoken to; as she'd learned from early childhood, filial piety was one of the most important Confucian virtues. So communication between father and daughter had been limited. But there was one thing that had drawn them together. No one else had known about it, except Scarlet— and she could be trusted. The secret was...books.

If Di-di had been the older of the two children, her father would have shared his passion for reading with his son. But as it was, Oriole was the one who'd benefited. She was the one who'd been— discreetly—invited into her father's study to explore his library, with its large collection of poetry, detective stories and supernatural tales. She was the one who'd learned the skills of writing verse and doing calligraphy with ink and brush. Her mother would not have been pleased, since she held the traditional view that girls didn't need to be educated; their duty was to learn the necessary wifely skills, like embroidery.

Oriole had managed to bring some of her father's favorite books of poetry and stories on their journey. These, and the portrait, were her precious mementos of him.

Their long journey had begun a few months ago. They were taking her father's coffin from Chang- an back to his hometown in Boling, five hundred miles to the northeast, for a proper burial at the ancestral grave.

Oriole, her mother and younger brother, together with a small group of maids and grooms, had been traveling by carriage and cart for more than a month when they reached the town of Puzhou. They'd ar- rived at the local inn, only to be warned by the innkeeper that it would be dangerous to continue.

There was a mutiny among the imperial soldiers stationed in the province, he'd explained. A small army, under the leadership of a hotheaded young rebel called Flying Tiger, had broken away and was now on the rampage, robbing villagers of food and possessions and generally taking the law into their own hands. A group of women traveling by them- selves would be particularly vulnerable—"asking for trouble," the innkeeper had said. He'd advised Oriole's mother, Lady Cui, to go and seek shelter in the nearby monastery. The guest quarters there were more fitting for a lady of her station than his own modest rooms, he admitted.

It hadn't taken Lady Cui long to realize that this was the same monastery to which her husband had donated a large sum of money, contributing toward its restoration; he'd also helped the present abbot obtain his ordination. Considering those facts, she was more than happy to follow the innkeeper's advice. She was certainly not as devout a Buddhist as her husband had been, but she was bound to be warmly welcomed at the Monastery of Universal Salvation because of Lord Cui's good deeds. The abbot would be well-disposed toward her.

Given the predicament they now found themselves in, they couldn't hope for a better solution. Lady Cui's mind was made up. The monastery it would be....

And that was what had brought them here, more than two months ago. All that time, her father's sealed coffin had been lying in a side room of the temple. The family couldn't go on, and they couldn't turn back; they were stranded. But at least they were safe, Oriole reminded herself. She had to try to accept the situation and not waste what was left of the afternoon moping around. Above all, she had to put yesterday's handsome student out of her mind. Maybe a bit of fresh air...

As if he'd read her thoughts, Pug yawned sleepily and began scratching his chin with a back foot, head cocked awkwardly to one side. He stood up from his cushion and stretched, looking expectantly at Oriole.

"No," she said firmly. "I'm not going to lift you down. You're not a baby! Do it yourself!"

His little legs were less than three inches long, but Pug had obviously decided to attempt the distance from bed to floor. He gave an energetic leap, turned in a half somersault and landed on the soft blue rug in a most undignified fashion.

"Oh, you poor darling!" Oriole giggled, but she checked herself when she noticed his decidedly ruffled expression. "Come here," she said, gathering him up in her arms and planting a kiss on his shaggy little head. "It's about time I took you out, isn't it? Come on, then."

They were out in the courtyard for quite a while, long enough for Pug to relieve himself and for the two of them to play a game of fetching the woolen ball. When Oriole finally returned to her room, she was surprised that Scarlet still wasn't back from her errand at the abbot's residence.

Lady Cui had been occupied lately with arrangements for a memorial service in honor of her dead husband. This would be performed by the abbot and monks. Though not a particularly keen adherent of Buddhism herself, Lady Cui, like many Chinese, was perfectly content to embrace its ceremonies and make use of its priests. Why not? She was a practical woman, and here she was—in a Buddhist monastery. More to the point, it was what her husband would have wanted.

She had sent Scarlet off after the midday meal to talk to the abbot about certain details—the date still hadn't been fixed, and neither had the fee. Lady Cui fully intended to pay the abbot however many

ounces of silver he requested. There was also the
question of the banquet, which she'd offered to provide the evening after the service. It would have to
be vegetarian, naturally—these Buddhists could be
so inconvenient!—but what dishes would be most
appropriate?

It was Scarlet's job to get definite answers to
these questions and then report back to Lady Cui.

But she'd been gone nearly two hours already,
Oriole thought irritably. What could be keeping her
so long? Having already resolved not to waste any
more time, she thought she'd try to complete her
painting of Pug. She didn't like leaving things unfinished; in fact, she would never have abandoned
the painting in the first place if it hadn't been for
her agitated state of mind. And all because of that—

"That man!" Scarlet exploded, bursting angrily
into the room. "Who does he think he is? What a
nerve!" She moved crossly about, picking things
up and setting them down again. "I'd like to teach
him a thing or two!"

"You're not making much sense," Oriole said
in a puzzled voice. "You're not talking about the
abbot, are you?"

"Of course not! I'm talking about that student of
yours!" Scarlet replied curtly.

Oriole was taken aback. She'd tried so hard to
forget all about him—but circumstances were con-

spiring to keep him constantly in her thoughts. Who was he? And what was he doing back at the monastery?

"Where did you see him?" she asked lamely, not wanting Scarlet to see her interest.

"At the abbot's. He was asking about a room."

"Why?"

The maid shrugged impatiently. "How should I know? Anyway, what's it to you?"

"Nothing," Oriole lied. "But at least you could tell me what upset you so much."

"Like I said, he's got a real nerve," she answered unhelpfully.

"Why? What did he say?"

"Well, first he followed me after I left the abbot's," Scarlet began in a rush, "and then he came up to me and said, 'Didn't I see you yesterday? With that young lady?' He didn't even wait for me to answer! He starts right in with all his personal particulars—his name, age, date of birth, family background. He even tells me his marital status!" Scarlet said scornfully. "Anyone would think I was a professional matchmaker!"

Oriole was silent. So it wasn't just her wild imaginings—something *had* passed between them. He'd noticed her, was asking about her. She felt dizzy with excitement. She might see him again, after all!

"So what's his name?" she asked.

"His name's Zhang Gong. His friends apparently call him Jun-rui, so he says," Scarlet answered stiffly.

"Jun-rui." Oriole sighed. "What a nice name."

"Well, I wouldn't go getting any ideas about this Mr. Zhang, if I were you," Scarlet warned. "It doesn't take much breeding to know that you don't go around giving your particulars to any old servant-girl! So he can't be much of a gentleman, can he?"

Oriole was forced to admit to herself that Scarlet was right. But she still felt torn between excitement and common sense. She didn't reply.

"What's more," Scarlet added, "your mother's just written to Heng asking him to come here as soon as he can. So it won't be long before your fiancé appears on the scene. Think about *that* for a moment!"

CHAPTER TWO

"THINGS ARE FALLING into place very nicely," Lady Cui said with satisfaction as she set her chopsticks and empty rice bowl down on the dinner table. She leaned comfortably back in her chair, motioning to Constance, one of her maids, to clear away the dirty dishes. "The service for your father will be a week from today," she told Oriole and Di-di. "On the fifteenth of the second month. The abbot says it's an auspicious date in the Buddhist calendar, and of course it's a full moon, too."

Since neither of her children made any comment, Lady Cui pressed on regardless, as was her way. "And thanks to Scarlet, I've now got several ideas for some rather unusual vegetarian dishes for the banquet. I thought I might get our kitchen girls to try them out on us beforehand."

Di-di, fearing, perhaps, that his mother was about to embark on a long description of culinary delights—inevitably boring to a ten-year-old—excused himself from her quarters to go and play a game of dominoes. Oriole used the brief interruption to turn her mother's attention to a subject of more immediate concern.

"Scarlet told me you'd written a letter today, Mother."

"Oh, yes, the letter," Lady Cui answered briskly. "I knew there was something else I wanted to talk to you about." She called out to Scarlet to bring them a pot of jasmine tea. "It's high time we started making definite plans for your marriage. We can't possibly leave the monastery, not until conditions improve. But there's nothing to stop your cousin Heng from joining us here. I'm sure the abbot could help us prepare a good wedding ceremony."

"Have you already sent the letter?" Oriole asked despondently.

"Scarlet took it over to the gatehouse this afternoon," her mother replied. "It'll be on its way as soon as there's a rider available. Even then, it will take three or four weeks to reach the capital. And no doubt Heng will have plenty of things to sort out before he can leave. So we shouldn't count on him arriving much before autumn."

The longer the better, Oriole thought grimly. It wasn't that she particulary disliked Heng, but it seemed so...so unjust that she should have no choice about who she was going to marry. She'd simply been *told* that Heng was the man—and of course no one had bothered to consult her about what *she* wanted. In fact, she'd never been given the *chance* to find out what she wanted. She was already twenty years old, but she'd had no experience of love or romantic attachment of any kind. The only young man she'd ever spent time with was Heng, and he was her maternal cousin. They'd played together as children, and they'd seen each other fairly often as they were growing up. But did that make him the right husband? True, he was ambitious and he had a good job in the city; he would certainly be able to provide for her. But was that enough? Was that all there was to marriage? It seemed to her that she and Heng had little in common and that he'd become rather coarse as he got older. Furthermore, he'd put on a *lot* more weight than she thought becoming. She'd read about love in poems, and though she didn't know what it was really like, she was sure she'd never find out with him.

Oriole was aware that she shouldn't be arguing with her mother, but she nonetheless plucked up the courage to speak her mind.

"Mother, I really wish you'd reconsider," she began. "You know I don't want to marry him and that I'd never be happy..."

At that moment Scarlet came in with the tea tray and poured them both a cup; sensing the tension in the air, she quickly retreated back to the kitchen.

"Oriole," Lady Cui said sternly once the maid

had left the room, "we've been over this a hundred times. It's not a question of what you want. Heng is your fiancé, and this is something that was arranged years ago, between your father and his. It's the way things are done. You don't imagine your father and I chose to marry each other, do you? Of course not! Our marriage was arranged for us, and we got on with it, that's all. Why should things be any different for you?"

"But I don't *love* him!" Oriole said vehemently.

"Love? What does love have to do with it?" Lady Cui spoke with obvious scorn. "Heng is a good match. He's from a good family and he's got a promising career. What more do you need?"

It was useless, Oriole reflected unhappily. Her mother refused to listen to her, refused to understand.

"You know the expression 'Marry a daughter, out with the water'?" Lady Cui continued. "Well, it's as simple as that. You'll marry the man and make the best of it. And I don't want to hear any more of your nonsense. I've got no intention of having an unmarried daughter on my hands for the rest of my days!"

She took a sip of tea and gave Oriole a penetrating look. "You're not yourself," she remarked. "You're a little flushed. What have you been doing all day?"

"Oh, not much," Oriole replied wearily. She was

hardly in the mood for conversation after her mother's uncompromising words. "I started a painting...."

"Painting won't get you very far in life!" Lady Cui asserted. "If I were you, I'd devote a little more time to your embroidery—and to thinking about the wifely virtues. A good wife must have a—"

"Yes, yes, I know, Mother," Oriole said impatiently. "You've told me many times. Do we have to go over it again?"

"I think we do." Lady Cui was adamant. "We'll go over it until if finally sinks in. Now, what are they, the four wifely virtues?"

With a sigh Oriole began her catechism. "A good wife must have a good character. She must have good looks. She must be pleasing in her speech. And she must be able to do fine handiwork."

"Excellent," Lady Cui said with approval. "Now remember, it will be your duty to please your husband and to obey him, just as you obeyed your father. The sooner you accept this, the better it will be for you and everyone else. Do you understand?"

Oriole nodded halfheartedly.

"Embroidery is a good discipline," her mother added. "You need to do something useful with yourself. You might as well start your wedding quilt. I'll see about getting some red silk for you tomorrow."

Lady Cui then sent Oriole off to her room to sketch out a design for the quilt so she could begin work on it as soon as the silk was purchased. A wedding quilt was the most important piece of embroidery a girl would ever do, and it involved many months of intricate work.

Lady Cui sat there in solitude for a while, thinking—and remembering. She herself had embroidered a very fine quilt; she'd slept under it on her wedding night all those years ago. And now here she was making plans for her own daughter's wedding. She frowned; she simply couldn't understand Oriole's attitude. Why was the girl so troublesome? Why did she ask so many questions? All this talk about love and happiness! It was high time Oriole faced reality and accepted her obligations.

Lady Cui had been a widow for little more than a year, but now she looked back on her marriage as if it had been decades ago. Although she'd been the First Wife, she'd had to make room for three others. They were all still in Chang-an, at the Cui household; to Lady Cui in the monastery near Puzhou, they seemed so far away. It had been up to her husband to decide which of his wives would share his bed each night, and of course there had been jealousies and squabbles among the women. But somehow they'd managed to live under the same roof without too much conflict. The worst had come later, as her husband got older. Like other men of his time, he'd believed that "younger blood" would help restore his own youthfulness, and he had therefore started summoning various of the maids to his room at night. Some of them were only junior maids, she remembered bitterly, hardly more than children. And Scarlet was among them. She shuddered. The humiliation had been almost unbearable.

She was fairly sure Oriole hadn't known about the maids. And certainly not about Scarlet. But if she spoke harshly to her daughter about marriage and wifely duties, it was only for the girl's own good. One day she, too, would have to put up with circumstances such as these—every wife did—and the sooner she learned her place in life, the easier it would be for her to cope.

Being a widow was not such a hardship compared to the trials of married life, Lady Cui reflected.

WHILE SHE WAS GRINDING the stick of ink on her inkstone, Oriole considered the motifs she might use for the wedding quilt. Apart from the character for "double happiness," which was a must as a symbol of wedded bliss and which probably ought to go in the center, there were numerous other symbols to choose from. Mandarin ducks, for example, since they represented faithfulness in marriage. Or butterflies, another symbol of joyful married life. Or two fish, signifying a contented partnership. She could use morning glory, too, which represented marital felicity, and have it twisting around the other motifs; it could look quite attractive, she thought, but would entail a lot of stitching.

On second thought, maybe the duck-and-lotus design would be more appropriate. Together they were supposed to represent happiness in marriage, but Oriole preferred to see the duck and lotus as two quite separate entities. Heng was a bit like the duck, she decided—a little on the plump side with a tendency to waddle and always nattering about something or other, like a duck quacking. She, on the other hand, was the lotus—slender, delicate, her perfumed petals unfurling and reaching out...

She dabbed her brush in the ink crossly. This was ridiculous! How could she be expected to feel any enthusiasm for Heng as a fiancé? For marriage? Even for this quilt? She knew her mother was disappointed in her, but there was nothing she could do about it.

Something had happened to her recently, something that made her feel like a different person. She remembered the sensation she'd felt yesterday—the way her heart had jumped with the look that passed between her and this man called Jun-rui. Then there was her excitement when Scarlet had told her that Jun-rui was back at the monastery, not to mention her profound gloom over the letter to Heng. Unfamiliar though these feelings were, they had an urgency about them. They would not be silenced.

Oriole glanced down and found that she'd painted, in deft brush strokes, a plump duck, its tail feathers splayed awkwardly up in the air and its head beneath the water, the ripples radiating outward to the edge of the paper. Quite a humorous little sketch. But sobering, too. She could dream, she could examine her feelings as much as she liked, but it wouldn't change the future that had been determined for her. There was no question of turning these arrangements and expectations upside down; merely *attempting* to do so would create a series of ripples—like the ones she'd painted.

Duty, obedience, respect, the wifely virtues—these were the things her mother had drummed into her for as long as she could remember. They were an integral part of the traditional Chinese way of life. She had a duty to her parents, which came before everything else. She must respect their wishes. She must think of her family reputation. She must do nothing to blacken their name. Her father had engaged her to Heng more than seven years ago; she must marry him whether she liked it or not.

And it could be worse, Oriole conceded. Some poor girls were married off to wrinkled old men they'd never even seen before, men old enough to be grandfathers, men who already had several wives. At least *her* fiancé was young and unmarried. Yes, it could be worse…couldn't it?

SCARLET CAME into Oriole's room to find her sitting at the tea table, brush in hand, surrounded by numerous crumpled sheets of paper.

"What on earth are you doing?" she asked in surprise. "I thought you'd be in bed by now."

In some ways Scarlet was really more like a big sister to Oriole than a servant. She had first come to the family as a junior maid more than ten years ago, and she knew almost everything there was to know about Oriole—her moods and frustrations, her strengths and her shortcomings. She was the one person Oriole confided in. There were times, though—like now—when Oriole chose to keep certain things to herself. She told Scarlet about the quilt, but said nothing about the inner turmoil she'd just been experiencing.

"So what happened after dinner?" Scarlet asked, sounding concerned. "There sure seemed to be a storm brewing. That's why I thought I'd better keep out of the way."

"Oh, I was asking my mother about her letter to Heng," Oriole replied in a deceptively calm manner. She put down her brush and looked Scarlet in the eye. "Nothing was said that hasn't been said before. I told her I didn't want to marry him, and

she told me I had no choice. And that's about it.''
She let out a sigh.

"Your mother is a hard woman at times," Scarlet observed. She sat down beside Oriole at the table. "But she only wants the best for you. Anyway," she continued, "she hasn't got much choice, either. She's duty bound to carry out your father's wishes. And you know what she's like." Scarlet mimicked Lady Cui's voice. "'Everything's got to be done *properly*. Everything must be done by the rules.'" She grimaced. She'd spoken in a joking tone, but they both knew the seriousness of what she was saying. "You're up against tradition here— that's the problem. It goes back thousands of years. And it's not going to change, so why fight it? Mind you—" she gave Oriole a sympathetic glance "—I admire you for trying!"

Scarlet was such a comfort, Oriole reflected. So practical and matter-of-fact. She always managed to make things seem less difficult somehow. And she knew so much more about life in the outside world; on several occasions she'd been able to offer invaluable advice. Oriole found it a great consolation to know that, even when she was married, Scarlet would still be there. She would *always* be there; the fact of the matter was that Lady Cui had paid good money for her and had no intention of ever giving her up. Scarlet was no better off than a slave. It was her destiny to be a maid of the Cui family for life.

"What would I do without you?" Oriole said fondly, not expecting an answer. She straightened and stretched up her arms, her long silk sleeves slipping down to reveal the soft creamy skin of her forearms. Her two white-jade bracelets, carved into plum-blossom sprigs, slid from her wrist toward her elbow, clinking together musically as they went.

"I feel like getting a little fresh air," she said on impulse. "I'm sure it would help me sleep. I need to do *something* to take my mind off those ducks and lotuses, or I'll spend all night having bad dreams about them!"

"Good idea," Scarlet agreed. She stood and smoothed down her red silk jacket and trousers. "Why don't we go to the Flower Garden? We haven't burned any incense today, and we really ought to. I'll clean up the mess you've made in here while you go and get your padded robe. You'll need it—there's a real chill in the air tonight." She started picking up the balls of crumpled paper and feeding them into the brazier one at a time, watching them burn. "I was quite cold earlier when I was coming back from the monks' refectory."

"What were you doing there?" Oriole called out from the dressing room. "I thought you'd been in the kitchen."

Scarlet wiped the inkstone, using a piece of soft rice paper, then put it away in Oriole's writing chest, together with the brush and ink stick.

"No, I had to go out to get a recipe for your mother. I bumped into Lucky just outside the dormitory and we got talking."

"Lucky?" Oriole asked curiously, lifting the brocade curtain and peering around the dressing-room doorway. "Who's she?"

"He, actually." Scarlet smiled. "He's a servant—that student's servant! I'll tell you all about it on the way to the Flower Garden. Come on, let's go. I'll get a lamp. You bring the incense."

Scarlet fetched an extra jacket for herself from her room in the maids' quarters at the far end of the courtyard. Soon they'd left the west wing altogether and were walking along the stone path that led to the temple. Scarlet told Oriole in hushed tones that the student and his young servant had been given small rooms next to the monks' dormitory, to the northeast of the temple. She'd evidently gleaned a lot of information during her conversation with Lucky, and she answered all of Oriole's questions to the best of her ability. Still, she couldn't help wondering whether it was wise to encourage her mistress's interest; after all, nothing could come of it.

No, she told Oriole, Lucky didn't know how long they were staying at the monastery.

Yes, Mr. Zhang—all right, Jun-rui—was from a good family. "Good" as in highly thought of. His father was a government minister who'd died of an illness at the age of fifty. His mother had died a year later. Of grief, Lucky said.

No, Jun-rui wasn't particularly well-off.

Yes, he spent a lot of time studying. Very fond of poetry, according to Lucky. And good at painting and calligraphy.

Music? Yes, he played the zither.

Physical exercise? Yes, he liked riding.

What color was his horse?

Scarlet gave her an incredulous look. "For goodness' sake, Oriole! Don't you think you've asked more than enough questions about a complete stranger?" She laughed. "You can't expect me to know *everything* about the man! Next you'll be asking me what color silk trousers he wears under his robe! Or how many girls he's—"

"Don't!" Oriole warned her with surprising fierceness. Seeing that Oriole was far from amused, Scarlet quickly wiped the grin off her own face.

"Look, we're here now," she said, diplomatically changing the subject. "We might as well go in and do what we came for."

Oriole held the oil lamp while Scarlet lifted the stiff latch of the heavy wooden gate that led into the garden. The gate creaked and groaned unnervingly as they pushed it open, and the two women stopped and looked at each other for a moment, as if wondering whether they should feel afraid. The tension was broken by Scarlet's sudden giggle.

"Don't you just love the ghostly sound effects!" she joked. "Maybe the garden's haunted!"

"I'm sure the whole monastery's crawling with ghosts," Oriole agreed, smiling. "But at least we don't have to worry about human intruders. That noise is enough to drive anyone away!"

The Flower Garden certainly looked eerie in the bright moonlight. The trees and ornamental rocks stood out darkly against the luminous blue-black sky. In the far corner of the garden, Oriole could just make out the pavilion, dwarfed by the towering bamboo, and nearer, the dark water of the little lake, now splashed with silver. Several stone paths twisted their way around the garden, like silvery-gray snakes gliding through black undergrowth. Everything was bathed in moonlight; Oriole imagined that a skillful artist had highlighted, in delicate brush strokes of silver-white and gray, the bare willow branches hanging down over the water, the stone balustrade of the arched bridge crossing the lake, and the glazed tiles on the high wall surrounding the garden. She felt as though she'd walked into a mysterious and beautiful painting.

Scarlet, as usual, brought her back to earth. "Come on," she grumbled. "I'm cold just standing here."

They took the middle of the three paths, the one that led straight to the lake. But instead of following the path as far as the bridge, they turned to their right to climb a little hillock, on top of which was a paved area with a stone incense table. Behind the table stood a cluster of huge ornamental rocks with plantains growing among them.

Oriole drew three sticks of incense from her wide sleeve, lit them at the brazier and held them out in front of her with both hands. She lowered her head and began her prayers.

"This first stick of incense is for my father," she chanted. "I pray that he is in heaven. The second is for my mother. I pray that she will stay in good health. The third is for..." She hesitated, then turned to Scarlet. "Who should this be for?" she asked. "For my brother or..."

"For you, I think," Scarlet replied confidently. "Let me do it." She cupped her hands around Oriole's so that they could pray together. "This third stick of incense is for Miss Oriole," she chanted solemnly. "I pray that she will soon have a good husband."

Oriole was puzzled by Scarlet's prayer and wondered how she of all people could use the word "good" where Heng was concerned. But doubtless it was well-meant, and a good husband had to be worth praying for.

They stood in silence for a few moments, then gave two deep bows before placing the smoking incense in a bronze pot on the table. Oriole took a deep breath of the fragrant burning musk and gazed up at the clear dark sky with its brilliant moon and array of glittering stars. A sudden breeze jangled the wind chimes hanging from the temple eaves, which loomed high above them behind the garden wall. Oriole felt strangely peaceful. She could happily have stayed there for hours, but it was already so late....

"I don't want to go at all, but I suppose we must," she said with reluctance. "If my mother realizes I'm not in my room, she'll be sending out a search party!"

Scarlet picked up the lamp. They had just begun their descent when they heard a soft deep voice coming from behind them. "A night of moonlight..."

They froze. Oriole could hear the rustling of her silk robe as it settled against her legs, and her heartbeat drumming in her ears. She felt slightly dizzy.

"It's him!" Scarlet whispered urgently. "I know his voice!"

Oriole put her finger to her lips, silencing the maid. She turned slowly around, wide-eyed and listening.

After a brief moment, the rich voice came again:

A night of moonlight.
The shadow of blossom quietly falls.

The moon's light is pure and white.
My moon goddess gently calls.

"It's a poem!" Scarlet whispered, unable to restrain herself.

"Of course it's a poem!" Oriole whispered back impatiently. "What else would it be? A recipe for moon-cakes?"

"Well, I don't like this." Scarlet frowned, and her voice grew a little louder. "It's not right. Being in the garden in the dead of night, with a strange man..."

Before she could say another word, a tall figure stepped out from behind the rocks.

CHAPTER THREE

ORIOLE COULDN'T TAKE her eyes off him. He was
standing there silent and still, half in moonlight,
half in shadow. The perfection of his classic features and slim build made him seem more like a
god who had suddenly descended from the starry
sky than just a man. The deep black of his silk
jacket and hat and his leather boots appeared to
recede into the dark background, while the folds of
his white gown caught the moon's rays and leaped
forward with dazzling radiance. His smooth forehead and straight nose glowed pale in the moonlight, while the rest of his face lay in shadow. As
Oriole stared at Jun-rui, a thin mist of incense
smoke wafted between them.

She wanted desperately to say something to him,
but he seemed too distant and unapproachable.
What could she say without sounding ridiculous or
trivial?

She noticed a tugging at her sleeve and was
vaguely aware of Scarlet whispering that they ought
to go. But that was impossible! She felt compelled
to stay; her eyes refused to leave him.

He moved suddenly and took a few steps toward her. Now Oriole could see his eyes clearly—they were bright and burning and seemed to be imploring her to do something, say something.

Finding herself face-to-face with a man, and such an attractive one, Oriole began to tremble. But she was determined to speak and tried to calm herself enough to decide what to say. If Jun-rui had spoken to her in verse, why shouldn't she reply likewise? She was clever at improvising, and after just a few moments' thought, came up with a short poem that made no secret of the passion so recently kindled in her young heart. Without taking her eyes from his, she spoke, softly and earnestly:

> In her orchid room alone, she sighs.
> The bloom of youth will soon depart.
> She asks the man with burning eyes
> To pity her, and give his heart.

Scarlet made an impatient snorting sound by way of comment, and the silence that followed would have been highly embarrassing for Oriole if she hadn't seen the smile that spread across Jun-rui's face. He was regarding her with a look of gentleness and...unmistakable invitation. Oriole felt her nervousness dissolve and a strange warm sensation invade her entire body. She boldly took a step toward him, and at that same moment he moved toward her. His hands tucked inside his wide sleeves, he bowed to her. In fact, he was just about to speak when Scarlet abruptly intervened.

"Look, this has gone quite far enough!" she said insistently, placing herself between the two of them. Her face was stern under the lamplight. "If you don't come with me this instant, Oriole, I'm going straight to your mother to tell her all about it. And I don't think she'd be very pleased, do you?"

This threat had the immediate effect of totally deflating Oriole's romantic inclinations. Abashed, she stared at Scarlet and realized that the maid was in deadly earnest. Her mother *must not* find out about this midnight encounter; the consequences were too terrible to imagine. Oriole had visions of being cast out of her family or sent to a convent or sold as a concubine. At the very least, she'd be locked in her room and subjected to endless lectures and scoldings by her mother. It didn't bear thinking about. But there was still this longing inside her. She stole another glance at Jun-rui. His hands were tightly clenched in front of him, and he looked utterly crestfallen but said nothing. Her heart went out to him at once. Still, what could she do?

"I'm sorry," Scarlet said firmly, taking Oriole's arm, "but I meant what I said. Now, are you coming or aren't you?"

Oriole allowed herself to be led away as though she were sleepwalking, down the stone steps to the bottom of the hillock and then along the path snaking its way to the garden gate. She turned around repeatedly until Jun-rui was no longer in sight. Each time, she saw him standing there frozen, the luminous white of his robe shining against the dark gray of the rocks, his face turned always toward hers.

It was only when they reached the outer wall of the west wing that Oriole awoke from her trancelike state. She shook her arm free of Scarlet's and glared at the maid with resentment.

"Why did you have to go and spoil everything?" she demanded. "My mother would probably never have found out. I'm sure she's fast asleep."

"That's not the point," Scarlet replied. "Anyway, it wasn't too long ago that *you* were talking about a search party and how we had to go back."

"The point is," Oriole declared hotly, "you're a sneak!"

Scarlet looked hurt and walked on without answering. As they approached the women's quarters, they both heard a muffled yapping.

"It's Pug," Scarlet said anxiously. "We'd better hurry, or he'll wake up the whole monastery!"

The yapping got louder as they drew nearer, and it only stopped when Oriole called the dog's name softly from outside her door.

Once inside, she received a warm welcome. Pug first bit playfully on the thick-soled socks Oriole always wore indoors, then dashed over to fetch one of the embroidered shoes she'd taken off and left by the door on entering. The shoe was at least half his size, but he tried nonetheless to impress his mistress by tossing it up in the air. When the attempt was unsuccessful, he pounced on it instead, then lay across it with a triumphant expression, as though he'd bravely captured his prey. Oriole and Scarlet couldn't help laughing at his antics, and with the laughter, Oriole softened.

"I'm sorry," she said gently to Scarlet. "It was mean of me to call you a sneak. But it shocked me, you know, to think you'd tell on me like that."

Scarlet was pensive for a moment. Then she motioned Oriole to sit on the bed, telling her to listen without interrupting because there was something she needed to explain.

"You know what I said about those student-types this afternoon when we were talking?" she began. Oriole nodded.

"Well, if your young man is one of those, then it's for your own good to steer clear of him, wouldn't you say?"

Oriole wanted to disagree, but her good sense got the better of her, and she nodded again, reluctantly.

"So far, so good," Scarlet said under her breath. She hesitated a moment before continuing. "I didn't want to tell you this, but I think I'd better— after what happened tonight." Oriole looked at her expectantly. "Well, you know how I didn't get a good impression of Mr. Zhang the other day when he was telling me all that stuff about himself? Like he was using me as a go-between, trying to fix something up between you?" Oriole murmured a quick yes, urging Scarlet to get to the point.

"Well, now—after what Lucky said—I don't know *what* to think!" Scarlet admitted. "Lucky says Mr. Zhang isn't like that at all. In fact, with his friends, he's got a reputation of *not* being one for the ladies—ever." Oriole stared at her, astonished.

"No, no. It's not what you think!" Scarlet hastened to reassure her. "He's not one for the boys, either! Lucky ought to know!"

Oriole breathed a sigh of relief.

"He's had plenty of chances to play around, apparently—he just doesn't!" the maid went on. "And his friends all tease him about it. He's got this thing about Beauty and Perfection, and no one's good enough for him—that's what Lucky says. The boy's read too much poetry, if you ask me," she added, her practical self coming to the fore. "Nobody's perfect. Any fool knows that!"

Oriole opened her mouth to speak, but Scarlet quickly resumed. "Wait," she said. "You know you asked me why he stayed at the monastery?" Oriole nodded dutifully. "He stayed because of you." She paused, presumably for dramatic effect.

Oriole frowned, confused and definitely flustered. She had no idea how to respond to this statement.

"Suppose he's not just playing around? Suppose he's serious in his intentions?" Scarlet asked her in a no-nonsense tone of voice. "You fall in love with the man. Before long you go creeping off to his room at night—" Oriole gasped and was about to protest. "A long, drawn-out love affair. And then what?"

There was a silence while Oriole considered the matter. After a while she looked at Scarlet miserably. "And then Heng turns up and I marry him."

"Exactly," Scarlet agreed. "So you see, either way—whether he's a no-good student or the paragon Lucky says he is—you *can't* get involved with him. And if you do, you leave me no choice but to be a sneak and tell your mother. For your own good," she added.

Scarlet's message had come through loud and clear, and Oriole felt bitterly disappointed about the way things were turning out. But there was nothing, really, she could do. Nothing she could say. Scarlet, on the other hand, had one last comment. "Pity, though," she said. "You'd have made a nice couple."

It had been a long and emotionally exhausting day for Oriole. Scarlet helped her get washed and changed into her silk nightgown, then settled Pug at the foot of the bed and went off to her own small room. But tired though she was, Oriole couldn't sleep, and she lay awake, gazing into the darkness. Twice she heard the night watchman on his round—made every two hours—of the monastery grounds, and the *toc-toc* of the hollow wooden stick he carried as he struck it with a small wooden beater. Her mind raced, thinking about Jun-rui and everything Scarlet had said.

THE NEXT FEW DAYS dragged along with painful slowness. Oriole had little inclination to do anything, and even the daily rituals, such as her makeup routine or incense burning, seemed pointless. She managed to finish her painting of Pug and do two others—of the garden by moonlight—and she struggled to apply herself to designing her wedding quilt. But nothing seemed to matter. She was aware of an emptiness inside and a feeling of permanent melancholy. Things that would normally have lifted her spirits—like blossom-covered trees in the spring sunshine or Pug romping playfully in the courtyard—no longer cheered her.

She'd taken Scarlet's warning very much to heart and had therefore avoided the Flower Garden ever since her midnight encounter with Jun-rui. She and Scarlet now burned incense every night at a makeshift table in the courtyard. And restricting herself to the women's quarters meant she was in no danger of running into him again. Lady Cui had given strict instructions that no male over three feet in height (with the exception of Di-di, of course!) should be allowed anywhere near the place—except under very special circumstances.

Still, the fact that Oriole hadn't seen Jun-rui didn't stop her from thinking about him. But her thoughts were no longer agitated, the way they'd been before. What she felt now was more of a deep sadness, which she kept to herself; she didn't even talk to Scarlet about it.

Oriole found it all rather tragic—to have met someone who had such an overpowering effect on her, someone who seemed equally drawn to her, and then, after a fleeting moment, to be compelled to shut him out of her life completely. Why? she asked herself. Because of what, exactly? She knew the answer. It was because of tradition. Propriety. The social order. Her parents' wishes. As Scarlet said, that was just the way things were. Nothing she could do about it.

Oriole knew all that. She knew she had to abide by her mother's dictates, her father's plans. Regardless of what her heart tried to tell her.

Her resignation, however, didn't make her sadness any easier to bear. She was sleeping badly and had lost her appetite. Her complexion became paler with each day that passed, and her eyes grew dull and listless. Her mother remarked on one occasion, "You're not looking well, my dear. Go out and get some sunshine this afternoon—it will do you good." But otherwise, Lady Cui was far too busy with preparations for the funeral service and the banquet to follow immediately afterward to take much notice of her daughter's condition.

Scarlet, by comparison, was well aware of the change in Oriole. Being a simple and straightforward young woman, she couldn't begin to understand the complexities of Oriole's emotions. In her practical way, she tended to think that people should just get on with life and not waste time yearning for things they couldn't have. But she was also devoted to Oriole; she could see that her mistress was ailing and wanted to do whatever she could to help. So she brewed herbal remedies designed to improve appetite and restore vitality. She gave Oriole frequent massages. She freshened the room with different aromatic essences and newly cut blossoms. She sat with Oriole at night to try to soothe her into sleep. But if she ever tried to talk, Oriole would shake her head gently and say, "Not now, Scarlet." Oriole was just like the girl in her poem, Scarlet reflected—sighing, alone in her orchid room.

IT WAS RAINING. A light summer rain. She was standing on the marble bridge in the garden, looking down at the lotus flowers and the raindrops plopping onto the black water. She looked up into the bright moon. She saw the fair-skinned moon goddess there; she saw the three-legged toad; she saw the hare standing on its back legs under the cassia tree, busily pounding the elixir of immortality. She saw the Old Man under the moon, holding a skein of red thread in his hands. He tossed the thread down, down toward her. The goddess, the toad, the hare, they all smiled.

Through the rain, she heard beautiful music. Softly plucked strings. She moved blindly, her bare feet following the sound. He was sitting on a low stool, a zither in his lap. The music stopped. He took her by the hand and led her into a small room. They stood facing each other.

"You're wet," he said. Her red silk robe, sodden, clung to her body.

"You're wet, too," she said. His white gown gaped open. There were drops of rain on his chest.

"We must get you dry," he said, undoing the wide sash tied under her bosom.

He placed his hand on her throat. He moved his hand down inside her gown and held her breast. Her body quickened. Their lips touched. His breath was sweet. Her thighs trembled and parted. His hand glided over her stomach and downward. His hardness pressed up against her. She tasted his tongue. She swooned. She let out a low groan....

"IT'S THE FIFTEENTH!" Scarlet said brightly the next morning, coming into Oriole's room and pulling open the heavy brocade curtains around the bed. Oriole groaned. Her eyes flickered open briefly, then she rolled over under the embroidered quilt. To Scarlet her drawn face showed all the signs of yet another restless night; it certainly didn't look as if Oriole wanted to get up.

Scarlet tried not to feel discouraged. She moved briskly into the dressing room and started rummaging around in one of Oriole's clothing chests.

"I'm sure I put it in here somewhere," she muttered to herself. "Your special mourning gown," she called out, in case Oriole was curious. "Oh, yes, here it is. I'm going to hang it outside to air. Not that I mind the smell of camphor," she added as she passed through the room to the courtyard with Pug at her heels, "but it's very creased."

Wide awake by this time, Oriole lay under the quilt, overwhelmed by a sense of shame. It made no difference that she'd been dreaming about mythological beings of the moon—the fair-skinned goddess with her hare and toad, or the Old Man with his red thread. She knew perfectly well that the Old Man was said to use his thread to join together lovers who were destined to marry.... The romance of her dream was all very well. It was the rest of it that bothered her. Even now, her body was tingling and aching for his next caress. She was filled with self-loathing. How could she, always so chaste, be guilty of such strong physical desires? How was it possible for her to have had a dream like that? There must be something wrong with her! How could she face Scarlet? Scarlet would be able to tell. Everyone would! How could she hide it from them, the truth of this terrible dream? They'd see it written all over her face. She hugged her knees to her chest and cried quietly into her pillow.

Scarlet was back in no time, putting coals on the brazier to boil a pot of water. "I've got the whole day mapped out," she said purposefully to the motionless lump curled under the quilt. "First, I'm going to give you a nice hot bath in orchid oil. Then, a choice breakfast of rice-cakes, vegetables fresh from the garden and candied fruit. After that, you can help me with the sacrificial food for the service." She tested the water—not hot enough yet—and searched in the tray of essences for the orchid oil. The room was peaceful in the early-morning light.

"We'll need to prepare quite a few bowls of cakes and fruit. Vegetables, too. Oh, and the flowers," Scarlet continued, as if thinking aloud. "I could do it myself, but it would all look so much nicer with your artistic touch," she said sincerely.

There was a lot to be done. Apart from the altar table behind the coffin, there would also be two smaller tables on either side of it, all of which were to be covered with food offerings. The memorial service was a big event in itself, since it marked the end of the Cui family's official period of mourning. The fact that it coincided with such an important festival in the Buddhist calendar, however, made it even more special—the fifteenth day of the second moon was, after all, the day on which Buddha Sakyamuni entered into nirvana. In every Buddhist monastery, this was an occasion for grand ceremony. So Scarlet knew that everything must be done to perfection.

A gentle bubbling came from the brazier, and Scarlet put on a second pot of water, then crossed to the bed.

"You'll need to have a good long sleep this afternoon," she advised, putting her hand on what she guessed was Oriole's back, buried under the pretty rose-colored silk quilt. "Or you'll never last out the ceremony."

Oriole's curled-up shape flinched slightly at Scarlet's touch, and a stifled sob escaped her. Surprised as she was to discover that her mistress was crying, Scarlet immediately assumed that the tears must be for her father; it was only natural that tonight's funeral service would make Oriole think of him more than usual. A girl needed her mother at a time like this. But when had Lady Cui ever been a comfort to her daughter? The woman was too busy running everyone's lives to notice what was right under her nose!

She rubbed Oriole's back soothingly. "Don't worry," she said softly. "You'll feel better after a nice hot bath. And it's a beautiful day today. Come on," she coaxed. "Turn around. Please."

Oriole turned slowly, but her face remained hidden. Scarlet drew down the quilt and peered at her closely.

"You look terrible!" she exclaimed, the words spilling out before she'd had time to check herself. Not only was Oriole extremely pale, she was blotchy around the nose and mouth, and her eyes were red from crying. Her long black hair was disheveled and stuck to her cheeks in matted strands.

So her fears were well-founded, Oriole thought, beginning to panic. Obviously Scarlet could tell what kind of dream she'd had, and before long everyone would know about her wicked thoughts. Her lips quivered, and she felt the tears rush to her eyes again.

"Now, now," the maid soothed. "You miss your father. Of course you do. I can understand that. Especially today." She reached for the portrait of Lord Cui on the side table and placed it in Oriole's hands. "But tonight we're going to make sure he goes to heaven, aren't we? With the help of the abbot—and a hundred or so lusty old monks whose tongues'll be hanging out the moment they see you, no doubt!" she added, smiling mischievously.

Oriole, enormously relieved that her secret was safe, sat up and gave Scarlet an impulsive hug.

Soon afterward they were behind the painted screen and Scarlet was adding orchid oil to the steaming water in the large porcelain bowl. Oriole was slipping out of her silk nightgown and pinning up her hair, ready for her bath. Her movements were slow and her eyes had an absent glazed expression.

Scarlet threw her a long searching look—a look Oriole didn't even notice. "By the way," she said once Oriole was squatting in the large bowl and splashing herself with the perfumed water. "I'd better warn you. Mr. Zhang will be there tonight. Apparently he asked the abbot if he could come to the service, and the abbot checked with your mother to see if it was all right. I expect she felt sorry for him—both his parents are dead, remember? At any rate, she agreed. That's what she told me this morning."

Oriole stopped her splashing and glanced nervously up at her maid.

"It's nothing to worry about," Scarlet reassured her. "But if you don't want to do or say anything you might regret," she cautioned, "just keep your distance!"

CHAPTER FOUR

LADY CUI SCOURED the side hall of the temple for any sign of her daughter. The hall was thick with incense smoke and thronged with saffron-robed monks.

At that very moment, the abbot—dressed in a sumptuous ceremonial robe of yellow embroidered brocade and wearing a high yellow tiara decorated with red tassels—was intoning the Lotus Sutra in front of Lord Cui's coffin and simultaneously ringing a hand bell. Several high priests were marking the rhythm of the abbot's chanting by lightly tapping a large wooden fish. From time to time, the huge gathering of monks broke out in chorus, accompanied by a group of musicians. The resonance of so many male voices, heightened by the sound of drums, cymbals, bells, chimes and bronze clappers, was stirring stuff, Lady Cui noted approvingly. Enough to drive away any number of demons and see her husband's spirit safely on its way to paradise.

But why wasn't the girl here yet? It was a service

for her own father, after all; you'd think she could have made the effort to get there on time!

Still, Oriole had done an extremely good job of decorating the altar tables, Lady Cui conceded with a touch of pride. The vases of blue and white silk flowers were set off strikingly against the glowing orange and gold of the fresh fruits—persimmons, kumquats and pears—and the vivid greens and purples of such exotic vegetables as kohlrabi, sugar beet, shallots and spinach. These were all beautifully displayed in painted porcelain bowls. There was also a colorful array of smaller dishes containing dried or preserved foods—honeyed bamboo shoots and ginger, hemp-seed dates, lotus and melon seeds, pistachio nuts, candied fruits and the aromatic seeds of the Korean pine. The girl definitely had a good eye for detail and such a way with color. What was keeping her so long? If she didn't show up soon, someone would have to be sent off to fetch her.

The ceremony had begun soon after midnight, when the full moon was already high overhead. It was a perfect night, clear and bright and not as cold as it might have been for early spring.

The abbot had been there to greet her when she arrived. In fact, he'd presented her almost immediately with this protégé of his—the young man who had asked permission to participate in the service, to honor his dead parents.

Lady Cui had felt she could hardly turn down the request of someone as eminent as the abbot.

And especially not if it involved a man the abbot called his protégé. She had therefore given her consent and told the abbot that Mr. Zhang would be most welcome.

As it happened, the protégé seemed pleasant enough.

"A nice-looking young man," she'd remarked to the abbot, when Jun-rui had gone off to burn incense at the altar. "A student, I suppose? Judging from his attire."

"Indeed," the abbot had answered. "A most accomplished young gentleman. Mr. Zhang is spending a little time here at the monastery before traveling on to Chang-an for the examinations. There are so few cultivated young people around here, you know, Madam. Mr. Zhang asks if he might be permitted to make the acquaintance of Miss Oriole?"

"Mm, perhaps," she'd replied evasively. She was not at all keen on the idea and quite relieved that the abbot hadn't pursued it. He'd soon offered to escort her to the side hall, and on the way there told her of reports that rebel soldiers had been sighted at Puzhou. But he didn't think there was any immediate cause for concern, and the service could certainly go ahead as planned. Once in the hall, he saw her to a seat near the coffin in the area reserved for the principal mourners; shortly afterward the ceremony had begun. In the ensuing smoke and noise, Lady Cui had been constantly on the lookout for her daughter. She'd just decided to send Constance to go and find her when Oriole suddenly made her entrance. She was leaning on Scarlet's arm, the two of them framed in the doorway.

The incantations ground clumsily to a halt, and a hush fell on the assembled company. The shaved head of every monk turned to look at the apparition illumined against the dark doorway. Lady Cui rose from her ornate chair near the coffin, wondering for a moment if she was seeing a ghost.

And Jun-rui, from where he stood half-hidden behind a lacquered pillar opposite the doorway, was mesmerized by Oriole's beauty. She was earthly perfection personified.

There was nothing contrived about her appearance, he observed. No cosmetics, no hair ornaments, no decoration of any kind, apart from two white jade bracelets on her wrist. Nor was she decked out in silken finery; instead, she wore the loose-fitting gown of a mourner, a coarse off-white sackcloth with frayed edges. Her long black hair was in a simple braid that hung down her back.

It was her face that haunted him. Jun-rui gazed at her longingly. Her face was radiant, luminous as moonlight, soft as white pear blossom. Her eyes glowed like black jet. Her lips looked as sweet as ripe berries. He hungered for a taste. He felt his body stir. His arms slid around to embrace the pillar as he watched her.

Though unaware of Jun-rui's admiring looks, Oriole felt acutely uncomfortable at having so many eyes on her, watching her every move. She knew from experience that monks were quite likely to behave this way. They came to the monastery for all kinds of reasons and from all walks of life—not always reputable ones, either. And they so seldom saw females of any description that a city beauty such as she was guaranteed to set them off. Scarlet had once joked with her about the monks—"What do they remind you of, anyway? All those shiny little bald pates peeping out?"—but Oriole hadn't really found her remark amusing.

"Let's do something *now*," she whispered urgently to Scarlet. "I can't stand it, being gaped at like this!"

"Head for the altar," Scarlet whispered back. "We have to burn incense first. Then we can sit down, out of the way."

The monks stepped aside as the two of them walked slowly down the center of the hall toward the altar table. Oriole heard plenty of lewd whispering as she passed, and one brazen monk even brushed deliberately against her leg. Fortunately, though, the abbot soon resumed his chanting, and order was restored.

Eyes downcast, Oriole moved solemnly past the coffin. It had been sealed and coated with several layers of red varnish long ago, to make sure no hint of decay ever escaped from inside; now it was also covered with sheets of oiled paper, and a white pall had been laid on top. Huge candles were ranged on the altar table behind the coffin, and the brightly colored pennants and banners that hung from the ceiling cast long flickering shadows all around. When Oriole had finished praying for her father, she placed the burning incense in a casket filled with sand, which stood in front of her father's spirit tablet. This was a rectangular piece of wood, standing upright. Lord Cui's name and other information about him were written on the tablet in a single column of characters, from top to bottom. There was also a large portrait of him in the center of the altar.

Oriole felt desolate and alone. Her grief for her father, her sense of emptiness and loss over Jun-rui and, more recently, her shame about the dream all became confused in her mind and weighed on her heavily. Feeling suddenly faint, she tottered forward, and Scarlet quickly took her arm again and guided her toward the mourners to sit with Lady Cui, Di-di and the maids.

Oriole sat there for hours, her eyes wide open and fixed on the coffin. The voice of the abbot droned on and on, interrupted by occasional bursts from the monks and musicians. There was more burning of incense and of paper money, too, and later the sacrificial food was presented. From time to time, the mourners wailed and lamented in high-pitched tones, rocking their bodies to and fro.

Gradually the smoke-filled air began to gleam with the first pale rays of dawn, and the abbot intoned the final scripture, expressing confidence that Lord Cui's spirit was well and truly at peace. Soon afterward, when the monks had shuffled sleepily out of the hall, Scarlet stood up and stretched stiffly, then took her wide-eyed but exhausted mistress back to the women's quarters.

Lady Cui lingered a short while with the abbot to express her gratitude. The two of them were just about to leave the temple building when a guard from the monastery's main gate burst rudely through the wooden doors and rushed up to the abbot. Lady Cui gave the man a withering look, but the abbot was clearly alarmed—the guard was ashen-faced and out of breath and had evidently been running.

"What's wrong?" the abbot asked him. "Come on, man! Speak up!"

"It's the rebels!" the guard gasped, catching his breath. "They're at the gate, Your Reverence! They've got us surrounded! Flying Tiger says to tell you," he panted, "if you don't hand her over—

Miss Oriole, that is—he'll kill us all! Every last one of us!''

THE ABBOT'S FOOTSTEPS echoed as he paced the length of the large reception room, while Lady Cui sat perched on the edge of a carved wooden chair, wringing her hands and blurting out every minute or so, ''What are we going to do?''

There was no question about the truth of the guard's words. The rebel camp could be seen from any of the monastery's towers. It was only about half a mile away, and on closer inspection, you could even glimpse the smoke from their fires and the bright colors of their battle banners.

Lady Cui and the abbot, still dressed in their ceremonial clothes, had come directly to the abbot's private residence after receiving the dreadful news. Flying Tiger had apparently heard in Puzhou that there was a young woman—daughter of an important government official—staying at the monastery. He'd heard she was a real beauty, too, and as he'd told the sentry, he'd decided to take her as a wife.

It was perfectly clear to Lady Cui that there would be no banquet that evening, and she felt quite wretched when she thought of all the preparation, all those wonderful dishes going to waste. But for the time being, there were more pressing matters to deal with. For the past hour, she and the abbot had considered their predicament from every conceiva-

ble angle, but had failed to come up with a solution
of any kind.

"What are we going to do?" Lady Cui wailed
yet again.

The abbot suddenly stopped his pacing and sat
down next to her, his stiff robe bunching into awkward folds as he did so.

"Madam," he pronounced, "we have done our
utmost to solve this dilemma, and we have failed.
It seems to me," he continued gravely, "that we
are left with no alternative but to summon the
young lady in person and see what she has to say."

Lady Cui grimly nodded her agreement.

"We could also send for my protégé—Mr.
Zhang," he suggested. Lady Cui now looked doubt-
ful.

"He may not be a man of the world, exactly, but
he's got a good head on his shoulders," the abbot
argued. "He might just think of something we've
overlooked." He turned to Lady Cui, his wrinkled
face lined with worry. "We must face the facts,
Madam. We need all the help we can get!"

The abbot had soon dispatched two junior novices to summon Miss Oriole and Mr. Zhang with
instructions that they were to brief the young people
beforehand. In this way, he hoped to avoid any
more hysteria than was absolutely necessary and to
enable the young lady to get her weeping over and
done with before she came to his residence. They

must all think clearly and calmly if they were not to perish at the hands of these murderous rebels!

Jun-rui appeared on the scene promptly, his hat askew and his gown crumpled, as though he'd got out of bed in a hurry. His face was anxious and his manner agitated. He joined the abbot in his restless pacing and talked with him in hushed tones, while Lady Cui continued to rock back and forth, wringing her hands.

There was a long wait for Oriole, and when she finally arrived with Scarlet, her eyes were red and watery, and she was clutching a silk handkerchief. Lady Cui leaped up at once and rushed over to her, seizing her arm and crying out in a shrill voice, "My poor girl, what are we going to do?"

Oriole had been devastated when she'd first heard of the rebel leader's terrible request. But after the initial shock and subsequent tears, a strange feeling of calm had descended on her. She realized that, because of her, many lives were at stake. Instead of shrinking back in despair and locking herself away in a small tragic world of her own—as she had done for the past week—she knew she had to meet the challenge of this fearful responsibility. Seeing her mother, always so self-controlled, in such an emotional state, had given Oriole an added jolt and made her all the more determined to get a grip on herself and not surrender to despair. She patted her mother's arm soothingly and turned from her to the abbot, and then, with genuine surprise, to Jun-rui.

"Um—" the abbot hesitated "—a young friend of mine. Mr. Zhang. You two have met in passing, I believe," he said to Oriole. She and Scarlet exchanged a quick glance. "A week or so ago when I was showing Mr. Zhang around the monastery?"

"Oh, yes," Oriole said, blushing. Their other meeting—in the Flower Garden—would, to her relief, remain a well-kept secret. She must not allow herself to think of what had passed between them that moonlit night. She must keep her eyes away from him.

The abbot turned to Jun-rui to complete the introductions. "Mr. Zhang, this is the young lady I was telling you about. Miss Oriole. Daughter of Lady Cui."

Jun-rui gave her a troubled smile and made a deep bow. His expression was one of tender concern.

"I'm sure you are well aware of the gravity of the situation," the abbot said soberly, addressing his remarks to Oriole. "This Flying Tiger, as he calls himself, has demanded an answer by noon today. I haven't met him in person, but I gather that he's a real villain. Not a man to be trifled with. As you know, for the past few months he's been terrorizing the entire county. Stealing from the villagers and—forgive my bluntness—violating their womenfolk.'' He coughed apologetically. "We can only assume that if his demand is not met, he will do as he says—burn the monastery to the ground and kill us all in cold blood!''

The abbot's position was not an enviable one. He alone was responsible, and if any harm were to come to the historic building or any of its occupants, his name would be disgraced for all time. He heaved a profound sigh.

"But why my daughter?'' Lady Cui complained bitterly. "Why does this barbarian want her for a wife?''

The abbot regarded the widow with a combination of wry amusement and pity. "They say familiarity breeds contempt, Madam,'' he answered enigmatically. "Look at her, and see for yourself. She is a young woman of exceptional beauty. And even in this backwater news travels fast.'' He cast an admiring eye over Oriole. "More to the point, Madam, where is the man who would *not* want her for a wife?''

Jun-rui shot the abbot a look of yearning, then quickly averted his eyes, apparently embarrassed. Lady Cui, meanwhile, was following the abbot's advice and scrutinizing her daughter's face. Hmm. Pretty, yes. But as for "exceptional beauty,'' she couldn't quite see it. The girl's eyes were bloodshot, and her complexion had lost some of its youthful bloom. It was just Oriole. What was all the fuss about?

The abbot cleared his throat. "We're straying from the matter at hand," he observed. "We must tr—"

"Excuse me, Your Reverence," Oriole interrupted boldly, "but I must speak." She looked sympathetically at each of them in turn and could see they were all exhausted after the long service, and consumed with fear over the present danger.

"Listen!" she exhorted them. In the far distance was the muffled beating of battle drums and gongs, and the occasional muted cry. "It's me he wants," she said in a resigned voice. "You wouldn't be in this mess in the first place if I wasn't here." She raised a hand to silence their protestations and motioned them all to sit.

The way Oriole was taking control of the situation was really quite impressive, in Scarlet's opinion. Where was the pale invalid she'd been nursing all week? And where had this sudden strength come from? It was all a bit of a mystery.

"I haven't had much time to think about this," Oriole began, "but as far as I can see, there are only two alternatives open to us. That's assuming we rule out the possibility of the monastery defending itself against the enemy."

"I'm afraid so," the abbot said. "There must be several hundred of them, to about 120 of us. And only one of our monks is a trained fighter. Hardly a fair contest!"

"Well, then," Oriole continued, "obviously the first alternative is to give in to Flying Tiger's demands and hand me over to him."

"That's out of the question!" Lady Cui exclaimed. "Think of our family name!"

"I am, Mother," Oriole replied coolly. "Our family name won't be much good to us if we're all dead, will it? At least this way," she said, counting off on her fingers, her bracelets clinking emphatically, "*you* will be safe. And Di-di. And my father's coffin. And the monks. And the monastery. There! That's five good reasons."

"But the disgrace!" Lady Cui moaned, choking back a sob. "Our family has always been beyond reproach. No crime. Not even a second marriage! How can I possibly hand you—my daughter—to a rebel?"

"Even if I *was* disgraced," Oriole reasoned, "you'd still have Di-di. And when he's older, he'll be able to make a good marriage and carry on the family line."

"No," Lady Cui repeated adamantly. "The disgrace would be on us all. I can't allow it!"

"In that case," Oriole said with a pained expression, "I suppose it'll have to be the second alternative."

"And what is that, my dear?" the abbot asked her kindly.

Oriole lowered her eyes and released a tragic sigh before replying. "To hand me over to him...as a corpse!"

In the stunned silence that followed this shocking utterance, the young man's groan sounded especially loud. All eyes turned to Jun-rui, and even Oriole looked up in surprise. Lady Cui stared at him curiously. His cheeks reddened, but he returned their gaze without flinching.

"I'm sorry," he said in that deep voice Oriole remembered so vividly, "but the second solution is even more outrageous than the first!"

Oriole gazed deeply into his eyes, despite her earlier resolution to avoid doing so, then spoke to him earnestly. "This rebel—we know he asked for me. But he didn't say anything about dead or alive, did he? I'd rather hang myself right now and get it over with than spend the rest of my life in shame and dishonor!"

"No," Jun-rui repeated, getting to his feet. "You will not do it. Not while there are people here who want to protect you."

His muscles were tensed and he looked so fearless that Oriole could imagine him delivering her from any number of adversaries. She suddenly thought of her dream and felt an urge to touch him, to be enfolded in his strong embrace.

"This fine talk is all very well," Lady Cui said impatiently, instantly rousing Oriole from her amorous imaginings. "But we're back where we started. We still haven't decided what to do. Can't anyone think of something?"

For a while all was quiet in the room except for the soft creaking of Jun-rui's leather boots as he paced the wooden floor. A spray of bamboo leaves rustled gently against the latticed window, and golden orioles called from the bare branches of a maple tree in the abbot's garden. A dull rumbling of battle drums vibrated in the distance. Oriole's eyes followed Jun-rui.

"I've got an idea," she said. They all turned to her.

"Yes?" her mother asked eagerly. "Tell us!"

"It might not come to anything," she admitted. "But why don't we at least try asking around in the monastery to see if anyone else can help? Apart from us, there are dozens of monks living here—"

"Not forgetting the novices and lay brothers and a few guests," the abbot put in.

"Yes." She nodded. "Well, one of them just might come up with an idea—especially if there was a sizable reward to be gained from it. I mean, saving a wealthy family from ruin would really be worth something, wouldn't it?"

"Hmm, an incentive of some kind..." the abbot mused. "What exactly would that reward be?"

"I've thought of that," Oriole said. She gave the abbot a steady look. "It's only logical that the reward should be me. Promised as a bride to any man who can save me from the hands of Flying Tiger. With a handsome dowry, of course," she added emphatically. "But my mother would have to agree to it—and give her word."

Lady Cui frowned. She twisted the large amethyst ring on her finger while weighing the proposal in her mind. Her daughter married to a defrocked monk! The idea was appalling! Such a drop in social status—and all that chanting and vegetarian food! Besides, what about Heng? The girl was already engaged to him. How could she now be promised to someone else? Lady Cui decided to cross that bridge when she came to it. After all, the danger was now, and Heng might as well be on the other side of the world for all the help he could give them. And as Oriole herself had said, her idea would probably come to nothing. What harm could there be in giving it a try?

Lady Cui sat up straight with an imperious air. "I agree," she said solemnly. "I give my word. If any man is able to prevent this...this rebel from taking my daughter, I promise I will accept him into my family."

"A wise decision, Madam," the abbot said approvingly. "Now, there's no time to lose. We only have two hours to come up with an answer for Flying Tiger. I'll send my novices at once to pass the word around the monastery, and we'll just have to be patient and see if there's any response. In the meantime," he advised, "I would suggest that the ladies return to their quarters. I will, of course, inform you of any new developments," he assured Lady Cui.

Oriole was suddenly overwhelmed with fatigue; the strain of their present danger was taking its toll. She also felt painfully aware of the fact that Junrui was absorbing her thoughts once again, and if she was to heed Scarlet's warning, she should remove herself from his presence as soon as possible. She got to her feet, waiting dutifully for her mother so that they could return to the west wing together. Scarlet stood respectfully behind Oriole, also waiting. But Lady Cui seemed dazed and slow to respond. Jun-rui, meanwhile, went back to pacing the floor, deep in thought.

The abbot was bustling past him to call for his novices when Jun-rui caught hold of his brocade sleeve.

"Wait, Your Reverence," he said quietly. "There's no need to go anywhere."

He then turned to Oriole and spoke to her in a strong voice that filled her with hope and confidence. "I might be able to help." His troubled expression had lifted, and his eyes were now filled with the warmth she remembered from that night in the garden. "I've got a plan," he said, looking at her intently. "And I think it might work!"

CHAPTER FIVE

IT WAS A WEEK later. Scarlet was preparing Oriole for the festivities taking place that evening. The banquet that Lady Cui had originally promised the abbot had now become a banquet to celebrate the success of Zhang's plan—and to acknowledge his reward. Marriage to Oriole. Acceptance into Lady Cui's family, as her son-in-law.

"Pretty as a picture!" Scarlet remarked happily as she ran the ivory comb through Oriole's long shining hair. She threw an admiring look at the glowing face reflected in the silver mirror Oriole held. "And by the time we've done your hair and got you all dressed up, you'll be an absolute knock-out!"

Oriole flushed at her maid's praise. She put the mirror down on the dressing table and fingered the ornaments they'd selected to adorn her hair—the pendants with their strings of turquoise and white-jade beads, the golden hairpins decorated with the flashing blue of kingfisher feathers, and the gold coronet with its cluster of delicate flowers set in lapis lazuli.

The whole afternoon had been devoted to getting Oriole ready for the banquet that evening. First, a leisurely bath in rosewater. Then a prolonged makeup session, which had begun with the application of a facial astringent made from the dried yellow stamens of lotus flowers. Oriole's skin tingled pleasantly, and her cheeks glowed like peony petals.

Scarlet had insisted that cosmetics and coiffure both be done by daylight, and the late-afternoon sun was still streaming in through the latticed windows.

"Just think!" Scarlet exclaimed, pausing a moment in her combing. "Only a week ago you were about as down in the dumps as I've ever seen you—not eating, not sleeping, and moping around with a long face as though the world was coming to an end. You really had me worried, you know!"

Oriole swiveled around on the rosewood stool. "I'm very sorry, Scarlet," she said sincerely. "I really appreciate the way you've looked after me—I don't know how I'd have managed without you. I must have been such a pain!" she groaned. "So miserable and so wrapped up in myself!" She winced slightly, remembering those lonely days. "But it all seems ages ago now," she said cheerfully.

"Yes," Scarlet agreed. "And today, you're as good as married to Mr. Wonderful! Must be that third stick of incense that did the trick." She winked. "You know, my prayer for Miss Oriole?"

Oriole gave a little laugh, but a thoughtful expression soon clouded her face. "There's something worrying me, though."

"For goodness' sake!" Scarlet answered quickly, a note of exasperation in her voice. "Some people are never satisfied! Here you are, all set to marry the man of your dreams—which seemed completely impossible only a week ago, I might add—and now you're finding something else to be gloomy about!" She raised her eyebrows curiously. "So what is it this time?"

"It's my mother," Oriole said with a sigh. "For the past few days, ever since Jun-rui's friend arrived at the monastery, in fact, she's been avoiding me."

"Hmm..." Scarlet frowned. She thought for a moment. "Maybe you're just imagining it," she said. "Your mother's had a lot on her mind lately, what with all that worry over Flying Tiger, and then the banquet to think about. She probably just hasn't had time for you, that's all."

"Well, she's had plenty of time for Di-di," Oriole countered. "Only this morning, they spent a good hour in the Flower Garden, taking his pet canary for a walk!"

Scarlet pulled up a wooden stool and sat down next to Oriole at the dressing table. "Even if you're right,'' she began, ''even if she is avoiding you, I don't see what the problem is. I mean, you must be pretty glad she's decided we'll stay on at the monastery for a while and not go rushing off to Boling. That *must* be because she's thinking about you and Jun-rui.''

''Yes, but every time I try asking her about him she brushes me off,'' Oriole complained. ''She won't tell me when she's going to announce our engagement—formally, I mean. If it's tonight, I'd be going in red, wouldn't I? But if it's not, I'd look a complete fool turning up in all my bridal gear! That's why I decided on the blue-and-gold outfit instead. Why can't she just *tell* me?''

''Look, I don't know why,'' Scarlet said. ''Maybe she just wants it to be a surprise.'' She freed a tangle in Oriole's long hair and smoothed it down with her hand. ''But whatever the reason,'' she continued in a reassuring voice, ''I'm sure you've got absolutely nothing to worry about. She's going to announce it sooner or later—and my guess is, it'll be tonight. You've just got to be patient. I mean, she can hardly change her mind now, can she? And she wouldn't have arranged for Mr. Zhang to move into the west wing after the banquet if she didn't already consider him part of the family.''

Oriole thought about Scarlet's argument carefully and decided it made sense. But patience didn't come easily under the circumstances. Every day of her mother's evasiveness was another day without Jun-rui. Only an official engagement would make it possible for the two of them to spend time together; at present they were unable to meet, even with a chaperon. Oriole wasn't sure how much longer she could tolerate this frustrating state of affairs—to be so close to him and yet so far away. She wanted to spend time with Jun-rui, she wanted to share her life with him.... Well, just getting to know him would be a good start, she admitted to herself. They knew so little about each other; despite that, she felt so sure of her feelings. How was this possible? She remembered her dream and the red thread. Could it possibly be her destiny to marry Jun-rui? Were marriages really made in heaven?

"Your mother's asked me to fetch Mr. Zhang tonight and bring him to the banquet a bit early," Scarlet said, interrupting Oriole's thoughts. "Speaking of which," she added briskly, standing up with her comb at the ready, "we'd better finish with your hair or you'll never make it to the banquet yourself! And you wouldn't want to miss out on an evening in the company of the great hero, now would you!" she said with a laugh.

For the maid to refer to Jun-rui as "the great hero" was no exaggeration, Oriole reflected proudly while Scarlet gave her hair a final combing.

Not only had he delivered her—not to mention her family and the entire monastery—from death and dishonor, he'd also rid the whole county of a vicious band of rebel soldiers who'd inflicted great suffering and hardship on a frightened population. Even though Jun-rui might not have performed any acts of physical courage himself, his ingenuity had saved the day—and because of that, his fame had spread quickly throughout the region.

Oriole went over the sequence of events, starting with that terrible morning after the service. Jun-rui had been pacing the floor of the abbot's reception room. It had occurred to him in a flash of inspiration that if the monastery was unable to put up a fight from within, the enemy must be attacked from outside. He had remembered that his friend, Du, who had taken up a military career and was now a general, had been stationed at Pu Pass, only fifteen miles away. If they could get a letter through to the general, Jun-rui was sure he would come to their rescue, since Du was an old friend of his and a sworn brother.

There were two obstacles to surmount, Jun-rui had told them. One was how to deliver the letter, and the other was how to hold off Flying Tiger until Du—known as the White Horse general—could arrive with his army.

The abbot had immediately proposed one of the monks, a trained fighter with a martial arts background, as a messenger. Monastic life bored this monk stiff, and he would certainly welcome any chance for adventure.

As for Flying Tiger, Jun-rui calculated, they should try to hold him off for three days, until the nineteenth; the journey to Pu Pass would take the monk a full day, and he would have to wait until dark before setting off if he was to succeed in breaking through the enemy lines. Then they had to allow another day for Du to march his army down to the monastery. The problem, Jun-rui had said, was how to delay a man as ruthless and determined as Flying Tiger.

"Ouch!" Oriole cried suddenly. "You're hurting me!" Scarlet had already scooped Oriole's hair into a mass at the back of her head and pinned it up. She was now taking individual strands and looping them one on top of the other to give the style more body, and she'd been a bit rough with the last hairpin. When she'd promised to be more careful, Oriole relaxed again and studied Scarlet's handiwork in her small mirror.

Yes, Flying Tiger. It hadn't been so difficult, after all, she remembered, to come up with a scheme for putting him off—although it had involved the abbot in telling a lie! He had met with the rebel general at noon on the sixteenth and told him that although the young lady had agreed to become his wife, she was still in mourning for her father. This, of course, was not true, since the Cui family's official period of mourning had ended the day before. He'd reminded the rebel that taking a bride dressed in white would bring bad luck. If, however, Flying Tiger would wait three days—by which time the young lady's period of mourning would be over—she could then be sent out to him in the red wedding finery of a proper bride, with a handsome dowry, as well. Flying Tiger was not to know he'd been tricked and had agreed to the abbot's suggestion.

But before daylight on the nineteenth, General Du made a surprise attack, defeated the rebel army and brought it to heel, then beheaded its leader. And that had been the end of Flying Tiger and the terrible ordeal.

Lady Cui had invited Jun-rui's friend to the banquet, but he had declined, explaining that he needed to return to his post. He had left the monastery that morning, promising to be back for the wedding.

"There!" Scarlet declared with satisfaction, stepping back to admire the intricate coils and loops of Oriole's hair. "I think it'll hold. We'll do the finishing touches after you're dressed." She glanced out the window and noticed that dusk was beginning to fall. "Goodness, I'd better run!" she exclaimed. "I promised to help your mother with a few things before I get Mr. Zhang. I'll come back and give you a hand with your clothes while they're having their private little drink together!"

It was the first Oriole had heard of this "private drink," and she turned to Scarlet intending to ask for an explanation.

But Scarlet was too busy hurrying out the door to notice the curious look on Oriole's beautifully made-up face.

THE NIGHT SKY was already studded with stars when Scarlet went over to the dormitory building to get Jun-rui, and they made their way back to the west wing by lamplight. The large and elegant reception room of the guest quarters, where the banquet was to be held, glowed with the soft lights of many oil lamps, candles and painted lanterns.

Lady Cui sat waiting for the young man at a big round table laid for eight. Each place was set with a pair of ivory chopsticks and a bowl, plate, saucer, spoon and tiny teacup all made of the finest painted porcelain from Kiu-Kiang. Twelve dishes of cold delicacies were arranged around the table.

Lady Cui stood up at once to greet Jun-rui when he came in, and after a lengthy exchange of bows and civilities, she persuaded him to sit on her right, the place reserved for the guest of honor. The abbot would sit on her left, she explained, as the second-most honored guest. She promptly ordered Scarlet to bring a flask of warm rice wine and two wine cups from the kitchen so she could drink a toast to Mr. Zhang. Leaving the room, Scarlet overheard

Lady Cui beginning her vote of thanks with, "Mr. Zhang, it goes without saying how eternally indebted I am to you—we all are—for coming to our res…" but the rest faded as she closed the door behind her. Coming back in with the wine a few minutes later, she heard Jun-rui saying earnestly, "I'd do anything for her, Madam!" but the two of them fell silent as Scarlet approached.

She poured the wine, then stood patiently behind Lady Cui's carved chair while they drank. Lady Cui nodded for the cups to be refilled; Scarlet did so, then waited again. The wine was strong, and after the third cup, Jun-rui's face was decidedly flushed, but the drinking showed no sign of coming to an end. Scarlet finally had to resort to faking a little cough to remind Lady Cui to dismiss her so she could hurry back to Oriole.

She could've sworn that Jun-rui gave her a friendly wink as she turned to leave. He looked cheerful and confident tonight—and why shouldn't he? He'd made no secret of his deep infatuation with Oriole. And judging by his remarks on the way to the reception room, he was fully expecting the big announcement to be made at the banquet after everyone had arrived. Scarlet thought he was right. What better occasion could there be for Lady Cui to seal the contract between her daughter and Jun-rui than at a banquet in the young man's honor? No wonder Jun-rui was pleased with life, Scarlet told herself. Once betrothed and conveniently installed in the study in the west wing, he'd see plenty of his sweetheart. And it wouldn't be long before Scarlet was obliged to give Oriole a few basic lessons in love!

When she got back to Oriole's room, she found that her mistress had already started getting dressed. Oriole had put on her silk undertrousers and a low-necked white silk inner robe embroidered with turquoise and gold peonies. She was now struggling with a wide turquoise sash, which she'd wound several times around her body below the bosom. Twisting awkwardly, she was trying to fasten it behind her, muttering and cursing irritably.

"Oh, Scarlet, thank goodness you're here!" she exclaimed. "Help me with this—I really can't manage it on my own!"

"Sorry I was so long," Scarlet apologized, tying the sash capably in a matter of seconds.

"What kept you?"

"Your mother," Scarlet answered briskly, disappearing into the dressing room and coming out with a beautiful robe of shimmering turquoise brocade embroidered with gold thread.

"Is Jun-rui with her?" Oriole asked, impatient for news of him. "Are they having their drink?"

"Drinks is more like it." Scarlet laughed, helping Oriole into the robe. "He was quite merry by the time I left!"

"What were they talking about?" Oriole asked as the maid guided her over to the dressing table to fasten on the final hair ornaments.

"Oddly enough," Scarlet told her, "they weren't doing much talking at all. Except when I went out to get the wine. But I did hear Mr. Zhang say something about *you*."

"What?" Oriole asked eagerly.

"Oh, something about how he'd do anything for you!" Scarlet teased, pinning a beaded pendant beside Oriole's temple so that it hung down in front of her ear.

Oriole felt warm inside when she heard this— and even warmer when she reminded herself that it wouldn't be long before she saw him. Her heart beat with anticipation.

"It was funny when I went to his room." Scarlet reached for the other pendant. "Guess what he said?"

Oriole frowned slightly. It sometimes irked her to realize that Scarlet could more or less come and go as she pleased while she herself was terribly restricted—and that Scarlet could spend time alone with the man *she* was to marry. "I can't imagine," she answered with a touch of resentment. "What did he say?"

"'How do I look?'" Scarlet laughed, impersonating Jun-rui's rich voice. "That's what he said! You see, he hasn't got a mirror, so normally he has to ask Lucky if his hair's sticking up or if his hat's crooked." She fastened the second pendant and turned Oriole's head to make sure both pendants hung evenly.

Oriole was smiling despite herself. "How *does* he look?" she asked.

"*Very* nice!" Scarlet answered at once. "Not that the clothes are any different, mind you—he's wearing the usual white gown with the black robe over it. But I'd say he and Lucky have been doing a bit of laundry—everything's so clean and fresh. And he's got a snazzy belt on—yellow leather decorated with horn." She picked up the coronet and turned it thoughtfully this way and that.

"It's not the clothes, though. It's something about him. He looks different tonight. So...so..."

"So what?" Oriole demanded, her curiosity well and truly aroused.

"So yummy!" Scarlet teased. "He looks good enough to make your mouth water."

She fitted the coronet carefully in the center of Oriole's head, then placed a gold brocade shawl around her shoulders. The effect was dazzling.

"And so are you!" she said, genuinely struck by Oriole's beauty. Her mistress might have been a princess, she was so stunning. "You look terrific! You and Mr. Zhang make a very handsome couple."

They finally set off, Scarlet carrying a lamp and

tucking Pug under her other arm. She was going to leave him in a warm corner of the kitchen so he wouldn't be lonely during the long banquet ahead. It was only a short distance to the reception room in the west wing, and as they walked Scarlet chatted about Jun-rui's nervous anticipation earlier in the evening and some of the things he'd said to her. She described her joking response when he'd asked what would be served at the feast: "Oh, a bit of moldy rice, a couple of plates of slimy vegetables and some stinking bean curd like old socks!" Her sense of mischievous fun was contagious, and she and Oriole arrived at the reception room in high spirits.

As soon as they entered, Oriole cast her eyes excitedly around the table, looking for Jun-rui. She was evidently the last to arrive. The abbot and the three high priests, who had all conducted the service, were already seated. So was Di-di, obviously bored with all the adult talk. And there was her mother, dressed in a handsome gown of black brocade. Jun-rui was sitting next to her.

He got up clumsily the moment he saw her and swayed rather than walked toward her, making an exaggerated bow. Scarlet was right, Oriole noted with wry amusement. His cheeks were flushed and he was unsteady on his feet—definitely on the way to being drunk!

She was watching his every move keenly, and as

he made his bow she could see him fishing around inside his sleeve. With some effort, he straightened, then leaned forward and discreetly pressed something into her hand. It was the first time she'd felt his touch, and although their fingers brushed for only an instant, her hand positively tingled afterward. He was gazing at her so intently that she felt the blood rush to her face and a trembling seize her legs. His dark eyes were slightly bleary and kept blinking in a strange way, but Oriole could almost hear them speaking to her. *Come to me,* his eyes were saying, *Come to me now.* Her fingers closed tightly around whatever he'd placed in her hand. It was something round, something cold and hard that grew warmer even as she held it. She had the foresight to slip it quickly into the little drawstring purse hanging from her belt before she got caught up with the other guests.

"Ah, it's the young lady herself!" the abbot was saying jovially. "Come over here, my dear, and let me have a good look at you." The old man rose, as did the others at the table. "My, my!" he remarked approvingly to Lady Cui. "She looks splendid! Absolutely splendid! Well worth waiting for, eh, my boy?" he said with a chuckle, turning to Zhang and giving him a paternal wink. The high priests shared in the abbot's little joke, nodding their bald heads knowingly.

Scarlet watched the proceedings from a respect-

ful distance behind Oriole. Everyone was in such obvious good humor she couldn't help noticing that Lady Cui alone looked aloof and uncomfortable. Scarlet began to feel a little ill at ease. Lady Cui cleared her throat awkwardly and asked her guests to be seated, sending Constance to bring more rice wine and extra cups.

Oriole took her place next to Di-di, across the table from Jun-rui. She imagined an invisible thread running between the two of them, binding them together, keeping their eyes fixed on each other. She heard the conversation and laughter echoing around her, as though from a long way off, and she lifted the wine cup to her lips mechanically, as though in a dream. They were going to drink to her and Jun-rui—they must be. Celebrating the engagement, and then…

Lady Cui's stiff, almost rasping, voice silenced the pleasant hum of conversation.

"As you all know," she began austerely, "the Cui family owes an enormous debt of gratitude to my guest of honor, Mr. Zhang." A murmur of appreciation passed around the table. "It is for this reason," she continued, "that I am now honored to welcome Mr. Zhang into my family, as a son."

The abbot rubbed his hands together with delight, and a look of warm excitement flashed between Oriole and Jun-rui. The suspense was almost too much for her to bear.

"Oriole and Di-di," Lady Cui said after a brief pause, fixing her eye sharply on her daughter, "I want you both to lift your wine cups and drink to the good health of Mr. Zhang. From now on," she said without any hint of a smile, "you will look on him as a brother!"

CHAPTER SIX

ALL THE GAIETY and excitement of a moment before was instantly crushed, and a confused silence fell on the room. Wine cups, which had been raised to drink to the joining of the young couple, remained suspended in midair. No one drank.

Oriole herself was completely stunned. A "brother"? What was her mother talking about? Surely there must be some mistake. A misunderstanding. Her mother must have been addressing Di-di and said "brother" in the sense of brother-in-law, since that was what Jun-rui would be to him after the marriage.... But that look her mother had given her, that sharp cold look. There was no mistaking that! She knew her mother well enough to understand its meaning—it was a warning. It said, *This is what I've decided, and you will do as I say.*

Oriole felt anger rising in her, a tightness gripping her chest. Her mother was breaking her promise! After everything that had happened! After everything Jun-rui had done for them! And without a word of explanation. Oriole's throat was dry and burning, but she refused to obey her mother's request that she drink to her "brother." She put her wine cup down on the table in defiance. What right did the woman have to play with the lives of others in this way? Who did she think she was, to cause such suffering, to dash their hopes so cruelly, hers and Jun-rui's?

Yes, what about Jun-rui?

Oriole was suddenly ashamed. She'd been so overwhelmed by her own shock and outrage that she'd momentarily forgotten about him. If she was angry, how angry must he be, wronged like this and publicly humiliated?

When she could finally bring herself to look at him, she saw sadness rather than anger on his face. He looked like a man who had just received the most painful news, a man who was grieving. His handsome brow was deeply furrowed, and his eyes were misted over; he stared solemnly into the wine cup clenched in his hand.

Tears started to well up in Oriole's eyes. How she felt for him! He was so powerless against her mother, so totally unable to defend himself against the wrong she'd done him. However unjust the situation, it was inconceivable that a young man like Jun-rui could challenge a woman like Lady Cui, a woman of such high rank and social standing. Oriole knew Jun-rui had no choice but to try to come to terms with her mother's decision. What else could he do?

She glared at the austere woman sitting opposite her, hard and cold in her stiff black brocade, with her graying hair combed tightly back from her proud forehead. Could there be anyone else so... unfeeling, so dispassionate? At that moment Oriole hated her mother intensely and loathed everything she stood for. This was something she would never forget and certainly never forgive.

The abbot had been pulling uncomfortably at his embroidered cuffs. He did not wish to appear ungracious or to offend his hostess in any way, but he felt sure that everyone would be looking to him to clear up this confusion. If *he* couldn't confront Lady Cui, who could? Reluctantly he gave a nervous cough to attract her attention.

"Er, Madam, if I might be so bold as to point out..." he began hesitantly. "The young couple...I think you are forgetting—"

"With all due respect, Your Reverence," Lady Cui cut in, "I am forgetting nothing. I am especially not forgetting my late husband and the marriage he arranged between our daughter and my nephew, Heng. Seven years ago, to be precise," she added curtly.

This latest revelation struck like a bolt of lightning. The abbot and high priests were openly shocked, and Jun-rui's involuntary start caused him to knock over his brimming wine cup. Oriole was mortified; it was bad enough that her mother had tricked Jun-rui and turned him down. But now here she was, making the situation ten times worse by announcing Oriole's engagement to Heng—a man for whom she had no feelings whatsoever. Announcing it, furthermore, in front of the man she'd been *promised* to, the man who deserved her love! And at a banquet in his honor! Surely things couldn't get any worse....

Lady Cui, apparently oblivious to the strong reactions she'd caused, motioned to Constance to mop up the spilled wine and then turned to Jun-rui.

"So, now you see, Mr. Zhang, why it is quite impossible for me to give my daughter to you in marriage." She returned his dejected look with a wry smile. "After all, one horse cannot wear two saddles, as the saying goes! But that doesn't mean to say I'm not deeply grateful to you for what you've done. Perhaps there's some other way I could repay you?" Her eyes narrowed as she toyed with the costly amethyst ring on her finger. "With gold, perhaps? Just think! With enough wealth at your disposal, you'd have your pick of any number of girls from good families!"

Oriole was sickened and felt a shudder running through her. Things *could* get worse! Now her mother was trying to bribe him!

"Thank you, but no," Jun-rui answered, his voice slow but unfaltering. He could barely conceal his distaste. "There's only one thing I want, and that's your daughter. If you're refusing to let me marry her, why should I want your gold?''

Lady Cui shrugged dismissively. "Well, you can think it over." She clapped her hands decisively. "Right now I think we're all ready to eat! Constance! Scarlet!''

There was no need for her to say more than this. The maids jumped to attention at once. Wine cups were immediately refilled with warmed wine, and the first course—a tureen of steaming hot-and-sour soup—was brought in from the kitchen and put down in the center of the table. Lady Cui had planned the meal with the utmost care, to provide the greatest variety of taste, texture and color. Twenty courses were to be served in a carefully determined order—two larger, more substantial dishes alternating with two lighter ones.

The second larger dish of the evening, known as "food for the saints"—or "Buddha's fry" to the kitchen maids—was always a hit with the Buddhists. Or so Lady Cui had been told. It consisted of eighteen different vegetables representing the eighteen Buddhist saints. Some of the ingredients—such as dried tiger lily and wood ear fungus—were Oriole's particular favorites, and she'd been looking forward to savoring them. But as it was, her appetite had deserted her completely. The few mouthfuls she managed to force down almost choked her. Even the two vegetarian pièces de résistance, which came toward the end of the banquet, were totally wasted on her: the so-called "roast chicken," molded from flour and sesame oil; and later, the "cold fried fish," made of bean curd, with a small dried prune for its eye. Naturally the abbot and high priests made all the correct appreciative noises as each new course appeared on the table. And even Oriole had to admit that the meal was a work of art; the food was delectable and the presentation exquisite. Considering that the banquet had been postponed for a full week, it was an achievement in itself that Lady Cui had produced so many fresh-looking and appetizing dishes. Thanks to the inventiveness of the kitchen-girls, the effectiveness of the monastery's food cellars and the good sense of Lady Cui, there had been very little waste.

But if the success of the occasion was measured by the amount of food consumed or the gusto with which each course was eaten, the banquet would have to be called a failure. Despite desultory attempts at small talk between Lady Cui and the abbot, a depressed mood prevailed throughout the dinner, and one dish after another was removed from the table, virtually untouched.

For Oriole the entire evening was nothing but an ordeal. It was all she could do to remain sitting there in her mother's presence. Every time she thought of the betrayal, she had to bite her lip and fight back the tears, and several times she came dangerously close to giving vent to her anger and disappointment in a flood of bitter reproaches. She didn't dare look at Jun-rui again, not after having seen his pain; she was afraid she'd break down completely if she did. Even the sound of Jun-rui's desolate voice on the rare occasions he was obliged to speak—to answer some question or other put to him by Lady Cui—pierced her to the heart. She knew it was cowardly of her, leaving him to fend for himself without once giving him a sympathetic glance or commiserating smile. But just keeping a grip on herself was almost more than she could manage.

It was a huge relief to Oriole when the maids cleared away the last course and poured out the green dragon-well tea, marking the end of the meal. Surely even her tactless and insensitive mother would see that her guests were more than ready to leave and bring the evening to a rapid close? Oriole drank the clean-tasting tea gratefully, feeling it ease the dryness of her parched throat.

It wasn't long before Lady Cui was summoning Constance and Scarlet to assist her with the customary formalities of seeing off visitors. *Finally!* Oriole thought. She was to be released from this terrible ordeal and would soon be alone with Scarlet, her only friend. At least then she'd be able to unburden herself.

But it was not to be.

"Scarlet," Lady Cui commanded, "I'd like you to accompany Mr. Zhang to the west-wing study and make sure he's got everything he needs. And, Constance," she continued, throwing a stern look at her daughter, "perhaps you could see Miss Oriole safely to her quarters."

ORIOLE HAD INSISTED they collect Pug from the kitchen before going back to her room. Quite apart from the fact that she didn't want to leave him there all night, she badly wanted to cuddle him and feel his soft warmth. Pug's constant loyalty and devotion would, she knew, be a great comfort in her present despair and loneliness.

Constance was older than Scarlet and far more malleable, and it didn't take much persuasion to convince her to leave as soon as the oil lamp in Oriole's room had been lit. Oriole explained that she was quite capable of getting herself to bed, and anyway, she wanted to be alone.

Once Constance had gone, Oriole stared bleakly around her at the shadowy room in which she'd spent most of her time these past weeks. She realized how very alone she was, and all the anguish she'd been suppressing during the long dinner came flooding back. So nothing was going to change, after all! This was it, until her marriage sooner or later to her dreary cousin, and a dreary life together ever after, no doubt. Hardly something to look forward to.

She marched over to her dressing table and snatched up her mirror, gazing bitterly at the dim reflection of her face. How absurd she now felt, decked out in all this finery. What a fool she'd been to believe that tonight would be a cause for celebration. She pulled the beaded pendants and coronet roughly from her hair and threw them down. They lay there on the dressing table gleaming faintly in the lamplight, mocking her.

And what about Jun-rui? What would he be to her after tonight? A man she'd briefly met? A radiant ghostly figure in a moonlit garden? A fading memory?

No, Oriole told herself with conviction, he would never be that. His memory would never fade. She would always feel about him as she did now. She was sure of that. The strength of her own feeling surprised her, and she realized she'd never really asked herself how she *did* feel about him. She'd known how proud she was of him. She'd known how he was always in her thoughts. But until this moment, she'd never been aware of the *power* of her feeling for him. Regardless of what the future held, she would always keep him in her heart. With a shock she wondered if this was love.

Suddenly she remembered the secret gift he'd given her at the banquet. She hadn't even had a chance to look at it; she'd only felt it and noticed the curious way it grew warm in her grasp. Impatiently she unfastened the little drawstring purse from beneath her sash, pulled it open with trembling fingers and carefully dropped the precious contents into her upturned palm. Hurrying over to the oil lamp, she saw there, in the soft light, a ring of the purest and whitest jade, perfect in form and color. It was very large for a ring—the size of a tiny bangle—and it was beautiful. She understood at once that it was a token of Jun-rui's love for her. The ring in itself was a sign of constancy and never-ending union, and the jade, a symbol of strength and purity. Again, she felt the cold stone grow warm in her hand.

On impulse she rushed to her embroidery box and rummaged around for a thin piece of white ribbon. She would wear the ring around her neck, tucked inside her robe, close to her heart. No one need ever know it was there. It was a keepsake, a memento. It was her only way of being close to him. And true to him. She would treasure it always.

She lit the candles on the side table and settled herself on the large brocade cushion, gathering Pug into her arms and burying her face in his warm coat. She didn't feel the slightest bit sleepy; there were still far too many emotions churning around inside her. One moment it was anger toward her mother, and the next sadness and tears. A feeling of calm came to her only when she remembered the jade ring and considered, with a sense of triumph, that even her mother couldn't stop her and Jun-rui from loving each other. But then, just thinking of her mother inflamed her rage all over again, and the cycle was repeated.

It was in one of these bouts of anger and bitterness that Oriole heard a quiet tap on the door. Pug didn't growl, which told her it must be Scarlet; sure enough, a moment later the maid had slipped into the room as silently as a ghost.

"My poor feet!" she groaned, taking off her shoes and leaving them by the door. "I don't think I've sat down once in twelve hours! 'Do this, Scarlet, do that, Scarlet.' God, what a night!" She flopped down next to Oriole and began massaging her tired feet. "So how are you feeling?" she asked. Under the circumstances, Oriole thought her tone particularly uncaring.

"What do you mean, how am I feeling?" she exploded. "How do you think I'm feeling? How would you feel if you were me? You sit there complaining about your feet when my whole *life's* in ruins!" Now that she'd started, there seemed no stopping the release of pent-up emotions. "I hate her! She's a witch! She's vicious! She's hardhearted and cruel! She's a liar, a mean deceitful liar! I'll never believe anything she says again! And if she thinks she can tear me away from Jun-rui, she's wrong. She can call off our marriage, she can break her promise, she can lie and cheat as much as she likes—but she can't come between us. I'll always belong to him, always. And there's nothing she can do about it! He loves me, and I..."

At this point Oriole was sobbing too much to continue, and it was some time before she quieted down. Pug regarded her with a mournful expression, while Scarlet still seemed totally preoccupied with her own aches and pains. What use was it, anyway, Oriole asked herself, all this ranting and raving? And what good was a memento? It was *him* she wanted, flesh and blood! How could she pretend otherwise? How could she settle for anything less?

"I know," Scarlet said softly after a pause. She was now flexing and pointing her stockinged feet and looking at them thoughtfully.

"Is that all you've got to say?" Oriole asked between sniffs. "I thought you were my friend! What do you mean, 'I know'?"

Scarlet reached behind her for a bottle of camphor oil and rubbed some into the back of her neck. She raised and lowered her head as she rubbed, to help relax her neck and shoulder muscles. "I know your mother's everything you say, and worse," she explained. "I also know Mr. Zhang's head over heels about you. And I know you feel the same."

Scarlet was now moving her head from side to side, still massaging the base of her neck with both hands. The constant swinging movement of her head was making Oriole quite dizzy, and she still felt hurt by the casualness of Scarlet's words and behavior.

"Don't *you* know a lot!" she said sarcastically. "You're really a great help, Scarlet—but not to me!" she added childishly. This was enough to make Scarlet stop what she was doing and look Oriole in the eye for the first time. The maid's jaw dropped instantly in surprise.

"Good grief!" she exclaimed in horror. "Your face! It's all wet and smudged. Like…like a painting left out in the rain!"

For a moment Oriole didn't know how to react, and she bent her head miserably. It was hardly the sympathy and compassion she'd hoped for.

"Listen, I know how disappointed and angry you must be," Scarlet said kindly, tucking a finger under Oriole's chin and forcing her to look up. "Anyone would be. But there's no sense in crying about it anymore. Besides, you're not planning to take this lying down, are you?"

Oriole was confused. "What else am I supposed to do?" she asked uncertainly.

"Heavens!" Scarlet snorted impatiently, rolling her eyes toward the dark ceiling as if seeking divine help. "You're as bad as *he* is! Completely helpless! No wonder there are all these stories about students and their sweethearts dying of broken hearts. Why don't they ever do something about it, instead of lying around moaning and complaining all the time? It's pathetic.''

"But what *can* I do about it?" Oriole asked again, nettled by Scarlet's scathing remarks. "I can't marry him, can I? Not when my mother's forbidden it."

"No, you can't," Scarlet agreed. "But what's to stop you from being with him all the same?"

"Scarlet?" Oriole gasped, her eyes wide with shock. "You can't mean—"

"Oh, yes, I can," Scarlet interrupted. "Let's face it, your mother's made things much easier for you. First she decides to stay on for a couple of months. Then she moves him into the west wing, just around the corner! Now you'll be able to visit him as often as you like without anyone being the wiser. You'll have to do it at night, though," she cautioned.

Oriole's head was swimming and her heart was fluttering wildly. There was nothing she wanted more than to be with Jun-rui. But alone with him in his room? And against her mother's wishes? She wasn't sure she had the courage on either count. And why was Scarlet changing tack? It was Scarlet, after all, who'd as good as dragged her away from Jun-rui that night in the garden and then given her that long lecture.

"I don't understand," she murmured. "What about all those things you said to me before? You know—how I have to forget Jun-rui and marry

Heng and all that? Why are you suddenly saying it's all right for me to do the opposite?''

Scarlet dabbed at Oriole's smudged face with a silk handkerchief. "I think the situation's changed quite a bit since then, don't you?" Her voice was quiet but confident. "You were promised to Jun-rui, and your mother had no right to go back on her word. It was a wicked thing to do, and she shouldn't be allowed to get away with it. But of course she *will* get away with it because she's Lady Cui and no one can do anything to stop her. Still," Scarlet added, with a defiant look on her face, "that doesn't mean to say we have to give in without putting up any kind of a fight!"

Oriole wasn't fully convinced. "But what will it achieve?" she asked doubtfully. "I mean, Heng won't just disappear, will he? In the end I'll still have to marry him."

"Yes," Scarlet answered. "But I don't think you'd be asking that question if you'd heard some of the things Mr. Zhang was saying in the study not so long ago. If it wasn't about doing himself in, then it was about how he'd have to leave the monastery first thing in the morning. Luckily I managed to talk him out of both!" Scarlet concluded briskly.

Oriole was appalled at what Scarlet had just said, and alarmed to realize the depth of Jun-rui's feeling for her. Even the mere thought of his going away was devastating. She couldn't let it come to that.

"How did you talk him into staying?" she asked Scarlet. "What did you say to him?"

"Exactly what I said to you," Scarlet replied. "That it was time to do something and not take no for an answer! I feel sorry for him, you know," she said warmly. "He's such a nice young gentleman. He's taken this very hard, and yet he's always thinking about you and not wanting to make things worse for you than they already are. But what a ditherer!" She smiled, shaking her head. "I can see I'll have to run quite a few messages between the two of you if anything's ever going to get off the ground!" She rose to her feet and stretched, letting out a yawn. "So...what do you think?"

Though still confused, Oriole was clear on one thing. "I know I don't want him to leave," she declared passionately.

"He'll be glad to hear that, at least," Scarlet said, fluffing up the padded quilt on Oriole's bed.

Later, when Oriole was in bed and Scarlet was putting on her shoes at the door, she gave Oriole a final word of caution. "You know what's at stake, don't you?" she warned. "We're going to have to be very careful."

OVER THE COURSE of the next few days, Scarlet went to and fro so many times between Oriole's room and Jun-rui's study and gave so many hours of counsel and encouragement that she began to wonder which would be the first to wear out—her voice or her cloth shoes.

It wasn't that Oriole's feelings toward Jun-rui had weakened or that she wanted him any less than before, but she was consumed with worry and indecision and couldn't bring herself to take the plunge. She knew how terrible the consequences would be—for her, anyway—if she became involved in an illicit affair and got caught. It was not the same for Jun-rui; he'd be able to walk away as if nothing had happened, while she'd be left to face the consequences on her own. This was what she feared most, and the huge gulf between her desire for him and her fear of what might happen made her behave in a most capricious way, quite unlike her normal self. Scarlet, who'd always thought of her mistress as being direct and true to her feelings, found it all extremely puzzling.

When Scarlet had taken Jun-rui to his study after the banquet, she'd managed to talk him out of his gloom and despair by suggesting he might succeed with Oriole if he tried a little "persuasive wooing." She'd even provided him with specific instructions. So the following night, when Oriole and Scarlet were in the Flower Garden burning incense, Jun-rui played a haunting and soulful melody on his zither. Oriole had been so drawn to the sound that she'd crept to the window of his study to listen. Scarlet could tell that her mistress was deeply moved, particularly when Jun-rui played the song "The Phoenix Seeks Its Mate."

The next morning Oriole asked Scarlet to deliver a note to Jun-rui, and Jun-rui had immediately composed a letter and poem in reply. Oriole had flown into a sudden rage on reading his amorous words, insisting that such sentiments were totally inappropriate in a brother-sister relationship. But soon afterward she'd nonetheless written a poem for Jun-rui, which Scarlet duly took over to him. He'd been ecstatic when he read it and told Scarlet that the poem's hidden meaning was a rendezvous in the Flower Garden that very night. Since Scarlet couldn't read, she was obliged to take his word for it and to believe that his interpretation was correct; in any event, she was glad that something finally seemed to be happening.

At midnight she'd accompanied Oriole to the garden—only to witness her mistress angrily rebuffing Jun-rui's advances and marching off in a huff. Scarlet felt great pity for Jun-rui, who stood there alone, looking hurt and bewildered.

The following day Scarlet heard from Constance that Mr. Zhang was ill and that Lady Cui had already sent two physicians to examine him and prescribe some medicine. When Scarlet relayed this information to her mistress, Oriole had seemed genuinely upset and immediately written out a prescription of her own for Jun-rui. Scarlet had pointed out that Oriole should be the first to realize his "sickness" wasn't one that could be cured by medicine, but Oriole had insisted her prescription was "special" and must be delivered at once. It consisted of several ingredients, she'd said—including cassia flowers, vinegar, angelica and ginseng—and it was guaranteed to be effective. Sure enough, much to Scarlet's surprise, Jun-rui made an instant recovery the moment he read the prescription. Scarlet only understood why when he read it aloud to her, laughing as he did so. It wasn't a prescription at all, but a note promising that Oriole would come to his study that night.

No wonder he had such a big grin on his face, Scarlet thought crossly. She felt more than a little foolish at Oriole's deception and hoped there would soon be an end to her games and indecision. Still, it was good to see some color in Jun-rui's cheeks again, and to watch him walking excitedly about his room, full of cheerfulness and optimism. She found herself praying fervently that this time he wouldn't be disappointed.

LATER THAT SAME NIGHT, well after the first watch had ended, Scarlet crept to Oriole's room with just a dim lantern to light her way. They had already arranged that she'd accompany Oriole to the study and then see her back to her quarters later on. Not a particularly happy prospect for Scarlet, to be waiting around in the cold for goodness knew how long, with nothing to do to pass the time. But someone had to keep an eye out, and who else could be trusted with their secret?

To make matters worse, it had begun to rain, and she'd already hurried back to her room once to fetch an oil-paper umbrella. She had no intention of catching pneumonia for the sake of a lovers' rendezvous!

"Oh, well," she said to herself. "Let's hope it's third time lucky!"

Softly she pushed open the door to Oriole's room, expecting to find her mistress dressed in her padded outer robe, ready to set off. But Oriole was nowhere in sight.

Suddenly there was a splashing noise behind the painted screen and then Oriole's voice calling out in a nonchalant tone, "Is that you, Scarlet? Give me a hand, would you? I'm going to bed!"

CHAPTER SEVEN

SCARLET'S PATIENCE was beginning to run out. She had to bite her lip and count to ten before she dared make any response. "How can you be going to bed?" she asked in a controlled voice. "What about your rendezvous tonight? You haven't forgotten about it, have you?"

There was complete silence. Scarlet could picture Oriole behind the painted screen, standing absolutely still over the hand basin, a towel pressed to her face. Eventually she heard the rustle of silk, and Oriole came into the room to answer Scarlet to her face.

"Of course I haven't forgotten," she said defensively, "but I've changed my mind. I'm not going."

Scarlet's blood began to boil, and all thoughts of maintaining self-control abandoned her entirely. "I've had enough of this!" she shouted, throwing up her hands in frustration. "I'm sick and tired of all your dillydallying and all the games you keep playing! You're no better than your mother—changing your mind at the drop of a hat!"

"That's not fair!" Oriole protested. "Anyway, leave my mother out of it! It's got nothing to do with her. It's none of her business."

"I've got a good mind to *make* it her business!" Scarlet threatened. "What do you expect me to do? Just sit around and watch while you torment that poor young man? You'll be the death of him, the way you're carrying on!"

Oriole was visibly shaken by this last remark. Her face grew pale and her lip quivered.

"I don't understand why you asked him to stick around in the first place," Scarlet went on furiously, "if all you wanted was to make him suffer! I wouldn't be surprised if he *did* string himself up, after all you're putting h—"

"Stop it!" Oriole screamed, both hands blocking her ears. "I'm not listening to any more of this!"

"Oh, yes, you are," Scarlet insisted. "I haven't finished yet! You haven't stopped to think about him, and you haven't stopped to think about me, either! How do you think *I* feel? Running between the two of you like a messenger boy, back and forth, back and forth! And for what? Just so you can tell me you've changed your mind? Well, you can get someone else to run your errands for you from now on. I'm on strike!"

She looked quite comical, Oriole thought. Her short plump figure, dressed in red jacket and trousers with an old padded coat thrown on top, was stomping about the room. Even more ludicrous, she was waving an umbrella wildly in the air. Oriole stared at her pensively.

"Why have you got an umbrella?" she finally asked.

"Because it's raining, stupid!" Scarlet answered rudely. But almost before she'd got the words out, it struck her how ridiculous she must look with her outstretched arm pointing the umbrella straight up at the ceiling, more like an imperial swordsman than a lady's maid! She saw the funny side of the situation and glanced at Oriole; the moment their eyes met, they both burst into peals of high-pitched laughter.

"Dear, oh, dear!" Scarlet said, wiping her eyes after they'd calmed down. She was still smiling. "What a performance! Come on, we'd better be off. He'll be worried sick by now!" She paused a moment at the door. "Grab your jacket, then."

"I can't be bothered," Oriole sighed. "We haven't got far to go."

OVER IN THE STUDY—a small wooden building standing alone at the far end of the west wing, quite close to the temple and set in its own little garden— Jun-rui was beginning to feel too apprehensive to concentrate on the book he was reading. It seemed ages ago now since he'd heard the night watchman

passing by on his second round of the night, yet
Oriole still hadn't come.

Every so often he'd think he heard her soft footsteps on the wooden floor of the veranda, but whenever he went outside to look, no one was there. It
must have been the wind blowing in the bamboo,
or the invisible creaking and groaning of the old
building. Once he even thought he heard the jangle
of the pendants she sometimes wore hanging from
her sash, but it was only the wind chimes beneath
the temple eaves nearby. After that he'd stood in
the garden for a while, looking up at the dark
branches of the cypresses and feeling the rain on
his skin. He'd also looked up to the quarter moon,
praying silently to the moon goddess that Oriole
would come to him that night.

Back in his room again he closed the book and
gazed into the guttering flame of the candle in front
of him. He was like a man possessed; he thought
only of Oriole. He knew he loved her wholeheartedly, and it wasn't just because she was beautiful.
She was divinely beautiful of course—there was no
denying it—but she wasn't the only beautiful
woman he had seen in his life. There was something...different about her. Somehow her beauty
touched him in a way the others never had.

Whenever he was in her presence, he felt a
sweetness emanating from her, a gentleness of
spirit, a kindness and quiet warmth. He was also

impressed by her unselfishness and her courage. When Flying Tiger was demanding her as a bride, she'd said she would rather die than live in disgrace, and she'd been more concerned with her family's safety than her own. This showed great inner strength, in his opinion.

He had known from the start that she was someone he could talk to. She was a thoughtful person, he'd noticed, and intelligent into the bargain. Scarlet had told him all about Oriole's passion for reading and her literary accomplishments—not that he needed telling. He smiled to himself when he thought of the various notes she'd sent him. He knew from personal experience that she wrote a damned fine poem! And her calligraphy was firm and gently rounded, just as *she* was. He imagined her slender fingers, so deft and sensitive with the brush, and how masterfully they would explore his body, what pleasure they would give him....

He let out his breath in a long low sigh. Suppose she didn't come? She'd been so tantalizing recently, raising his hopes and then dashing them to the ground. He thought he could understand her fear, and he sympathized with her—but why would she doubt him like this? Didn't she realize how much he loved her and how he wanted to be with her to the very end? Whatever that end might be?

Feeling restless, he went out into the garden again, but there was still no sign of her. The rain was falling more heavily now, and the raindrops felt cold on his skin. He soon went back inside to sit at his desk.

Scarlet had told him not to neglect his studies, not to give up all his ambitions for the sake of a romantic attachment—which was easier said than done. Obviously she didn't understand the strength of his feelings. His every waking moment was devoted to Oriole; he dreamed about her every night. How could he concentrate on the ancient texts under such circumstances? The abbot, too, had warned him about earthly desires and the dangers of the flesh—but what could the old man know of such things? Despite all these cautions, Jun-rui believed in what he felt for Oriole, believed in it above all else. Other people might belittle this feeling by calling it obsession, blind infatuation, passion, weakness—but he didn't care. He believed in it just the same. And he knew it was love.

The guttering candle flickered suddenly and then went out, leaving Jun-rui in complete darkness. As he groped his way toward the bed to get another candle from the small carved camphor-wood chest beside it, he heard the swishing of silk outside his room, followed by a gentle knocking on the door.

Jun-rui had experienced this moment many times before in his imagination, but now that it was actually here, he felt as though his whole body was paralyzed. For some seconds he remained crouched in the blackness as excitement crept over him. He heard a muffled whisper from outside the door—"It's all dark. Maybe he's not here." The thought that she might go away without seeing him roused him to action. He quickly found a new candle and fumbled clumsily with the tinderbox in his attempts to light it, cursing his awkward fingers all the while. At last, when the candle was set securely in the brass candlestick, he hurried to the door and opened it.

"Phew!" Scarlet said, to break the awkward silence. "We were beginning to think you weren't home." She gave Oriole a little push forward. "Well, here she is. She's all yours!"

Since neither one of them showed any sign of taking the initiative, Scarlet decided to leave them alone to get on with it.

"Just open the door and cough loudly when you're ready to go back," she told her mistress. "I'll be out here somewhere. Waiting!" she added pointedly. The closed umbrella in her hand had dripped a dark pool of water onto the wooden floor.

Oriole was having second thoughts. She turned back and threw Scarlet an imploring look.

"Go on!" Scarlet urged, giving her another push.

Then without further ado she went scurrying away across the veranda. She raised the umbrella as she stepped down onto the paved path. She was heading for the small pavilion in the corner of the garden where she would find some shelter from the rain. Oriole followed Scarlet with her eyes until the maid had disappeared into the darkness.

She swallowed hard at the sudden realization that she was completely alone with Jun-rui. This was it! There was nothing for it but to see what would happen next.

As Jun-rui softly closed the door, she turned. They now stood facing each other, not moving, not speaking, but looking deep into each other's eyes. The intensity of his gaze was soon too much for Oriole, and she cast her eyes down, blushing. There were drops of rain on her skin. He reached for her hand and held it in his, moving his thumb gently across it, to and fro.

"You're wet," he said in a quiet voice.

Her eyes moved up his body slowly, from his white robe to the brown skin of his chest, which was beaded with raindrops. Still, she lacked the courage to look at his face.

"You're wet, too," she said faintly. She hardly knew her own voice; it seemed to come from far away, from deep inside her. Her knees felt weak—she knew exactly what he was going to say next.

"We must get you dry." He let go of her hand and reached around her waist to untie her long sash. She felt herself growing dizzy, and her knees suddenly buckled beneath her...

The next thing she knew, she was opening her

eyes to find herself lying on his bed, wrapped in a faded blue-and-white cotton quilt. It had an unfamiliar smell, quite unlike her own bedding, which Scarlet always infused with musk. She remembered the times she'd been near Jun-rui before and recognized it as *his* smell—the smell of a man. Compared to the fragrance of the world she inhabited, this scent was raw and physical. It excited her and she breathed it in hungrily.

He'd moved the candle to the camphor-wood chest and was sitting on the edge of the bed watching her, with the warm candlelight flickering on his face. She thought he'd never looked so handsome.

"I'm sorry," he said, patting the old quilt apologetically. "I told Scarlet I'd buy a new one, but she said not to be silly. She said it didn't matter."

"She's right," Oriole replied happily. "I love it."

She nestled deeper into the faded cotton, relishing his scent and feeling her own body grow warmer and more languid.

"I frightened you just now," he admitted with a concerned frown. "I was too quick, too impatient. It's just that I've been waiting for this for so long, I couldn't stop myself. I certainly didn't mean to grab at you like that. It's probably a good thing you fainted when you did." He stared down at his hands as though he was ashamed of them. "I don't know what you must think of me..." he whispered.

Oriole felt safe and utterly content. As she lay there listening to the rain pattering on the trees outside and watching the candlelight dancing on Junrui's anxious features, she wondered how she could ever have doubted him. How she could ever have been so cruel as to make him suffer. With all her heart she wanted him to feel as happy as she did that very moment. She felt a new flood of passionate longing course through her veins. If she wanted him and he wanted her—what could be simpler? How could there be anything wrong with it?

She touched his cheek with one hand. "Don't be sad," she entreated him earnestly. "You must know by now what I think of you. I've loved you since that first time I saw you—"

He had moved his head down toward her as she spoke, and now his mouth was on hers, silencing her words. He spoke to her with his kisses, gently at first, his lips brushing lightly against hers, and then more passionately, his tongue finding its way between her parted lips and exploring the sweetness of her mouth. It felt strange to her at first, but soon she was eagerly tasting his tongue with hers and shivering with pleasure as his hands caressed her neck and shoulders. He moved a hand downward, inside her gown, but then seemed to hesitate.

"Yes," she breathed, lifting the quilt and trying to pull him toward her. She couldn't understand why he sat up suddenly with his back to her, but then she realized he was pulling off his leather boots. A girlish giggle escaped her. He had soon turned and quickly slid under the quilt beside her. He wasn't laughing.

She noticed the fire in his eyes and was aroused again. She kissed him with mounting passion as he slipped his hand inside the fold of her gown and felt her breasts, and when his kisses had moved down her throat and he had taken her nipple into his mouth, she felt an indescribable burning sensation deep inside. His full hardness pressed against her thigh.

Although she'd never experienced any of this before, she seemed to know instinctively what was coming next and felt herself growing moist in excited anticipation of what was to follow.

His hand glided down over her stomach and moved lightly there in a circular motion under her sash. She moaned softly with delight as he caressed her lower still and slid down to her silk trousers.

"Can I?" he breathed imploringly in her ear.

She made no answer, but quickly untied the silk cord and eased her trousers down over her trembling thighs. He had rolled on top of her in an instant and begun teasing her with his arousal. Before she had time to feel afraid, he gave a sudden thrust and she felt a stab of pain as he penetrated her.

He was groaning as he thrust into her again, and she felt a sudden warmth inside her. It was all over very quickly, and his body soon became limp. "Oriole... Oriole, I love you," he repeated softly, stroking her damp forehead.

He rolled onto his side and lay there studying her with a look of tender concern. She felt bewildered, confused, a little disoriented. She reached in her sleeve for a handkerchief and dabbed it between her legs with a growing sense of alarm.

"You've taken my virginity," she said to him solemnly, searching his face with her serious eyes. "Now everything's changed. Now I'm completely at your mercy. I..."

Her voice trailed away. She closed her eyes, her brow creased in pain. She couldn't finish what she was going to say.

"What's the matter?" Jun-rui asked gently. "I'm here. You don't need to be afraid."

"That's just the trouble," Oriole blurted out. "I *am* afraid! I'm afraid you'll leave me now, and then what will become of me? Who will I turn to?" Her eyes had filled with tears as she spoke; they trickled out and ran down her cheeks. He caught them on his finger and brought it sensually to his lips.

"I'm not going to leave you, now or ever," he said with conviction. "You must believe me. This is just the beginning." He kissed her so that she tasted her own salty tears, and she was immediately certain he meant what he said. She watched the flame of the candle casting shadows around the room as she settled comfortably in his arms.

After a while Jun-rui released a contented sigh and said to her teasingly, "I was beginning to wonder if we'd ever share the clouds and the rain, you and I, but—"

Oriole didn't know what he was talking about. "The what?"

"The clouds and the rain. It's an old expression for what we've just done here in my bed!" he explained, laughing. "Well," he added, in a slightly forlorn tone, "if I'm honest, it was more like a little shower than a real downpour! It can't have been much fun for you."

Oriole was still rather bewildered by what they'd done and didn't know what it ought to feel like. So she didn't reply.

"You must promise me you'll come here again—tomorrow night," he urged her, "and I'll try not to be in such a rush. It was all over almost before it started," he admitted sheepishly.

"You're wonderful," Oriole whispered, snuggling against his warm chest. "I feel so happy."

THEY MUST HAVE FALLEN into a deep sleep in each other's arms soon afterward. When Oriole blearily opened her eyes, the candle had burned itself out and she could see the pale glimmer of early dawn through the paper panels of the latticed window.

"Heavens!" she exclaimed, suddenly wide awake and sitting up in bed in a panic. "I've got to go! Everyone will be waking up, and they'll find out I'm not there!"

The two of them scrambled out of bed and hurriedly adjusted their disheveled clothing. Jun-rui straightened her sash and tucked it up neatly behind.

"Oh, no," Oriole groaned. "Scarlet! She's been out there all night! She'll be furious!" She looked around anxiously. "My handkerchief!" she remembered. "Where is it?"

She rushed over to the bed, lifted the quilt and started feeling agitatedly underneath it.

"It's all right," Jun-rui said, reaching into his sleeve. "I've got it. I'd like to keep it if you'll let me." He pulled out the handkerchief to show her, and she saw that it was dotted with her own virgin blood. She winced and was about to snatch it away from him when he took her hand and squeezed it insistently.

"It will remind me of you and our first night together. Please!" he entreated her.

She thought for a moment. As though to persuade her, he felt inside her robe for the jade ring on its white ribbon. He stood before her, the ring in one hand, her handkerchief in the other, and pressed his lips to hers in a last passionate kiss.

"Now we've both got something to remember

each other by when we're apart.'' He smiled, tucking the jade ring back inside her robe and returning the handkerchief to his sleeve pocket.

As he gazed into her eyes, a worried look crossed his face. ''You promise you'll come tonight? You promise you won't change your mind?''

Oriole nodded her head vehemently. ''I promise.'' Then, reluctantly, she made for the door, opened it halfway and gave a loud cough.

CHAPTER EIGHT

NOTHING HAPPENED, and even when Oriole coughed a second time, there was still no sign of Scarlet. Feeling a little worried, she cast her gaze around to make sure the coast was clear, then hurried to the pavilion in the corner of the garden. She was aware of a light dew on the stone path and surrounding vegetation, and a damp mist in the air.

Oriole could see Scarlet as she approached. The maid was sitting on a wooden bench inside the pavilion, her body slumped over the latticed balustrade that ran between the pavilion's four red-painted pillars. She was snoring fitfully. It was obviously not a deep or comfortable sleep, Oriole thought with a sense of guilt. The umbrella and lamp lay on the pavilion's stone floor, beaded with dew.

Oriole shook Scarlet gently at first and then a little more urgently. The maid shuddered and let out a prolonged snore. All of a sudden she sat bolt upright, her eyes wide open.

"Where am I?" she asked, glancing around at the unfamiliar surroundings.

"In Jun-rui's garden, remember?" Oriole answered softly.

Scarlet didn't reply, but bent stiffly to pick up the umbrella and lamp, then got slowly to her feet.

Neither of them spoke as they made their way furtively back to Oriole's room. Oriole darted the occasional look at Scarlet's face and deduced that she was in an extremely grumpy frame of mind. What was more, she was pale and her nose was red.

Scarlet sneezed loudly as soon as they entered the room and almost trod on Pug, who'd hurled himself excitedly off the bed and raced up to greet them. Ignoring him completely, she went straight over to kindle the brazier and heat some water, muttering to herself as she did so.

Holding Pug in her arms, Oriole came up behind the maid, trying to make peace.

"I'm really sorry, Scarlet," she began in a conciliatory tone. "I fell asleep. I really didn't mean to keep you sitting out there, waiting for me all that time."

Scarlet harrumphed crossly, keeping her back to her mistress. "You certainly got your money's worth last night, I must say!" Her shoulders suddenly hunched as she was overtaken by another enormous sneeze. "Thanks to you, I've gone and caught my death of cold!" she grumbled, feeling around in her pockets and sleeves for a handkerchief.

Oriole dashed into her dressing room and came back with one of her prettiest silk handkerchiefs, embroidered with yellow chrysanthemums. "Here," she said, handing it to Scarlet. "Use this. You can have it if you like."

Scarlet blew her nose noisily, but kept her back turned.

"Scarlet," Oriole persisted in her most apologetic voice, "I really am sorry. I promise it won't happen again."

Scarlet's curiosity was aroused. "What do you mean, it won't happen again? Aren't you going back?"

"Yes, of course I am," Oriole answered with a smile. "Tonight. But I won't keep you waiting so long next time, that's what I meant."

"I'll probably be dead by then, anyway!" Scarlet complained melodramatically.

Pug had started licking Oriole's neck, and his whiskers were tickling her chin. She couldn't help giggling despite Scarlet's bad humor.

"I'm glad someone's got something to laugh about!" Scarlet said sourly, sending her young mistress a reproachful look. Still, she couldn't help noticing the radiance of Oriole's face that morning.

"So why don't you tell me what you got up to in that study?" she asked.

Oriole blushed and averted her eyes, unsure how to go about answering this question.

"Did you do it or didn't you?" Scarlet demanded.

Oriole was taken aback. "Well," she hesitated, feeling acutely embarrassed, "we, uh, we did the clouds and the rain, if that's what you're talking about."

Scarlet raised her eyebrows, apparently impressed. "Mmm, quick work!" she said with a touch of sarcasm. "And you've even picked up the lingo! You're obviously a fast learner."

She saw that the pot of water was steaming on the brazier and carried it behind the screen to pour into the porcelain bowl. She put on a second pot to heat.

"You'll be needing a good wash down there, then," she said to Oriole in her usual down-to-earth fashion, adding in a rather hurt tone of voice, "Not that there's anything *I* can tell you that you don't already know."

Oriole followed her to the screen, disappointed that Scarlet was still determined to be so unfriendly and distant. She put Pug down and clutched at Scarlet's arm.

"Don't be silly!" she pleaded. "You know how ignorant I am about all of this! Apart from that little talk we had the other day, when you told me about 'jade stalks' and 'precious flowers' and those other odd words, I don't know *anything*—except that Jun-rui makes me happy and I want to be with him.

Why, if it hadn't been for you,'' she insisted, forcing Scarlet to meet her eyes, "I'd still be sitting here all miserable, wondering whether to go to him or not. *Of course* I need your help—more than ever!''

Scarlet gave a little sniff; she seemed to be softening.

"Now, tell me about this washing,'' Oriole said. "What do I need to do?''

Scarlet was pensive for a moment, then asked her mistress one or two probing questions. From the answers she got, she soon realized that the young couple hadn't taken any precautions in their first physical encounter. It was evidently high time, Scarlet decided, that Oriole was told a few more of the basic facts of life. She began by giving her a stern warning.

"You're going to have to be a bit more careful in future if you don't want to end up with a bun in the steamer! How would you go about explaining *that* to your mother, eh?''

Oriole's face registered alarm. Scarlet could see that she hadn't considered this risk at all and probably didn't know the first thing about safeguarding herself against it. She felt a bit remiss not to have prepared her better.

"Look,'' she said kindly, "don't you worry. We've got all day to talk about what you can do next time. But right now we need to make sure you're OK *this* time. Luckily for you, I've got a few tricks up my sleeve. We're going to need plenty of hot water—but water on its own won't be enough. I'll have to go out and get some moxa. You stay here and keep your eye on the pot. I'll be back as soon as I can.''

She stuffed the handkerchief up her red sleeve and bustled purposefully out the door with a parting sneeze.

As it happened, Scarlet was gone for at least half an hour—long enough for Oriole to do more thinking than was good for her peace of mind. In the cold light of day she began to wonder whether it had really been so wonderful, after all. She remembered the stab of pain, and the way she'd lain there listening to Jun-rui groaning; she remembered how detached she'd felt from the whole thing. Was it *supposed* to be like that—the clouds and the rain? Was that what her body had ached for? And now Scarlet had caught a bad cold and was talking about serious things like precautions and babies and the possibility of her mother finding out. She wondered whether love was worth it, if it caused all this trouble and anguish afterward.

Suddenly she recalled that she was supposed to be seeing to the water—the pot was already bubbling furiously and sending out clouds of steam. She quickly emptied it into the large bowl, then put still more water on the brazier.

This burst of activity succeeded in jolting her out of her negative thoughts. In the end there was no question about it—she would go to him that night as she'd promised. She would always go to him. They belonged together now. She remembered how she'd felt wrapped in his arms, safe and warm in his bed, and she was in the process of reliving his kisses and caresses when Scarlet walked back into the room carrying a small basket. Still half in a dream, Oriole stood there looking distracted, a soft smile playing on her lips.

"Come on," Scarlet said briskly, putting the basket on the side table and taking something out of it. "Let's get to work!"

She marched Oriole behind the screen, hustled her into the bath and explained how she must wash herself thoroughly with the special agar-agar jelly she'd managed to get hold of. It was a kind of gelatinous substance made from red seaweed, and it had certain contraceptive properties, Scarlet said, if properly used. It felt smooth and slightly sticky.

"You can do this each time," Scarlet told her. "Before and after."

Once the bathing was completed, Oriole was to dry herself thoroughly, put on a silk robe and go over to the bed; meanwhile Scarlet would light the incense and prepare the moxa.

Oriole had had moxa treatments from Scarlet for various ailments and therefore knew what to expect.

She went to the bed and lay on her back as Scarlet had instructed.

The brazier had heated the room a little, but Oriole was still cold in her thin robe, so Scarlet covered her with quilts, all except for her stomach where the first moxa was to be burned. The moxa was a soft natural substance made from Chinese wormwood and one or two other plants, and Scarlet had prepared it by rolling it into several small cones. Before touching it, she'd rubbed her fingers with ash from the incense stick to make sure they were completely dry; the moxa would then not stick to her skin.

When Oriole was comfortable and lying still with her midriff exposed, Scarlet located the first of the acupuncture points where she would burn the moxa. This was a point called Stone Gate, about one inch below the navel. Scarlet put a moxa cone there— having first applied a dab of water to keep the moxa in place—then lit the tip of the cone very carefully by teasing it with the burning stick of incense. Oriole soon felt the heat from the smoldering cone being absorbed into her body. Scarlet was careful to remove the moxa with a small pair of bamboo pincers before the cone had burned right down. This was to prevent scarring or blistering on Oriole's sensitive skin.

Next, Scarlet told Oriole to roll over onto her side so she could burn a second cone on a point about one inch above her right ankle. A third cone was burned on Oriole's hand. The whole process was repeated twice immediately afterward and would have to be done every day for about three weeks if the contraceptive qualities of the moxibustion were to be effective. Oriole had noted, from the fineness and pale yellow color of the moxa, that Scarlet had somehow managed to procure the best quality herbs.

She'd also noted that Scarlet had been sniffing throughout the long procedure and had periodically reached for a small towel to blow her nose, the handkerchief having quickly become unusable. Scarlet was obviously feeling quite ill, yet she'd lavished all this attention on Oriole for most of the morning—and without a single complaint. It seemed only right that Scarlet should be pampered for a change. As soon as the maid had removed the last burning moxa cone from her skin, Oriole slipped out from under the quilts and went to put on a padded robe.

"Go and sit at the table," she told Scarlet firmly as she tied the robe over her thin silk gown. "It's my turn to fuss over you!"

Scarlet had hardly slept the previous night. Her limbs were heavy and aching, and her head was throbbing. She had used up her little remaining energy in administering the moxa treatment; now she felt completely exhausted. She was only too happy to be told what to do and dragged herself over to the tea table, where she sat with her elbows propped on the inlaid wood and rested her head in her hands. Oriole, meanwhile, had collected a handful of dried orange peel and a paper sachet of white powder from her medicine chest. The powder was ground from a hard-to-find root; it was quite expensive but worked well against colds. She put the peel in a bowl of hot water to soften and then made a pot of strong black tea. When the orange peel was well soaked, she wrapped it in a linen bandage, which she wound tightly around Scarlet's head.

"I can't possibly go out looking like this!" Scarlet protested feebly. "What would people say?"

"It's all right," Oriole reassured her. "You don't have to go anywhere. As long as my mother doesn't send for you, you can spend the rest of the day here. You need to rest. I'll get Constance to bring us some lunch—she won't ask any questions."

She poured a cup of tea and tipped in a little of the white medicinal powder, waiting a moment for it to dissolve. Then she placed the cup in front of Scarlet.

"Drink this," she told her. "It'll clear your nose and get rid of some of your aches and pains. I'll go and find Constance."

It wasn't long before the two of them were seated cozily at the round table near the brazier, eating a simple meal of rice, vegetables and hot soup. The medicine had made Scarlet even drowsier, and she was nodding off before she'd even finished her soup. Oriole helped her to the bed and tucked her under the quilt—as though Scarlet were the mistress and she the maid. While she was sitting on the edge of the bed for a moment, looking at Scarlet's flushed but peaceful face, a thought suddenly struck her.

"You know, Scarlet," she said, laughing, "Jun-rui took off his boots, but he kept his hat on all night long! He was still wearing it when I woke up in the morning. Don't you think that's funny?"

But Scarlet had drifted off to sleep, and Oriole was left to enjoy the joke on her own.

THE DAY HADN'T PASSED too slowly for Jun-rui, after all. He'd been in bed most of the morning, sleeping off the excitement and exertion of the previous night. And in the afternoon, he'd got Lucky to clean his study while he sorted through the books and papers piled high on his desk. He realized that he'd allowed himself to sink into a disorganized and untidy state of existence over the past week or so, especially when he'd been ill. But now that his feelings of indecision and uncertainty were behind him, he wanted to make a fresh start—perhaps even get down to some serious study again. More important, though, he wanted his room to be presentable for Oriole's sake. He felt ashamed of the mess it had been the night before, especially since he knew what a refined and sensitive young woman she was. Yes, it was time to put his bachelor habits behind him, he thought, and pay a little more attention to the finer things.

Lucky, a trusted servant and always the first to share in his master's secrets, seemed to have an instinctive flair when it came to understanding female tastes and fancies. He was casting a critical eye at the now clean but bare-looking room. Eventually he made a suggestion.

"Some flowers for the young lady, sir?" he said, stroking his chin thoughtfully.

Jun-rui nodded with enthusiasm. "Good idea," he replied. "I'll do it myself. I think there's still some nice plum blossom in the garden."

Lady Cui had come by earlier in the afternoon on an unexpected "courtesy call," but finding him and Lucky in the middle of spring-cleaning, she'd fortunately kept her visit brief. He felt awkward in her company after the way she'd treated him; it had given him a deep mistrust of her that he wasn't likely to get over in a hurry. And considering that he'd just spent the night with her daughter, he found her visit all the more tense and embarrassing. He'd hardly been able to look her in the eye. He was sure, though, that she'd attributed his awkwardness to the bumbling social ineptness of the typical young scholar and had suspected nothing.

Now it was dark outside, and Jun-rui was sitting

at his desk with a book open in front of him—*The Sayings of Confucius.* He was reading it by the light of a candle, trying to memorize important passages. Though he was making a determined effort to keep his mind on his work, every so often his thoughts would wander and he'd find himself in the grip of a mounting impatience. Time seemed to be standing still, and he wondered if the third watch would ever come.

He admitted to himself that he was afraid Oriole wouldn't be back. He couldn't help remembering her bewildered confused expression when it was all over last night and how distressed she'd been about losing her virginity. Scarlet had made a point of telling him in one of their private chats that her mistress was totally inexperienced. She'd told him he'd have to be especially gentle in his lovemaking. Looking back, he was forced to admit that he'd allowed desire to run away with him completely. He hadn't been as careful or patient as he'd intended. He hadn't given her any warning, hadn't given her enough time. He'd thought more of his own pleasure than hers. She'd probably gone away with the impression that he was an uncaring and selfish brute; their union had probably been an ordeal for her, rather than a pleasure. And now that she'd had the whole day to think about it, she must have decided not to come back for more!

From the darkness of the garden he suddenly

heard the screeching of a magpie, and his heart lightened. It was a good omen. It meant that a lover would return. Jun-rui felt thoroughly ashamed of himself; how easy it was to doubt, he reflected. Why should he expect her to trust *him* when he was so quick to doubt her? He must have faith in her and wait patiently for her to come to him, like she'd promised. She would keep her word. He *must* believe in her.

He flattened his hands on the desk to stop their nervous twitching and tried to resume his reading. He'd read more than three-quarters of the book and had reached a section on virtue. It began:

> There are three things the superior man must guard himself against. In youth, when the physical powers are not yet settled, he must guard against lust....

Jun-rui paused for a moment to consider the whole question of what was lust and what was love. He was pretty sure he wouldn't agree with what the great master Confucius had to say on the subject. But he wasn't sure of his own thoughts, either. He was definitely having trouble sorting them out. The room was warm with the heat from his small brazier, and soon Jun-rui was drowsing away.

The wooden *toc-toc* of the night watchman passing behind the outer wall of the garden woke him from his slumber. It was only a few minutes later that he heard soft footsteps and then a light tap on his door. He also heard an odd growling noise coming from the veranda; when Oriole whispered, "Hush," it stopped. Jun-rui hurried to the door, curious as well as impatient. He discovered Oriole and Scarlet waiting there, Scarlet with a thick bandage wrapped around her head, and Oriole with a small furry thing in her arms—apparently a dog. In the dim lamplight, he couldn't tell which end of the shaggy creature was which—until the end closest to him began to growl again as soon as he took a step forward.

"Hush!" Oriole told the dog a second time. She seemed nervous with Jun-rui standing in front of her and didn't meet his eyes. "It's Pug," she explained in a rushed whisper. "I had to bring him. Scarlet said he was barking a lot last night, and we thought we couldn't risk him waking everybody up, especially not my mother! It's better if he's with me so I can keep an eye on him. You don't mind, do you?"

Jun-rui flashed her a reassuring smile. He liked animals and found Oriole's fierce little companion amusing. He was quite prepared to try to be friends with it. "Not at all," he replied. "The question is, does *he* mind? He doesn't seem to like me very much!"

"Just ignore him until he gets used to you," she

advised. "He hasn't met many men before—besides my father and Di-di—and he's probably just jealous."

She focused her whole attention on Pug for a moment and scolded him gently. "Now you be nice! It's Jun-rui. He's my friend. Hush now, there's a good boy!"

Jun-rui, meanwhile, was looking at Scarlet's impressive bandage.

"What happened to you?" he asked.

"She's got a nasty cold, thanks to me!" Oriole answered on Scarlet's behalf. "She ought to be in bed. I promised her I wouldn't stay so long tonight."

Scarlet wasn't her usual talkative self at all; she turned to go without having said one word.

"You run back to your room now and keep warm," Oriole told her. "And meet me here straight after the fourth watch, all right?"

Scarlet nodded and was gone.

THEIR SECOND MEETING was very different from the first. Although they both knew that their time together was short, neither of them felt rushed. There would be other nights.

When Oriole entered the room carrying Pug in her arms, she was shy and reticent. There were so many things she wanted to talk to him about, but the memory of their closeness in that very bed over there in the corner made her feel more awkward than before. It was hard to know how to begin. And Jun-rui wasn't very forthcoming, either. She wondered if he felt as uncomfortable as she did.

She'd noticed the instant she came in that the room was changed in some way and that there was a fresh smell in the air. Glancing about her, she immediately caught sight of the handsome blue-and-white vase on the camphor-wood chest, full of delicate plum blossom. She went over at once to admire it, with Jun-rui following. He began telling her where he'd picked the blossoms, then launched into a description of his and Lucky's busy afternoon. His efforts to beautify the room pleased her, and she began to relax. They were soon chatting freely, and Jun-rui was showing her some of the little curios he'd picked up on his travels. One was a small stone carving of a man and a woman whose smooth white-jade limbs were tightly intertwined. Oriole blushed when she saw it and her own limbs felt weak and tingling. Jun-rui told her that he often held the carving in his hand while he sat at his desk reading; he said he found the smooth rounded contours of the jade soothing and pleasant to the touch.

Oriole put Pug down on the bed and ran her fingers over the carving, which Jun-rui had placed in her hand. They were sitting side by side on the edge of the bed. Pug seemed to have decided that Jun-rui wasn't a threat and had curled up near them, blinking his eyes sleepily.

As Oriole looked at the two small figures and turned them over in her palm, she found it impossible to tell where one began and the other ended. They were so closely joined they'd become one rather than two. A single shape, in perfect harmony.

This made her think about Jun-rui and the two of them together. She'd felt so distant from the act with him, even when their limbs had been so closely entwined. It bothered her that she'd felt almost nothing and...

She suddenly heard Jun-rui ask what she'd been doing that day, which distracted her from the subject. She told him all about the moxa treatment Scarlet had given her and the "important matters" Scarlet had discussed afterward.

Jun-rui looked very shamefaced when Oriole had finished. "I know," he confessed. "I was careless. It won't happen again. And, of course, using this will help. Next time."

While he was talking, he had carefully taken hold of the white ribbon Oriole wore around her neck and pulled the jade ring from inside her yellow silk robe. His meaning was obvious, and no surprise to Oriole—she'd noticed from the start that the ring was much too large for her own slender fingers. But it was Scarlet who'd explained its actual use to her, that afternoon, after they'd both awoken from a deep sleep. A man wore a jade ring such as this one, Scarlet had told her, to prolong sexual pleasure and to delay "the bursting of the clouds."

"After all," Scarlet had added enigmatically, "a man tends not to be too pleased with himself when he sheds tears at the first sight of the gate!"

The gentle brush of Jun-rui's hand on her neck made Oriole's skin tingle with anticipation, and she leaned toward him almost without realizing it.

He stroked the side of her face and neck and looked into her eyes, which had glazed over slightly at his touch. Her lips had parted a little. He longed to kiss them, but made himself wait.

"You look so different without all that makeup," he commented, tracing his fingers across her forehead. There were no beauty spots and her eyebrows were only lightly painted. His eyes were following the movement of his fingers, as though he wanted to explore every tiny part of her.

She smiled at his ignorance. "This isn't my real face, you know. I've still got makeup on—it's just different from what I wear during the day. It's what Scarlet calls my evening face!"

"Don't do it next time," he urged her. "I want to see you as you really are. And your hair…"

He'd gently turned her head away from him and was pulling out her golden hairpins and tortoiseshell combs one by one until her black hair came cascading down and fell in a long stream down her back. He took it in his hands and held it to his face. It was soft and silky and smelled of rosewater.

"And what about *your* hair?" Oriole inquired boldly. She was curious, and the fact that she had her back to him and couldn't see his face gave her the courage to mention it. She smiled mischievously. "Or maybe you haven't got any! Maybe you're as bald as a monk underneath that hat you always wear!"

He let go of her hair and swiveled her around by her shoulders. His eyes were twinkling as he said, "Why don't you look and see?"

She rose instantly to the challenge by lifting off his tight-fitting black hat. Beneath it, she saw that his hair was brushed into a topknot and held in place by a piece of stiff black gauze. She felt around to see how the gauze was fastened—Jun-rui had apparently decided not to help her and was giving nothing away—and then she untied it and put it inside the hat. A single hairpin kept the knot of hair secure; when she pulled this out, his hair fell to his shoulders. It gave her a strange feeling, seeing him like this, with his face framed by jet-black hair. It excited her, and her breathing immediately quickened. She cradled his head in her hands, seeking his lips with her own.

"Wait," he breathed, moving away from her warm embrace.

He started very slowly to undress her, hanging

each piece of clothing carefully over the back of a chair—the shawl, the padded outer robe, the long sash with its hanging pendants, the yellow silk inner robe, the apronlike garment tied over her bosom, the silk trousers, even the thick-soled socks. When she was completely naked from head to foot, he explored her body thoroughly with kisses and caresses. Her skin was soft and creamy and faintly perfumed. But even though he found her intoxicating and yearned for their bodies to be joined, he still managed to keep his resolve not to lose control. He waited. He waited until she was so aroused she began tugging at his gown and trousers to remove them.

Then they lay together in the warm room, with the soft light of the candle dancing on their nakedness. And when they finally made love, it was because she wouldn't let him delay any longer. There was no pain for her this time—they were moving and moaning as one.

For a long time afterward they lay in each other's arms without speaking, but softly touching and stroking. Oriole felt serenely happy and could tell it was the same for Jun-rui; she didn't even need to ask.

The fourth watch sounded all too soon, and Oriole dressed as quickly as she could, since she didn't want to keep Scarlet waiting any longer than necessary. But when she looked at Jun-rui curled up

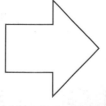

NO COST! NO OBLIGATION TO BUY!
NO PURCHASE NECESSARY!

PLAY "LUCKY 7" AND GET FIVE FREE GIFTS

HOW TO PLAY:

1. With a coin, carefully scratch off the silver box at the right. Then check the claim chart to see what we have for you—FREE BOOKS and a gift—ALL YOURS! ALL FREE!

2. Send back this card and you'll receive brand-new Harlequin Historical™ novels. These books have a cover price of $4.99 each, but they are yours to keep absolutely free.

3. There's no catch. You're under no obligation to buy anything. We charge nothing—ZERO—for your first shipment. And you don't have to make any minimum number of purchases—not even one!

4. The fact is thousands of readers enjoy receiving books by mail from the Harlequin Reader Service®. They like the convenience of home delivery...they like getting the best new novels BEFORE they're available in stores...and they love our discount prices!

5. We hope that after receiving your free books you'll want to remain a subscriber. But the choice is yours—to continue or cancel, anytime at all! So why not take us up on our invitation, with no risk of any kind. You'll be glad you did!

THIS SURPRISE MYSTERY GIFT CAN BE YOURS _FREE_ AS ADDED THANKS FOR GIVING OUR READER SERVICE A TRY!

DETACH AND MAIL CARD TODAY

THE HARLEQUIN READER SERVICE®: HERE'S HOW IT WORKS

Accepting free books places you under no obligation to buy anything. You may keep the books and gift and return the shipping statement marked "cancel". If you do not cancel, about a month later we'll send you 4 additional novels, and bill you just $3.69 each plus 25¢ delivery per book and applicable sales tax, if any.* That's the complete price—and compared to cover prices of $4.99 each—quite a bargain! You may cancel at any time, but if you choose to continue, every month we'll send you 4 more books, which you may either purchase at the discount price...or return to us and cancel your subscription.

*Terms and prices subject to change without notice. Sales tax applicable in N.Y.

there on the bed, so peaceful and drowsy, she wished with her whole heart that she didn't have to leave. She bent to kiss him goodbye and was about to slip out the door when she remembered Pug.

Pug had been so quiet and well-behaved all this time it was hardly surprising she'd forgotten he was there. Hurrying back to the bed to gather him up, she found him lying asleep in a little nest of his own making, with his head resting in Jun-rui's hat.

What had kept him so busy for more than an hour, she discovered to her dismay, was the job of chewing up—quietly, into countless tiny scraps— the piece of black gauze Jun-rui wore on his hair. No wonder he was sleeping so soundly now!

CHAPTER NINE

EVER SINCE her terrible shock on the night of the banquet, when Lady Cui had deceived her so cruelly, Oriole had done her utmost to keep out of her mother's way. This wasn't always easy. They were still part of the same family, after all, and still living under the same roof, only a few doors from each other in the women's quarters of the west wing. It just wasn't possible for Oriole to cut herself off from her mother's company altogether, whatever her feelings.

Lady Cui never referred to what had happened that night and continued to act as though nothing was wrong—which only made it more difficult for Oriole to accept. There had never been a confrontation between them on the subject, so Oriole's bitterness and outrage were left to fester. No matter how many times she went over it in her mind, she couldn't find a way of understanding—or excusing—what her mother had done. It became an unacknowledged barrier between them, one that showed no sign of disappearing with the passage of time.

Now that she'd made several nightly visits to Jun-rui's study and was becoming increasingly absorbed in him and more deeply in love with him, she was far too preoccupied with the present to dwell on the future. Constantly remembering that their love was only a temporary state of affairs would have destroyed her happiness with Jun-rui; she therefore made every effort to put their coming separation out of her mind. For the same reasons, she refused to think about Heng. He'd never replied to Lady Cui's letter and there'd been no news of him at all, so it was easy for Oriole to pretend they'd never been engaged, and that maybe he'd never even existed. On the rare occasions when the reality of the situation forced itself on her, she thrust it from her thoughts at once, pretending that it was nothing more than a bad dream. She refused to contemplate something as terrible as being without the man she loved. She truly believed she and Jun-rui were destined for each other, and everything about their being together seemed so natural and so right. How could she ever reconcile herself to losing him? She *couldn't;* that was all there was to it.

There were times, though, when she felt acutely uncomfortable about the lies and deceptions that now filled her life. It was as if she were simultaneously living on several different levels. Most of the time her thoughts were taken up with Jun-rui, with reminiscences of their past meetings and plans for the next—and that was when the secrecy of their liaison seemed inevitable and totally justifed. But then—when she was with her mother or Di-di or the abbot or one of the maids—she'd suddenly catch herself in the act of lying and would feel ashamed. She'd been brought up to believe that honoring and respecting her parents was a solemn duty, yet here she was, keeping the truth from her own mother. Whatever Lady Cui might have done, Oriole occasionally felt guilty that she herself had become such a liar and dissembler—that she'd gone to such lengths to protect her secret.

At other times, though, she experienced a sense of triumph to think that for once, she'd outwitted her domineering mother. And she'd managed, so far at least, to get away with it. Lady Cui would have been horrified if she'd had any inkling of what was going on right under her nose, and this knowledge sometimes gave Oriole a feeling of precarious pleasure. She was doing what *she* wanted for a change! If her mother imagined she was going to sit around moping until Heng turned up to claim her, then she was wrong.

Admittedly, though, when all was said and done, Oriole still felt distressed about deceiving her mother like this. She wished everything could be simple and straightforward and out in the open. But...if that meant losing Jun-rui, the situation would have to remain as it was, and she'd have to carry on with the lies and deceptions. What choice did she have?

It had reached the point that the only people she could be herself with were Jun-rui and Scarlet, because they were part of the secret. Being with anyone else made her uncomfortable. Not a happy state of affairs.

Oriole lay in bed one morning thinking about these things. She was tired, since she hadn't gone to bed until after two, but couldn't fall back asleep. She'd decided to get up and perhaps have a nap in the afternoon instead, when there was a brisk knock on the door and her mother breezed into the room, with Di-di at her heels.

Lady Cui cocked her head a little disapprovingly at finding her daughter still in bed. "It's almost lunchtime! What's the matter with you? Aren't you well?"

Her brisk unsympathetic tone of voice grated on Oriole's nerves. "I've got a headache," she answered, "but I was about to get up." To change the subject she asked quickly, "What have you and Di-di been doing?"

She'd noticed that her brother was carrying a roll of paper and a brocade bag when he came in. Now he was amusing himself with Pug, throwing the woolen ball for him to fetch.

"Go and do that outside," Lady Cui told the boy firmly. She had a very low tolerance for noise or distraction. Di-di was obviously glad of any excuse to escape into the sunshine, and he made for the door at once.

"We've been at the abbot's residence," Lady Cui said in answer to Oriole's question. "One of the high priests—the plump one called Lee—was giving Di-di a calligraphy lesson. We'll be going every morning from now on."

She settled herself at the tea table and watched Oriole climb out of bed and put on an embroidered gown. The girl had a tired, rather absentminded look about her, Lady Cui noted. She often seemed to be in a complete dream these days.

"You know, I can't seem to keep track of you and Scarlet lately," Lady Cui complained, narrowing her eyes. "One of you always seems to be in bed at the most peculiar times of day! And Scarlet's becoming quite forgetful of late." Oriole sat down across from her mother, but didn't attempt to offer any explanation.

"Speaking of Scarlet," Lady Cui continued, "how is she? She seems to have a nasty cold."

"Oh, she's much better today," Oriole assured her quickly. "She's had plenty of rest and she's definitely over the worst."

"Well, where is she now?" Lady Cui asked.

"She's over at the kitchens," Oriole answered. "I think she's getting the monastery's special recipe. For incense, I mean. We were going to try making some this afternoon."

Lady Cui gave a slight frown. "I trust you're still finding time to work on your embroidery?" she said. "It hasn't been much in evidence recently, and the quilt needs to be finished as soon as possible. Heng could show up at any moment, you know."

"Yes, Mother," Oriole answered glumly. "Don't worry. It's coming along nicely."

"Well, let me see it, then," Lady Cui demanded.

This put Oriole on the spot. She'd done nothing about the quilt since those first preliminary sketches, and the length of red silk her mother had given her was still lying in her embroidery basket, folded and untouched.

"You...you can't see it," Oriole faltered.

"And why not?" Lady Cui sounded vexed. She drummed her fingers impatiently on the table.

Oriole racked her brains for an excuse. She couldn't think of anything that seemed plausible. "Because I want it to be a surprise," she hedged. "Even Scarlet's not allowed to see it. I've told her to wait until it's finished."

"Well, you can at least tell me what it's like. What design did you choose?" Lady Cui persisted.

"Ducks and lotuses," Oriole replied curtly.

"Have you got all the thread you need?"

Oriole waited a moment before answering, trying to look as if she was considering it. "Yes, I think so. But I could use a brighter turquoise for the duck feathers.'' She found herself blushing at the white lies she resorted to in her effort to sound convincing.

"How long do you think it will take you to finish?'' her mother asked next, apparently not ready to end the interrogation yet.

Oriole was in the process of pretending to do some calculations when Scarlet fortunately arrived back from the kitchens, clutching a piece of paper. She bobbed a curtsy to Lady Cui and darted a glance at Oriole. Her mistress seemed reasonably composed, she thought.

"I hear you've been getting the monastery's incense recipe,'' Lady Cui said to her. "I'm surprised they let you have it—it's quite old, you know, and famous. They usually keep these things secret.'' She looked at Scarlet quizzically. "What's it got in it apart from sandalwood?''

"Um…musk, I think. But I can't remember the other things,'' Scarlet answered vaguely. It would have been pointless to consult the piece of paper, since she couldn't read more than one or two simple characters. She handed it to Lady Cui, who proceeded to read out loud.

"Here we are. It's got five ingredients. One and a half ounces of aloeswood. Five ounces of sandalwood. One ounce of storax. One ounce of onycha. Half an ounce of Borneo camphor. And half an ounce of musk.''

"That's six," Scarlet corrected her. "Six ingredients."

She might not have been able to read, but that didn't mean she couldn't count.

Lady Cui frowned. She didn't care to be contradicted, especially by a maid. "Apart from the sandalwood, I meant," she said crossly.

"How do you make the incense, then?" Oriole asked Scarlet. The question was intended to divert her mother and to diffuse the tension in the air.

"You grind all *six* ingredients until they're nice and fine," Scarlet said pointedly. "Then you strain them through a piece of gauze. After that you mix them with honey to make a paste. And then you wait for it to dry."

"Sounds simple enough," Lady Cui commented. "Give me some when it's done. I'm quite partial to the monastery's special mix. The abbot uses a lot of it. I've noticed how his rooms always have a particularly pleasant smell."

Di-di poked his head around the door at that moment and threw his sister a cheeky grin. She wondered why—until a few seconds later when Pug came scrambling over the threshold and raced across the matting, scattering a trail of dried leaves and twigs behind him. He was absolutely filthy.

"What have you been *doing* to him?" Oriole

gasped as the scruffy little creature lay down at her feet, panting heavily.

"Nothing," Di-di answered unhelpfully.

"Well, then, wipe that silly grin off your face and get your things. It's time for lunch." Lady Cui spoke brusquely to her son, then turned to Oriole. "What about you?"

"Oh, I'll have my lunch here. Scarlet can bring it to me." She was picking the bits of debris out of Pug's dirty coat and thinking irritably that she'd have to bathe him now.

Before Lady Cui stepped out the door, she paused to give her daughter another reminder.

"Don't forget your embroidery, Oriole. I shall look forward to seeing it soon!"

THAT NIGHT after the third watch had sounded Oriole crept over to the study as usual, with Scarlet accompanying her. Pug was tucked under her arm. He was clean again and no doubt looking forward to getting his teeth into the juicy bone Oriole had brought for him. Oriole wasn't wearing makeup, and her hair hung loose, as Jun-rui had requested. She'd decided to try out a new perfume that night, made from rose mallow; it gave her skin a subtle fragrance she thought Jun-rui would like.

When she got there, she found that he'd prepared a surprise for her. He'd put his zither on a long table and was sitting on a low stool behind it, waiting for Oriole to arrive so he could play for her.

His zither was one of his most treasured possessions and a particularly handsome instrument. It was made from paulownia wood, inlaid with birds and flowers in mother-of-pearl; it had jade tuning pegs and a jade bridge, and its seven long strings were made of silk of different thicknesses. Oriole had heard him play once before and felt a tremor of excitement at the prospect of hearing him a second time. He seemed to have a way of making the instrument speak that she'd never encountered before. He could make the strings sigh and moan or laugh and sing. That other time—before they were lovers—he'd played music that was so sad and haunting she'd felt like weeping. And then he'd played a tune so light and airy it had lifted her soul and filled her with tenderness. No wonder they called it the instrument of love!

The room was cozy in the candlelight, and a fresh branch of blossom stood in the blue-and-white vase. Oriole sat there on the bed listening to Junrui play "The Phoenix Seeks Its Mate"—the song that had moved her so much the night she'd first heard it, the song that had drawn her close to his study window. She found herself remembering the dream she'd had about the goddess and the Old Man under the moon with his red thread, and Junrui playing the zither in the rain. He had touched her in that dream, and she'd been ashamed when she awoke. It seemed so long ago now, as though it had happened in a previous life. Who would have thought it possible that one day she'd be here sitting on his bed, so familiar with him and his caresses and always hungering for more....

He'd stopped playing and was staring at her intently.

"You look so faraway," he said, a little perplexed. "What are you thinking about?"

She was startled, as though brought back to earth too suddenly. She wasn't sure she wanted to tell him about the dream—he might not understand. He might think badly of her. He might think it was too childish. Or hopelessly romantic. On the other hand, he was the one person she didn't want to keep secrets from.

"I was remembering a dream I had before we were together," she began.

"What was it about?" Jun-rui asked.

She took a deep breath and told him, concealing nothing. She even told him how strange it was the first time she'd come to his room, because she'd seemed to know exactly what was going to happen and what he was going to say. He didn't laugh at her or tease her about it; he just looked thoughtful, and once or twice opened his mouth as if he was about to say something but then changed his mind.

"What is it?" she asked him gently.

He hesitated a moment. "You probably won't believe this, but I had a dream, too. It was before I got ill, the night we met in the Flower Garden when you were so mad at me and went stalking off. Remember?"

Oriole blushed at being reminded of it. How could she have treated him so unkindly? It was surprising he'd wanted her at all after that.

"Yes, I remember," she said, staring down at the floor. "I wish it had never happened."

He took her hand in his. "It doesn't matter now," he said reassuringly. "I just wanted to tell you about my dream. It was when I'd come back from the garden. I was so miserable. In fact, I'd given up hope altogether. It was cold, and I got into bed with all my clothes on and fell fast asleep. And then I had the most beautiful dream. The odd thing is, it was almost exactly the same as *your* dream, except that you were playing the zither here in my room and I was lying on the bed listening. I was half-naked. And when I woke up, I thought it had really happened. Then I realized I'd only been dreaming, and that was when I got so sick. I think I must have been the most disappointed man in the world—until your prescription arrived to cheer me up!"

He squeezed her hand and noticed that her eyes were brimming with tears.

"I always thought we were meant for each

other," she said passionately, "and now that you've told me about your dream, I'm even more convinced. Why else would we both dream about the red thread?"

"Yes," Jun-rui agreed. "It's a sign that we're destined to be together. That's what it ought to mean, anyway. But the fact of the matter is…you're already engaged. So where does your cousin fit into all this?"

"I don't know," Oriole answered with an unhappy shrug. "I'd rather not think about it."

They were both silent for a while, overwhelmed by the hopelessness of their situation. They might feel they were meant for each other, but circumstances seemed to be dictating otherwise. Circumstances that were definitely beyond their control.

After a few minutes Jun-rui squeezed her hand again. He hated seeing Oriole look so sad.

"It's funny about the zither," he said, smiling. "I wonder why you were playing it in my dream?"

She smiled back at him, overcome by a sudden rush of love. The situation was hard for him, too, yet he never dwelled on his own troubles; he was always thinking about her happiness, instead of his own. She gazed into his dark eyes and stroked his black hair. Protesting their fate didn't do any good. They simply weren't strong enough to oppose it. How could the two of them—however much in love they were—take on the whole social order, of which Lady Cui was like some kind of formidable figurehead? It wasn't possible. She knew—as she'd known all along—that they had only one choice. Seize the moment and make the most of their short time together. It was too precious to waste.

Suddenly, she realized exactly what she wanted to do. Much to Jun-rui's surprise, she asked him to lie down on the bed, then loosened his gown and trousers to make him more comfortable. She settled herself on the low stool behind the table. Soon she began to play for him, better than she'd ever played before, her fingers rippling the strings of the zither so softly and fluidly that the notes merged into one another like a waterfall of sound. As Jun-rui lay there with his eyes closed listening to her, he could feel her love for him filling his body, her fingers dancing lightly on his tingling flesh. Her music was touching him, and he wished it would go on forever. Even when she'd stopped playing and had come over to the bed, he could still hear her music echoing in his ears.

"There now," she breathed in his ear. "Your dream's come true."

And their union afterward was like a song's crescendo, followed by serene peace.

A WEEK OR SO LATER, when Oriole was about to leave the study after another of her amorous visits, Jun-rui thrust something into her hand and mum-

bled a few words to the effect that she might like
to look at this sometime. It was a hard rectangular
package wrapped in a grubby piece of linen. She'd
stuffed it up her sleeve so that she'd have both
hands free for holding Pug and had slipped away
without asking what it was. She'd gone straight to
bed when she got back to her room early that morning and had thought nothing more about the linen-
wrapped package until much later in the day, when
she suddenly remembered having hidden it in her
embroidery basket.

Curious, she fished it out and carried it to the
sandalwood table. The late-afternoon sunlight
streamed in through the paper panels of the latticed
window, and from the courtyard came the sound of
sparrows twittering. Unwrapping the linen, she saw
an old book with a tattered blue-silk cover and a
title written in faded gold characters. After puzzling
over the writing for a little while, she managed to
make out what it said. If she understood it correctly,
the title read, *Strange Positions for the Flowery
Battle,* and there was a subtitle beneath in smaller
characters that read, *On the Art of the Bedchamber.*

Battles? In a bedchamber? Intrigued by the title,
Oriole opened the book at random to see if she
could find out what it was all about. The book fell
open at an illustration, and as soon as she saw it,
her cheeks flushed bright red and she broke into a
hot sweat. She quickly slammed the book shut,

fumbled for the silk handkerchief in her sleeve and began dabbing her cheeks and forehead nervously, wondering if she was imagining things. Had she really seen what she *thought* she'd seen? And if so, what had induced Jun-rui to give her something as explicit as that?

When she'd calmed down a little, she decided she'd try looking at the book again just to make sure. It fell open at a different illustration, but this one was every bit as immodest as the last. She'd never in her life seen pictures like these, and her automatic reaction was to avert her eyes, but then she forced herself to take a closer look. Her breathing had quickened and her skin was damp with perspiration. She wiped her face again, clutching the handkerchief tightly in her moist palms.

On closer inspection the picture proved to be even more blatant than she'd first thought. It showed a woman, totally naked apart from her embroidered shoes, sitting on a folding chair with her legs propped over its wooden arms, exposing her private parts for all the world to see. Her peculiar arched position made her stomach appear large and bulbous, and her breasts were bulging down over it in a very unattractive fashion, Oriole thought. A naked man was striding toward this woman—his jade stalk, as Scarlet had called it, leading the way—with his hands outstretched and a wicked leer on his face. Behind the man and woman was a large painted screen of an elaborate mountain landscape.

Oriole moved her eyes to the page opposite, where there was some writing. She could tell it had been hand-copied—like the illustrations, which were drawn and colored by hand. She read the heading, which said, "Picture 21: Hitting the Butterfly," and then the paragraph that followed: "The painted screen is warm with spring and delights the hankering lust of the crazed lovers. She sits leaning backward in the chair with her dainty feet spread, letting him thoroughly explore the fragrance of the Flower. Now it is time for him to display his marksmanship."

Oriole paused for a moment, puzzled, and looked back at the picture to see if she'd missed something. Where was this flower? And what did it mean about marksmanship? He was totally nude—not exactly dressed for archery! And there was no sign of bows and arrows....

Gradually, Oriole began to understand. It couldn't mean flower as in "precious flower," could it? It surely wasn't referring to the woman's...? Oriole was shocked. Scarlet had used all these odd expressions when they'd talked—like "jade stalk" and "turtle-head" or "pleasure pavilion" and "red grotto." But Oriole had never expected to come across such words in a book. Nor the graphic pictures to go with them! It was all a rather rude awakening.

She'd been too busy peering at the picture to notice a shadow outside the window.

She turned back to the text to read the second paragraph; maybe this would throw more light on the picture—and teach her some new words.

"The Red Heart is clearly visible and is offered straight to the precious lover. He does not tire of hitting the mark and piercing the bull's-eye. Now he comes forward, then he retreats. Untold times they engage in this bloody battle. The hoofs of the Horse trample left and right. The Butterfly flutters—now far, now near. Look! The arrow has entered!"

"Arrow, my eye!" Oriole muttered, pushing the book away in disgust. She didn't care to think any further about what it was describing. "What a load of rubbish!"

Out of the corner of her eye, she saw a shadow flitting past the window; almost immediately there was a tapping at the door. She scrabbled desperately around for the piece of linen so she could cover up the book—it wasn't something she wanted to get caught with! But she'd left it too long to call out, "Wait!" because whoever was outside had already opened the door and stepped into the room. Oriole just had time to throw the cloth over the book. She was now standing at the table, clutching the book to her chest, afraid that the look on her face would give her away. Almost at once, though, she heaved a huge sigh of relief. Thank goodness—it was only Scarlet!

Scarlet, however, was regarding her in a very odd way, which made Oriole feel quite uncomfortable.

"Why are you staring at me like that?" she asked nervously.

"I've been watching you from the window," Scarlet replied, continuing to stare at her. "It's a long time since I've seen you so wrapped up in a book. Must be a good one!"

"Oh, not really," Oriole said, trying to sound casual. "It's just something my mother gave me about…uh, embroidery."

"Pull the other one!" Scarlet said with a snort, moving toward the table and giving Oriole a knowing look. "It's not as if you need to have any secrets from *me*. Why don't you just tell me? Come on—I'm curious!"

The two of them were now standing face-to-face, and it was impossible for Oriole to hide her embarrassed blushes from Scarlet's discerning eye. She glanced away, then down at the covered book, wondering what to do about her awkward predicament. She could, of course, just tell Scarlet to mind her own business. But that wouldn't stop her from wanting to know exactly what this mysterious book was, and Scarlet could be pretty persistent. Anyway, Scarlet did have a point; Oriole acknowledged that she shouldn't be hiding things from her, not after what Scarlet did to help her each and every day. Besides, the book had aroused her own curiosity enough that she wouldn't mind hearing what Scarlet had to say about its flowery writing and explicit pictures.

"Go on," Scarlet urged. "Tell me."

Although she wasn't sure how to set about describing the book, Oriole looked Scarlet in the eye and tried to keep her voice steady. "It's a book Junrui gave me. I don't completely understand it, but it's about battles and butterflies and archery, stuff like that...."

Her voice trailed away. She realized she wasn't making much sense.

"What on earth are you talking about?" Scarlet asked in surprise.

Oriole tried again. "Well, it's got pictures of people totally naked, sitting on chairs and—"

"I think you'd better show me," Scarlet interrupted.

Oriole sank onto a sandalwood stool and pushed the book across the table to Scarlet, having first removed the cloth. She lowered her eyes when she saw the maid about to open it. From the sound of rustling pages, interspersed with occasional comments like, "Oh, my!" or "That's a good one!"

she deduced that Scarlet was in the process of leafing through it.

The rustling sound suddenly stopped. Scarlet poked her and said in an amused tone, "I bet you haven't tried this one yet."

Although she'd been striving to remain aloof from the whole thing, Oriole's curiosity got the better of her, and she turned her head to find out what Scarlet was referring to. Scarlet was staring at a picture of a naked woman hanging from a clothes rack with a man standing in front of her, his "jade champion" well and truly engaged. Though Scarlet looked as if she was having difficulty keeping a straight face, Oriole's reaction was more surprised.

"No, Scarlet. Of course I haven't tried that one! What do you think I am? This is just a book—real people don't do those things!" she said indignantly. "And besides, how could I? There isn't a clothes rack in the study."

That was finally too much for Scarlet. She bent almost double, clutching her sides, screaming with laughter. "A good thing, too!" she managed to blurt out between guffaws. "I mean, he's only got to push a bit too hard and the whole contraption will topple over and that poor woman'll land flat on her back!"

It was an alarming thought, but also kind of funny. Oriole couldn't help smiling.

"Tell me what the words say," Scarlet said when she'd stopped laughing.

Oriole told her the picture was called "The Magpie on the Branch"—which gave Scarlet another attack of giggles—and then read her the two paragraphs that followed. Scarlet found it all highly entertaining, and she especially enjoyed the part that said the man couldn't reach "the Peony on its high perch" without the help of a stool, because his legs were too short!

"Read me this one now," Scarlet said, turning back to a page where there was a picture of a man and a woman making passionate love in a large porcelain bath full of water.

As they turned the book's pages and encountered one astounding position after another, Oriole started to find the pictures less shocking. Not so inhibited now, she was able to ask Scarlet questions about what she saw.

Scarlet had said that not all young ladies were lucky enough to have maids as knowledgeable as *she* was to help them with their love lives. That was why books like this were quite commonplace. They were like sex handbooks, designed to teach innocent young couples—especially women—the art of the bedchamber. Jun-rui must have lent her the book to give her some new ideas and add to her pleasure. Real people *did* do these things, Scarlet assured her. That was the point!

Oriole was beginning to find the book quite intriguing and could see that it opened up a whole new dimension of experience and exploration. What she and Jun-rui had done together paled by comparison. There certainly seemed to be a whole wealth of choice available! She'd had no idea!

When they'd looked through most of the book together, one thing still bothered Oriole. She couldn't understand why—when almost all the twenty-two pictures had only a man and a woman in them—two or three of them included a third person. This third person seemed to be helping out in some way. In fact, one picture had what looked like a maid lying at right angles to the woman, underneath the woman's waist, sort of propping her up and arching her back. As far as Oriole was concerned, her amorous encounters with Jun-rui were something just between the two of them, and she couldn't imagine why anyone else needed to be present at such an intimate moment. Eventually she asked Scarlet about this.

"Oh, it's done quite often," Scarlet explained. "There are lots of things a maid or boy-servant can do to help—like holding up clothing that's getting in the way, or stopping the clothes rack from falling over!"

She had another little laugh over this, but soon stopped and said to Oriole in complete seriousness, "Maids are often invited to join in, you know. I always guessed you'd prefer to get on with it by yourselves. But I'd be more than happy to help if—''

"That's quite all right, thank you," Oriole interrupted, declining the offer firmly. "I think we can manage perfectly well on our own!"

CHAPTER TEN

THE WEEKS SPED BY with Oriole hardly noticing how quickly time was passing. Lady Cui continued to enjoy life in Puzhou and had repeatedly put off their departure for Boling. The last of the spring blossoms had long since shriveled and fallen, and the hundreds of deciduous trees in the monastery's many gardens had budded and come into leaf. The willows in the Flower Garden draped their glowing green branches over the sparkling lake. The lotuses burst into flower in white and glorious shades of pink. The weather had been growing steadily warmer, and the days were gradually becoming longer until now each day was full of burning sunshine, and darkness fell late in the evening. Birds announced the breaking of each new day with a vibrant chorus of song, then continued their contented twittering until the sun went down at night. The ducks and other waterfowl swam and splashed among the lotuses or settled at the water's edge to bask in the sunshine.

Scarlet and the other maids had folded all the winter clothing and bedding and packed them away in trunks and boxes, with liberal quantities of camphor to keep out moths. Summer clothing and coverlets had been aired and freshened in the warm sunshine. Bees buzzed lazily from flower to flower, and the occasional early cricket chirruped in a courtyard or garden. Di-di amused himself—when he wasn't obliged to work at his lessons—by catching the largest crickets he could find and putting them in tiny bamboo cages he'd made himself. His plan was to fatten them up for fighting if they didn't die on him first. Sometimes he caught a smaller cricket and fed it to his pet canary.

Pug was shedding badly and needed regular combing and brushing, which Oriole did every afternoon. The poor little dog was uncomfortable these days; he'd lie panting in the shade during the hottest hours. And he had no desire to run and play except toward late afternoon, when the day started to cool.

Jun-rui was by now so much a part of Oriole's life that she'd almost forgotten what it had been like before she met him. She couldn't imagine how she'd managed to get through those days. What could possibly have made them seem worthwhile? Had her life *really* consisted of long hours at the dressing table for makeup and coiffure, of embroidery and painting, of the occasional furtive dipping into books of poetry and tales of adventure? It wasn't that she didn't enjoy these activities, but how had they succeeded in filling all her days? How had she survived the monotony and the routine without ever having something to look forward to— as she did now?

Now, for example, she could happily spend an afternoon painting, because she knew that in only a few hours she'd be with Jun-rui again. She was equally happy to sit and sew—but not the quilt her mother was increasingly impatient to see. She'd been very busy for a while working on something for Jun-rui, though she hadn't told him about it yet. It was an undershirt, which she was embroidering with a dragon and a phoenix, symbols of good luck.

It couldn't be denied that their luck—hers and his—had held up pretty well, especially since they'd become, if anything, a little careless as the weeks went by. Now that everyone was going to bed later because of the long summer evenings, Oriole usually went over to the study around midnight and didn't return to her room until shortly after the sixth watch was sounded, at about five in the morning. They were spending more time together, but it never seemed enough; there was always so much to talk about, and their physical ardor showed no sign of weakening.

Ever since Oriole had looked through the handbook Jun-rui had given her—which he told her he'd picked up in the brothel quarter of Chang-an on one of his previous visits to the capital—they hadn't tired of experimenting with the various positions and techniques it described. Among the ones they'd tried, they had discovered a couple of favorites. Their appetite for each other seemed insatiable, and they lived as though they had all the time in the world to carry on with their sexual adventures.

One day recently, Oriole had plucked up the courage to ask Jun-rui something she'd been curious about for a long time, ever since their first night together. She'd felt so naive and clumsy, whereas he'd seemed so much more at ease—and she couldn't help wondering why. Sometimes she'd catch herself speculating about whether Jun-rui was the kind of man Scarlet had once told her about—the kind of man who went to the big city to learn the "facts of life." Jun-rui had often spoken of his visits to Chang-an and he'd mentioned the brothel quarter once or twice, so she wondered, somewhat obsessively, whether that was where he'd gained his experience. And if so, with whom? How many times? Had there been more than one woman? Before long, she'd find herself trying to picture what these women looked like, what they wore, how they did their makeup, how gifted they were at their profession... It pained her so much to think of Jun-rui with anyone else that she'd have to force herself to banish such thoughts. But they always made their way back, to hurt her all over again.

This was the first time Oriole had ever suffered from a lover's jealousy, and she found it a bitter experience. It seemed as though a kind of poison was spreading through her body, creating suspicion and turning her thoughts sour. For a while she couldn't give him her love as freely as before, and sometimes she even doubted the sweet words he spoke to her, wondering whether he'd already said them to someone else. Eventually she realized that this poison wasn't going to disappear of its own accord. She would have to tell him about it—or it would destroy her love for him.

When she finally did, he'd listened to her without interrupting. He'd held her close and called her his silly darling, asking her how she could possibly have thought that of him and why hadn't she mentioned this before.

He confessed that once, in the capital, his friends had bullied him into visiting one of the pleasure houses with them. Nothing had come of it, he said. The girl had been pretty and willing, but he'd felt nothing for her, so he hadn't wanted to do anything; it was as simple as that. He'd listened to her singing until she was red in the face, and she'd told him a great deal about the tricks of her trade. But there'd been no lovemaking, he swore. His friends had, of course, teased him mercilessly about having nothing to show for his night in the pleasure house.

He was looking at Oriole with such an open honest expression she didn't feel she had any cause to doubt him. She felt the poison drain out of her, and a sense of relief and comfort immediately flowed through her. She didn't believe he would ever lie to her; she didn't think he was even capable of it. The directness of his gaze, the love he always showed her—these were sufficient proof.

Her love for him was strengthened and renewed by this experience, and she promised herself she'd never hide her thoughts from him again. She didn't want to expose herself to this bitter poison a second time. Once was enough!

SOMETIMES IT FELT to the lovers as though the monastery had become their home, so that they were able to forget they would ever have to leave it. All those weeks ago back in early spring, Oriole's family had come to the monastery as a refuge from Flying Tiger and his band of brigands. But that had all been sorted out—almost three months ago now—and there was nothing to prevent Lady Cui and her entourage from continuing their journey and getting her husband to Boling and properly buried at long last.

But since Lady Cui was rather enjoying life at the monastery, she didn't feel in any particular hurry to leave. The coffin was in good shape. There were plenty of monks around to say daily prayers to honor her dead husband and safeguard his spirit.

And Di-di was making progress with his calligraphy lessons. Not only that, it was much too hot to travel now. Far better to wait until early autumn, when it would at least be a little cooler.

More to the point, there still hadn't been any news from Heng. For all they knew, he was at that very moment on his way to join them. And really, the Monastery of Universal Salvation was the ideal setting for the marriage ceremony. So why not just wait a few more weeks? By that time Heng would probably have arrived and the wedding could take place. The newlyweds would then be free either to return to Heng's house in the capital or to travel on with Lady Cui to the northeast—to spend the winter there, perhaps?

Lady Cui was pleased with life in general. And she was especially pleased to see the dramatic change in her daughter's behavior. There had been some difficulty a while back, what with all that romantic nonsense about love and marriage and wanting to choose her own husband. And then there'd been the whole business with Flying Tiger, and afterward all the sulking and black looks about not being allowed to marry that young student. But everything seemed to have resolved itself. Oriole had left those silly ideas behind her and finally come to terms with her engagement. She never complained about it now; furthermore, she was always totally in agreement with any suggestion made by Lady

Cui. It was really quite gratifying for a mother not to have to put up with all that resentment and argumentativeness. To know that everything was going to work out as planned.

You only had to look at Oriole to see the improvement in her. When Lady Cui thought back to early spring and the time of her husband's memorial service, she remembered how pale her daughter had been, how miserable and listless. She'd had the appearance of a girl who'd just been crying and needed a good night's sleep! And after that, Lady Cui remembered, when the girl hadn't got her way about marrying the abbot's protégé, there'd been a long period of time when she was just plain sullen, not to say hostile.

But to see her now, you'd hardly think it was the same person. Her face had filled out a bit, and there was definite color in her cheeks. She looked stronger and healthier. And she just seemed so much happier with life.

What exactly was it that made her seem different? Lady Cui wondered. It wasn't just the obvious physical changes. No, it had something to do with poise and self-assurance. Something to do with growing up—yes, that was it. Lady Cui realized that her daughter was no longer a girl; she had quite suddenly become a woman.

Of course, not *everything* was perfect. There were one or two niggling little things that irked

Lady Cui and offended her sense of order. One was that Oriole still kept irregular hours and often seemed to be eating, sleeping and bathing at odd times of the day. Another was the quilt. Lady Cui had lost count of the number of times she'd been told to be patient, to "wait and see" when she'd asked how the embroidery was progressing. It didn't seem to make any difference whether she was cross about it or cajoling or insistent. Oriole would always look at her with that imperturbable expression and those dreamy eyes and tell her to wait a little longer. The girl could be so infuriating!

Still, this business about sleep. She supposed it wasn't really worth fretting about. As for the quilt, she'd just have to trust that it would be finished sooner or later. At least Oriole wasn't making a fuss about the wedding any more. That was the main thing. One had to be grateful for small mercies.

THE NIGHT WAS HUMID, as well as hot, and Jun-rui and Oriole were sprawled on his bed, fanning themselves and feeling lethargic. They were both wearing their thinnest silk gowns—Oriole's was a pretty pale apricot color—and Oriole had her hair tied up to keep it off her neck.

Pug lay stretched on the floor in front of the open doorway, where there was the tiniest hint of a breeze. Occasionally he gnawed half-heartedly on a bone. It was really too hot for man or beast. Too hot to do anything much, except lie there and pant.

Oriole had lain beside Jun-rui in silence for some time. Suddenly she let out a long sigh and said in a slow breathless voice, "I'm so hot. Couldn't we have the window open?"

"It is," Jun-rui replied lazily.

"Well, the door, then?"

"It is," he drawled.

Oriole kicked her feet impatiently, then tried to lie still. After a few minutes she spoke again.

"Wouldn't it be lovely to go outside? Near some water? It's so stifling in here."

Jun-rui rolled over sleepily and fanned her with his bamboo fan. It was simple and crudely made, but much more effective than her own elaborate fan with its peacock feathers and fancy tassels. She felt as though she could breathe again. And even laugh.

"What's so funny?" Jun-rui asked, mildly curious.

Oriole touched a hand to his cheek and smiled at him mischievously. "Where's your book?" she asked.

"What? The handbook?"

Oriole nodded.

"Bottom drawer of my desk. Underneath the diaries."

Oriole slipped out of bed to fetch it and lit a candle on the camphor-wood chest. There was a bright moon that night, but not bright enough to read by. From the sound of pages being turned this way, then that, Jun-rui could tell she was searching for something in particular.

"Here, look at this," she said at last.

Jun-rui propped himself up and saw that the book was open at an illustration called "Willow in the Wind." It showed a woman sitting in the cleft of a willow tree, holding onto a sturdy branch to keep herself upright, and a man—naked except for his boots—taking her from the front. It was graphic enough to make Jun-rui feel some stirrings of interest, despite the heat.

"We haven't done this one," Oriole reminded him teasingly.

Jun-rui put down the fan and began rubbing his chin slowly. "Well, no," he agreed. "But—"

"Let's do it now," Oriole urged him, nudging his arm.

Jun-rui continued rubbing his chin, a perplexed expression on his face. The stirrings of interest were meanwhile making their presence felt and turning into something he couldn't ignore.

"Well, yes," he said with a vague smile. "But how? There doesn't happen to be a tree in here, you know."

"We'll go outside, silly!" she told him. Her eyes glinted wickedly. "We'll go to the Flower Garden, that's what. Plenty of trees there. Plenty of willows.''

Jun-rui's jaw dropped in astonishment. ''You must be crazy!'' he exclaimed, shaking his head. ''That would be risking everything. We'd be seen!''

''Not necessarily,'' Oriole replied, putting her hand on his chest, which was shiny and damp with perspiration. She stroked him persuasively, still with that glint in her eye. ''It'll be all right as long as we're careful. Everyone's asleep, and it'll be ages until the night watchman comes this way again—he's probably over at the gatehouse having a few drinks!''

Jun-rui wasn't responding to her enthusiasm, so Oriole squeezed his arm insistently. ''Just think how much cooler it'll be outside,'' she whispered. ''Especially by the water. Anyway, I'm tired of being here in your room night after night. It's about time we had a change of scene. Just once, Jun-rui, please. Just for a short while...''

She gave Jun-rui her sweetest, most imploring look. He seemed to be wavering.

''And what do we do about Pug?'' he asked, as though casting around for an excuse.

''We'll take him with us. I'll carry him. He'll be fine,'' Oriole assured him.

''You promise it's just for a little while?''

''Yes, Jun-rui, I promise.''

Before he could change his mind, Oriole handed

him his boots, put on her own shoes and threw on a slightly heavier robe. Then she blew out the candle. She picked up the dog and stood waiting for Jun-rui in the doorway. There was no need for a lamp; the full moon would light their way.

"Come on," Oriole said impatiently. She already felt cooler just standing in the open doorway.

To reach the Flower Garden they had to cross the studio garden first and go out by the wooden latticework gate. Then they had to follow the path behind the outer wall until it joined the main path coming from the west wing. This was almost opposite the gate to the Flower Garden.

They lost little time in getting there, clutching each other with nervous excitement and looking about them warily as they went. The worst part was opening the Flower Garden's creaky old gate; once inside they both breathed a sigh of relief. They took the path leading directly to the lake and carefully inspected the willow trees to see which was most suited to the purpose they had in mind. Oriole soon found one right by the water's edge; it was perfect, with a nice low fork. She asked Jun-rui to hold Pug while she settled herself in position. It was such a novel experience for them to be doing this outside—and they were both so jittery about every sudden noise—that it took a while to get things under way. Finally, though, "Willow in the Wind" was in full swing. Jun-rui soon found that having a

dog under his arm was cramping his style, so eventually he let Pug drop to the ground. Now he could give full rein to his passion.

For some time all was well. The lovers were deeply engrossed in their lovemaking, and Pug was fascinated with new smells and sounds. Everything was going fine, in fact, until Pug discovered the ducks. He must have disturbed a pair of them when he was snuffling around in a clump of rushes beside the lake. As soon as they began flapping and fluttering their wings, he started barking excitedly. Their struggle to get away from the intruder only encouraged Pug to give chase.

Oriole and Jun-rui were both alarmed by his barking, afraid someone might hear. They tried calling him back, tried telling him to be quiet, but the barking and wild racing around became even more frantic.

They were by now far too distracted to continue what they'd been doing. Jun-rui helped Oriole down to the ground and they quickly adjusted their clothing, giving each other anxious looks as they did so.

All of a sudden they heard a splash, and the barking came to an abrupt stop. Shortly afterward they heard a frenzied thrashing around in the water, and then the barking—softer now—began again from the other side of the lake. It grew farther away all the time.

Oriole bit her lip with the realization that Pug was now completely out of control. He was behaving in a totally unpredictable fashion, and there was no knowing what might happen if she didn't get him back at once. She glanced at Jun-rui in dismay.

In the distance they heard another bout of muffled barking. It sounded as though it was coming from near the gate.

"He's leaving the garden, the little rascal!" Jun-rui hissed at her. "Quick! We'd better get back to my room as soon as we can. I just hope that's where he's heading!"

DI-DI HAD BEEN FLUSHED and complaining of a headache all day, and Lady Cui—afraid her son might be coming down with something—had arranged for him to sleep in Constance's room. If anyone was going to play nurse, she preferred it to be one of the maids, rather than herself.

In the early hours of the morning, Di-di awoke with a high temperature and began crying for his mother. He refused to be comforted by Constance, and she couldn't persuade him to stay put, however hard she tried. Constance could predict that Lady Cui would be none too pleased about being disturbed in the middle of the night, but Di-di was becoming hysterical in his demands. Short of tying him to the bed, she could see no alternative but to give in to his wishes and take him to his mother.

Constance's room, like Scarlet's, was in the maids' quarters—between the women's quarters and the studio. To get to Lady Cui's rooms, they would have to cross two courtyards and pass by Oriole's room.

Constance gave Di-di a cool cloth to hold against his burning forehead and got him dressed in his gown and shoes. She was about to light the lamp, but when she saw how bright the moon was, she thought they could manage without. Di-di was blubbering pathetically all the while, more like a baby than a ten-year-old.

They were just passing through the small courtyard near Oriole's room when a small dark shape went hurtling past them and drew to a stop outside Oriole's door, whimpering and clawing at the wood. It was Pug. And that succeeded in silencing Di-di immediately.

"What are you doing out here in the middle of the night, you poor little thing?" Constance said kindly. "Just wait a moment, Di-di, while I let him in."

She quietly opened Oriole's door and closed it once Pug had gone inside, but then the whimpering and clawing started again from the other side of the door. Constance was puzzled by this; however, she didn't feel she could go away and leave the dog making such a racket. It would disturb Miss Oriole.

She went back to open the door. This time Pug

hopped over the threshold and went straight to Di-di, sitting at his feet and gazing up at him with doleful eyes. He was still whining pitifully. Constance stood there at a loss, but Di-di—sick though he was—reached down and picked up the dog. This at least stopped the whimpering.

Constance wondered what to do next.

"We can't take him with us," she said to Di-di. "We'll have to put him back in. You come with me."

She opened Oriole's door for the third time, and she and Di-di stepped inside. Almost as soon as they entered the room, Pug started whining again.

Constance couldn't think what was wrong with him and was by now becoming quite distraught.

"Hush, now," she pleaded in a whisper. "You'll wake Miss Oriole and get us into trouble."

In her agitation, she crept over to the bed to check that Oriole was still asleep. She very quietly drew aside the thick brocade curtain and peeked inside.

Much to her surprise, the bed was empty.

CHAPTER ELEVEN

LADY CUI WASN'T HAVING a good night. First, she'd spent hours tossing and turning in a sort of half sleep, and then she was well and truly woken by an irritating noise that sounded like barking—and after that, it was impossible to get back to sleep. She was lying there feeling hot and out of sorts when she heard footsteps and whispering outside her room. It was the middle of the night, and no one except the night watchman had any business being up and about, so she was understandably nervous—but she certainly wasn't about to show it.

"Who's there?" she called out sharply.

Much to her relief it was Di-di who answered. His voice sounded weak and small.

"It's only me, Mother."

What with all the drama and excitement over Pug, Di-di had almost forgotten how hot and feverish he'd been feeling, but as soon as he heard his mother's voice, it all came back and he started to blubber again. He was crying quite tragically by the time he and Constance went inside.

Lady Cui felt more annoyed than ever. First it

was the barking, and now it was her son in hysterics! How was a person supposed to get a wink of sleep? How many more disturbances would she have to put up with that night?

"You'd better have a good reason for waking me in the middle of the night!" she snapped. "Now, stop your sniveling and tell me what's the matter."

Constance bit her lip. It upset her to hear Madam speaking so roughly to her son, especially when he was feeling poorly.

Di-di stopped his crying for a moment. "I've got a headache and I'm hot and I feel sick," he told his mother.

"Come over here," she said brusquely. She felt his forehead and sighed—the boy did have a high temperature, no doubt about it. "You'd better get some water on the boil for tea, then bring me the medicine chest," she ordered Constance.

Reluctantly she heaved herself out of bed and pulled a silk robe over her nightdress. She was hurrying toward Di-di with the intention of settling him on her bed when she suddenly saw the shaggy rat-like creature in her son's arms. She let out a terrible screech. Pug responded with a low growl.

"What's that?" she asked Di-di nervously.

Di-di had stopped his whimpering and was staring quizzically at his mother. "It's Pug, of course," he replied, stroking the dog's head affectionately.

"Well, what's it doing here?" Lady Cui demanded crossly. This really was the last straw! Now her bedroom was being turned into a farmyard!

Di-di looked up blankly and didn't answer. Constance, meanwhile, had come back from putting water on the brazier in the kitchen nearby and was fetching the medicine chest from Lady Cui's cupboard. She froze as soon as she heard the question. She didn't pretend to know why Miss Oriole hadn't been in her room, but she certainly didn't want to see her in trouble. She prayed that Di-di would keep quiet.

"I said, what's it doing here?" Lady Cui persisted. "Why have you got it? Why isn't it in your sister's room with her?"

"It's him, not it," Di-di said stubbornly, glaring at his mother. He thought she looked a little like a witch at that moment, with her long loose gray hair and her red angry face. He was boiling hot and uncomfortable, and not getting the sympathy he'd come for. He was starting to feel a little mean.

"You still haven't answered my question," Lady Cui said suspiciously, peering at Di-di. "Something's wrong here, I'm sure of it. Now, are you going to tell me why you've got that dog in my bedroom, or am I going to have to send for your sister to tell me herself? Di-di? Constance?"

She glanced from one to the other, waiting for an answer. Di-di's lower lip began to quiver, and all at once he turned on his mother and said defiantly, "You can't send for my sister because she's not there, that's why!"

Lady Cui stiffened. "What do you mean she's not there? Of course she's there!" Her thoughts were racing. "Speak up!"

Constance decided it was time to intervene and said in a rush, "Well, you see, Madam, we went inside Miss Oriole's room to take her dog back because it was running around all over the place and crying for her, but she wasn't there, so we couldn't. But it's probably nothing to worry about. She's…she's probably just with Scarlet…."

Di-di looked scornfully at Constance, then hastened to put her straight.

"No, not with Scarlet," he said in a perfectly innocent tone. "At Uncle Zhang's again, I expect. To play chess." Since no one said anything, Di-di thought he'd better elaborate. "That's where Scarlet takes her. I saw them. Scarlet said I mustn't tell. She gave me cakes and crickets…" His voice trailed off.

Constance was totally flabbergasted, and Lady Cui immediately sank into the nearest chair with an expression of absolute horror on her face. Di-di was beginning to feel quite surprised himself to see both women acting so strangely. What could he possibly have said to get such a dramatic response? He turned anxiously to look at his mother again—she was now gasping, a bit like a goggle-eyed goldfish.

And when she finally stopped gasping, she started muttering to herself and hissing like a snake.

"What a stupid fool I've been all this time! How could I have *been* so stupid? How could I have failed to see what was going on? Right in front of me! The shameless hussy! She really had me fooled. Just wait till I get my hands on her, the deceitful little slut."

Di-di was by now huddled on the bed, clutching Pug for comfort, and Constance remained crouched by the cupboard. As soon as there was a break in the hissing and cursing, Constance went scurrying over to Lady Cui with the medicine chest and thrust it under her nose. This seemed to bring Lady Cui back to her senses. She took the chest and got to her feet.

"I'll see to my son," she said sternly to Constance. "I want you to go and get Scarlet and bring her here. Now!"

Constance just stood there, wringing her hands unhappily. She didn't want to see Scarlet in trouble any more than Miss Oriole. "But, Madam," she said tentatively, "she'll be asleep. It's only four o'clock in the morning."

Lady Cui gave Constance a cold stare. "I don't care what time it is," she said. "There are a few explanations needed, and I want to hear them *now!* Scarlet will be able to tell me what's going on. This time, I will *not* be told to wait!"

As Constance was about to disappear out the door, Lady Cui called her back and said shrilly, "And you can take that wretched dog with you while you're about it!"

CONSTANCE MADE HER WAY to the maids' quarters in a state of misery. She walked slowly, with her head bowed, feeling extremely abject and full of remorse. Through no fault of her own—quite unintentionally—she'd helped uncover a terrible secret and would now be responsible for several people getting into trouble with Lady Cui. And judging by Madam's reaction, it was going to be *big* trouble! She should've known better than to turn up at Lady Cui's quarters with Miss Oriole's dog—but what else could she have done? On reflection, Constance decided she should just have left him in Miss Oriole's room, whining and scratching at the door or not! At least then Madam wouldn't have found out about Miss Oriole not being there.

Constance was full of self-reproach. If only she was smart like Scarlet! Scarlet would never have made such a mess of things. Constance certainly wasn't looking forward to waking Scarlet and telling her that Lady Cui wanted to see her—and why!

But it was strange, she thought, what Master Di-di had said about his sister and Mr. Zhang. It must be true or why would he have said it? He could never have invented something like that! But when had it happened? How long had he known? And why did his mother believe him straight away when normally she was quick to ignore whatever he did and said? Maybe she'd had suspicions of her own to start with....

Constance knew she was out of her depth. It had been a complete and utter surprise to learn that there was something going on between Miss Oriole and the young student; she hadn't had the slightest inkling. So, who else knew and how they'd found out was even more of a mystery to her, and not worth guessing at.

All too soon she'd reached Scarlet's door. Taking a deep breath, she pushed it open.

There was still a good half hour before the sixth watch sounded—which was when Scarlet usually went over to the study to collect Oriole and escort her back to her room. So Scarlet was still sound asleep in her narrow bed under the thin cotton cover. Constance had to shake her quite vigorously to rouse her.

At first Scarlet was grumpy about being woken, but her grumpiness rapidly turned to alarm once Constance explained what had just happened. She quickly scrambled out of bed and got dressed, cursing under her breath. The only thing she'd said in answer to Constance's long tale of woe was, ''Well, we're really in deep trouble now!''

Constance hung her head, feeling horribly guilty.

"I'm so sorry, Scarlet," she began. "I feel really—"

"It's not your fault," Scarlet interrupted. "It would've come out sooner or later. I'm just surprised Di-di kept his mouth shut and we got away with it as long as we did." She was scratching her head and looking worried. "I've got to see Oriole, though—now. It can't wait. And I'd better take Pug with me, too. She'll be wondering where he is and worried sick about him."

"But Madam's waiting," Constance said anxiously, not wanting to inflame Lady Cui's wrath any further.

"Well, Madam can damn well wait a little longer, then, can't she!" Scarlet replied. "I've got to see Oriole. Before anything else."

She hurried off to the study with Pug, leaving Constance waiting nervously in her stuffy little room. She had to warn the unsuspecting couple they'd been discovered. She'd advise Oriole to go back to her room as quickly as possible—and to prepare herself for a big confrontation with her mother.

After she'd broken the dreadful news, it wasn't easy for Scarlet to get away. Inevitably there was panic. She hated leaving Oriole in the study and in floods of tears, but she knew she'd be pushing her luck to keep Lady Cui waiting a moment longer. She rushed back to her room, where she found Constance restlessly pacing the floor. The two of them bustled off to Lady Cui's quarters, not speaking much but darting the occasional nervous look at each other. After all the excitement and all her dashing around, Scarlet was feeling very hot and sweaty by the time they arrived at Lady Cui's door.

The two maids paused for a second to muster their courage.

"Well, here goes!" Scarlet whispered tensely as she knocked on the door.

"Good luck!" Constance whispered back in encouragement, smiling faintly.

They both knew that if there was anything Scarlet needed at that moment, it was luck.

LADY CUI WAS SITTING in her room on a highbacked wooden chair with a severe expression on her face and a dangerous look about her. Her fingers were tapping impatiently on the polished arms of the chair. Her mouth twitched as the maids came in, and she stared Scarlet up and down in an extremely haughty fashion. Scarlet kept her composure; she wasn't about to let Lady Cui get the better of her without putting up any resistance.

When Lady Cui finally spoke, it was not to Scarlet.

"You can leave us now, Constance. What I've got to say is for Scarlet's ears alone. Di-di's asleep in the back room, so there's no need for you to stay. I'll call for you later.''

She picked up the sandalwood fan lying in her lap and fanned herself briskly for a moment. Her eyes narrowed as she added, ''You did well, Constance, to bring this sordid affair out into the open. Very well indeed.''

Constance blushed. Madam's praise made her feel nothing but acute embarrassment. She bobbed a halfhearted curtsy and left the room as quickly as she could, feeling ashamed at abandoning Scarlet to the presumably dreadful fate that awaited her.

Scarlet was now alone with Lady Cui. The two of them stared at each other without flinching.

''I ought to have you whipped!'' Lady Cui said at last.

''What for?'' Scarlet asked incredulously. She thought it might be worth a try to act the innocent.

It was a bad move. Her question only infuriated Lady Cui even more.

''You know perfectly well what for!'' she snarled. ''I'm talking about my good-for-nothing daughter and that wretched student of hers. You're the one who fixed things up between them to start with! Go on, admit it!''

Scarlet blinked in a bemused fashion. ''I don't know what you mean. They're friends, that's all. She only goes there to pl—''

''What sort of fool do you take me for?'' Lady

Cui cried, her rage sweeping her out of control in an instant. "Play chess, indeed! I know perfectly well what she goes there for, the slut! Di-di told me he's seen the two of you creeping off in the dark, and he knows where you go. You're only making things worse for yourself by lying to me, you know. I want the truth!"

Scarlet gulped and gazed down at the floor, thinking desperately. There was clearly no sense in continuing to deny it; Lady Cui was already convinced of Oriole's guilt. Perhaps she ought to try getting herself off the hook by making it seem as though she'd had no involvement in any of this.

"The thing is," Scarlet began in an apologetic-sounding tone, "the first time Miss Oriole went to visit Mr. Zhang, it was when he was sick. You remember? And I thought she was giving him acupuncture. That's why I left them alone together. I didn't see any harm. How was I supposed to know that—"

While Scarlet was talking, Lady Cui had risen from her chair and seized a thin stick of bamboo. Without warning, she brought it down hard, hitting the floor right beside Scarlet and startling her so badly she stopped in midsentence.

"How dare you tell me such lies!" Lady Cui roared. She was red in the face and trembling with fury. "You've got eyes in your head! Of course you knew what they were up to! You've known all along. You've been deceiving me for weeks. You're no better than that whore who dares to call herself my daughter. The two of you deserve a sound thrashing!'' She paused for a moment to catch her breath, then added, ''And to think I trusted you—''

Scarlet let out a contemptuous laugh. ''Trust!'' she exclaimed. ''What do you know about trust? It's because you broke—''

Lady Cui raised the stick. ''I'll teach you to answer me back, you impudent hussy! A good beating's what you need, and I'm going to make sure you get it. Right now. Bend over, my girl!''

She brought the stick down even harder than before, and this time she was aiming for Scarlet. But Scarlet instinctively jumped aside, and when the stick hit the floor, she put her foot on it to prevent Lady Cui from lifting it up again. Scarlet had decided in that split second that she had no intention of submitting to a beating—not when the circumstances were so unjust. Eyes blazing, she glared at Lady Cui, then wrenched the stick out of her hand.

''Now, you listen here,'' she shouted. ''I've had just about enough of this! I've got one or two things to say to *you* for a change, so you just sit down and be quiet and listen!''

It was unheard of for a maid to speak like this to a Madam. Lady Cui was obviously dumbfounded at Scarlet's rebellion—and her unexpected forcefulness. She collapsed into her chair like a puppet, her mouth hanging open. Scarlet was tapping the stick angrily on the floor, feeling about ready to burst with all the things she'd been storing up to say to the hard-hearted woman sitting in front of her.

"Let's get something straight," she began. "You talk about trust, but you don't even know the meaning of the word! Everyone trusted you, everyone believed you meant it when you said that Miss Oriole and Mr. Zhang would marry after he'd got us out of that Flying Tiger mess. And why did they think that? Because you *promised,* that's why. But then you went and broke your promise and made everyone miserable, and now nobody trusts you anymore, and why should they?"

Since Lady Cui just sat there in stunned silence, Scarlet decided to go on because she still had plenty to say.

"And then, after breaking your promise, instead of giving the young man a big reward and sending him on his way, what do you do? You move him into the study practically next door to your daughter's room, you put temptation right there in front of him, and you say to him, 'Go on, there she is'.... Did you think anyone was going to fall for that 'welcoming Mr. Zhang into my family as a son' bit? How could you be so blind? I mean, what did you *expect* to happen? You must have known they were attracted to each other—anyone could see *that*. So you've got no one to blame but yourself that their feelings finally got the better of them and they ended up in bed together. They've been together every night for weeks, you know...."

Lady Cui was squirming in her chair and spluttering, apparently speechless, but she managed to get out a few words while Scarlet was catching her breath. "But...but...this is scandalous!"

Scarlet put the stick safely out of Lady Cui's reach and came back to face her again.

"For once I agree with you," she said, a little less angry now. Her tone was more like the sensible matter-of-fact one that Lady Cui was used to. "It *is* scandalous, the way things stand at the moment, and it's up to you to put them right. What's done is done, and there's no sense wishing it hadn't happened. What's needed now is for you to get them together properly and make everything respectable—if you get my drift."

Lady Cui clutched the arms of the chair and shook her head. She was having none of it.

"You'll pay for it later if you don't," Scarlet warned. "You've already let down your good name by not keeping your promise to Mr. Zhang. It was a breach of trust, a dishonor to your family—that's what the abbot said...."

Lady Cui looked up anxiously. If there was one thing she cared about above everything else, it was her family reputation. Scarlet had, of course, been completely aware of this when she'd attributed these comments to the abbot, with more than a touch of exaggeration.

"And quite apart from making the Cui family look bad now," Scarlet went on, "what about in the future? That Mr. Zhang's pretty smart. He won't be a penniless student forever, you mark my words. One day he'll be rich and powerful, I'm sure of it, and do you imagine he'll just forget the way you treated him here? I don't think so. And if he takes it to Court—which is quite likely, in my opinion— they'll find out how he did you such a big favor and you rewarded him with a knife in the back— by breaking your word about letting him marry Miss Oriole. And then, people will hear how you actually encouraged the romance between him and your beautiful daughter. If they hear all *that* in Court, things won't be looking too good for you, I'd say."

She paused for a second to catch her breath and then continued, "On top of everything else, it'll be public knowledge that you failed to keep your own daughter under control and that she made a real fool of you. No, if it went to Court, I certainly wouldn't like to be in your shoes...."

Scarlet sneaked a glance at Lady Cui to see if her words were having any effect; she thought she detected a worried frown on the older woman's face. She suspected Lady Cui was in the process of making up her mind—trying to decide whether to punish Oriole and her lover, or marry them off. Scarlet thought she'd add some more ammunition while she had the chance.

"They really do make a very handsome couple, you know, Madam, and he'd be a real credit to you as a son-in-law. If you could overlook their little fling and give your permission for them to marry, everyone would say you'd done the right thing. They'd compliment you on making an excellent choice of husband for your only daughter, and they'd respect you all the more for keeping your promise to him."

Lady Cui had stooped to pick up her sandalwood fan and was now gently fanning herself. Her frown had gone and a pensive look had taken its place. She regarded Scarlet shrewdly. "You're a fine talker, there's no doubt about it. But what you say doesn't alter the fact that my daughter has behaved no better than some good-for-nothing singsong girl and she deserves to be punished!"

Scarlet heaved a sigh and threw up her hands in frustration.

"Look, you've said all that already, so why say it again? You can't change what's happened. You might just as well patch it up as best you can and stop blaming—"

"Yes, yes," Lady Cui said hurriedly. "I'll do as

you say. I can see it makes sense, and anyway, I don't think I have a lot of choice in the matter. But don't expect me to be happy about it!"

"Of course not. That would be expecting too much." Scarlet muttered this last remark under her breath, but a little too loudly.

Lady Cui shot her a reproving glance.

"They love each other, you know," Scarlet put in defensively. *"That's* something to be happy about, don't you think?"

There was no answer from Lady Cui, apart from a soft harrumph. After a moment she shrugged. "I wouldn't know," she said in an odd choked voice.

Scarlet turned to her in surprise and got the impression she was genuinely upset. But true to form, Lady Cui regained her composure in an instant and resumed speaking in her normal brisk and businesslike fashion.

"In love or not, it makes no difference to me! I will not have a penniless student as a son-in-law. He'll have to go to the capital and take the examinations and *pass* them before he marries any daughter of mine! He can leave the monastery first thing tomorrow. You tell him this from me—I don't want to see his face again until he's out of those white student rags and wearing something decent. I expect him to have a proper job and the clothes to go with it. And what's more, I don't care how long it takes!"

Scarlet regarded Lady Cui closely for a moment. "I'll do as you say. I'll tell him everything you said and I'll make sure he does it. I give you my word. But there's something you need to do, too."

"And what might that be?" Lady Cui asked in her haughtiest voice.

"Write to Cousin Heng immediately to tell him the engagement's off—assuming he isn't already on his way here. If we're not careful, we'll have Miss Oriole marrying two men at once!"

Lady Cui sniffed, apparently not amused. "I'll do it," she said stiffly. "Right away."

CHAPTER TWELVE

NOT SURPRISINGLY Oriole was still in a state when Scarlet finally got back to her after the encounter with Lady Cui. All Oriole knew was that her world had suddenly come crashing down, and she didn't know what she was going to do about it.

She'd found it unbearably hard to tear herself away from Jun-rui that morning and go back to her lonely room. But Jun-rui had managed to impress upon her that the last thing they needed was to make the situation any worse by being caught in his room together. He tried his best to calm her, saying that for the time being they were in Scarlet's hands and must trust in her to argue their case. And if Scarlet failed to convince Oriole's mother that a marriage between the young lovers was the best way out of an extremely awkward situation, it would be up to him to try. Whatever the outcome, he would not be separated from her; that he promised.

Oriole sighed as she went over to the window to look for Scarlet. It was all very well for Jun-rui to say these things, but the reality wasn't quite so simple. They both knew there was no question of running away together—where would that lead, except to ruin and disgrace? So if her mother refused to let them marry, what other alternative was open to them, apart from separation?

And Oriole found it quite impossible to believe that her mother would ever agree to a marriage between her and Jun-rui. Lady Cui was already far too committed to the idea of marrying her daughter off to Heng. Oriole couldn't imagine anything that would make her change her mind. It seemed that she and Jun-rui had been hiding from the truth for much too long—and now that the truth was staring her in the face, she was forced to admit it looked bleak. She'd be foolish to pretend otherwise.

She patted Pug's head sorrowfully. He was lying very quietly in her arms, as though he knew he'd done something wrong. Early that morning Scarlet had thrust Pug at her in the study with the words, "Here's the little rascal responsible for your undoing!" At the time, Oriole had felt like strangling him. The anguish and anxiety he'd caused her—dashing off from the garden, making all that noise and then disappearing altogether—well, it wasn't something she ever wanted to go through again. But she'd already forgiven him. It wasn't his fault, after all; it was quite definitely hers. Making love in the garden—what an incredibly stupid idea that had been. Stupid and reckless. Why had she ever suggested it? Why had she insisted on pushing their luck when everything was going so smoothly? Anyone would think she'd *wanted* them to be found out! Was that possible? No, surely not!

Oriole felt confused and unhappy, and incapable of sitting still for more than a minute. As soon as she heard Scarlet's footsteps outside, she dashed for the door.

"You've been gone for ages! What did she say?" Oriole asked, impatient for news. "What's she going to do? Did she ask to see me? Will she send for Jun-rui? Did you get a beating?" Oriole paced nervously across the room.

"Hold on a minute!" Scarlet replied in a strained voice. When she'd slipped off her shoes, she left the doorway and walked slowly over to stand next to Oriole. She looked tired, but there was a sparkle in her eyes all the same.

"I may as well tell you right away and put you out of your misery," she said. Oriole held her breath. "Don't worry," Scarlet said reassuringly, her face breaking out in a warm smile. "She's agreed!"

Oriole sank onto a stool at the tea table and stared at Scarlet in disbelief. "To the marriage? You mean she's agreed to the marriage?"

Scarlet nodded.

Oriole continued to stare at her, pale and wide-eyed, utterly unable to believe that Scarlet was telling her the truth. Gradually, though, the words began to seem real, and as Oriole's excitement increased, the blood rose steadily to her cheeks until she was quite flushed. She couldn't contain herself a moment longer. She leaped to her feet and grabbed Scarlet's hands, jumping up and down as if she'd lost her senses.

Scarlet was smiling, but not as much as Oriole would have expected. There was something preventing her from sharing wholeheartedly in Oriole's happiness, and Oriole sensed this almost immediately. She quickly stopped her joyous movements and stood quietly looking at Scarlet, waiting for an explanation.

"You're right," Scarlet said, eyeing Oriole soberly. "It's not all good news. Your mother says she won't hear of you marrying a down-and-out student and says she doesn't want to see him again until he's got a proper job and all that."

Oriole was crestfallen but did her best to look at the situation in a positive light. "Oh, well, I suppose the delay won't kill us. It just means he'll have to go to the capital for the exams—but at least he's bound to pass them the first time around, not like some of those poor young men who have to keep on trying until they've just about got one foot in the grave! And we'll be able to spend some time together before he leaves."

"I don't think so," Scarlet said softly, giving

Oriole's hands a sympathetic squeeze. "She wants him to go quite soon, I'm afraid. Tomorrow, in fact."

Oriole was horrified. "Tomorrow? Why? Surely it could wait a couple of weeks? I mean, you can't expect a person to drop everything and go just like that!" She drew her hands out of Scarlet's and slapped them against her sides in exasperation. "Why is my mother always so difficult?" she asked crossly, not really expecting an answer.

"Your guess is as good as mine," Scarlet replied with a shrug. "But there's no point in looking for trouble, is there? If you want my advice, you should just accept her terms and do what she says, regardless of what you think about it. And if that means being parted from your sweetheart for a little while, then that's what has to happen. It's not the end of the world."

"But, Scarlet," Oriole said miserably. "It's not just a little while—it'll be months. It'll take him at least a month to get there, and then he'll—"

"I know," Scarlet interrupted firmly, "but that's the way it is. You'll just have to try and be brave about it and wait for him as patiently as you can. There's plenty we can do to keep ourselves busy in the meantime."

"Like what?" Oriole asked in a dejected voice.

"Like making a wedding quilt, for instance!"

Scarlet laughed, giving Oriole a conspiratorial wink.

But Oriole wasn't in the mood for humor of any kind. The brief and beautiful happiness she'd enjoyed on hearing that her mother had agreed to the marriage was completely overshadowed by the thought of being without Jun-rui for months and months. Her most immediate concern was how she'd manage to see him to say goodbye. She asked Scarlet about this.

"Well, I don't imagine you'll be having another one of your midnight get-togethers, now will you," Scarlet quipped. It was such a ridiculous notion that Oriole didn't even bother answering. "I guess it'd better be this afternoon. Your mother wants to see you before lunch, so we'll try and arrange it with her then."

Oriole's face fell at the prospect of a meeting with Lady Cui. It was the last thing she felt she could endure. But Scarlet tried to encourage her.

"Come on now, let's get some breakfast inside you—then you'll be better prepared to deal with the old fire-breathing dragon!"

LADY CUI KEPT the meeting with her daughter brief and to the point, and though she didn't actually say anything insulting to her face, she managed to convey—through facial expressions and tone of voice—what an incredibly low opinion she had of

Oriole's behavior. Oriole came away from it feeling hurt and angry, which was more or less what she'd expected.

In the end it was Scarlet who fixed up a legitimate rendezvous for Oriole and Jun-rui. Lady Cui had agreed to this meeting, which would take place late that afternoon.

Scarlet was resolute that at this stage neither Oriole nor Jun-rui should put a foot wrong; everything should be done in the proper fashion. They mustn't risk alienating Lady Cui and giving her a reason to change her mind, not when she'd finally granted them permission to do the one thing they'd wanted all along.

Lady Cui had instructed that the lovers meet in one of the west wing's reception rooms. She'd asked that Scarlet be present throughout, to make sure nothing untoward occurred. Scarlet was happy enough to go along with her request.

Since this would be their last chance to see each other before Jun-rui left the following day, Oriole was determined to look her best. When she got back from the unpleasant encounter with her mother, she immediately set about preparing herself for Jun-rui. First she had Scarlet do her hair in a very simple style, just coiled up at the back of her head and held in place with several ivory combs. Then she put on her makeup. She wanted to do it in very subtle tones this time, to reflect the sadness and seriousness of the occasion.

For the same reason she selected a rather somber-looking gown in a deep blue raw silk. Apart from her white-jade bracelets, she wore nothing decorative except for a pair of earrings and a necklace made of kingfisher feathers set in gold. She knew that the pale creaminess of her skin contrasted strikingly with the dark richness of her clothing, and the simple but bold jewelry gave her a dramatic air. The final effect was both dignified and stunning.

When Scarlet had finished Oriole's hair, she'd gone off, saying she had a few errands to do but would be back within the hour. She returned on time, as promised, at a few minutes to five, and they started for the reception room. The late-afternoon sun was still strong, and the light was harsh and glaring. On the way Scarlet complimented Oriole enthusiastically on her appearance.

Jun-rui was no less impressed. He'd arrived at the appointed room ahead of them, and they found him standing at the open window in a thoughtful pose, his arms folded inside his sleeves, his head down. But he looked up when they entered and drew in his breath with admiration.

"Oriole, you're so beautiful!" he said, hurrying impulsively toward her and clasping her hands in his. It had been quite a while since he'd seen her in daylight, elegantly dressed and made up like this.

She really was ravishing! "How will I ever manage to tear myself away from you?" he asked her, apparently making an effort not to be too downcast. "You're like one of those fox spirits, working your magic on me and keeping me under your spell. How will I ever get away?"

His words might be light, but there was a desolate edge to his voice and a sadness lurking in his eyes. Oriole could tell at once how wretched he was feeling and wished she could think of something to say, something that would make it easier for him. But how could she, when she felt equally wretched? She was utterly at a loss for words. Worse, she felt ridiculously shy and uncomfortable in front of her lover.

Scarlet, sensing the awkwardness between them, decided to step outside and leave them alone for a few moments, regardless of her promise to Lady Cui. What harm could it possibly do?

Oriole tried to muster her courage and speak, instead of standing there pathetically shy and tongue-tied. "It won't be for too long," she said bravely.

"No," Jun-rui agreed, looking down at their hands, which were still clasped together.

"You'll be back in no time—you'll see," Oriole told him in the most reassuring voice she could manage.

"Yes, I guess I will," he said doubtfully.

"It'll only be a couple of months—" Oriole

broke off abruptly and bit her lip. Her eyes filled with tears.

Who was she kidding? It was a month's journey to Chang-an and another month back. And the next examinations wouldn't be held until late autumn. They both knew he was unlikely to return much before the end of the year. And if her mother insisted that Jun-rui arrange a career for himself before coming back, it was going to be considerably longer. A lengthy period of separation seemed inevitable, and the empty months loomed before them like a dark abyss.

Jun-rui swallowed hard. He didn't want to shatter Oriole's attempts at optimism. Why make her any unhappier?

"Yes, you're probably right," he pretended. "Time goes pretty fast when you're—"

Before he knew what was happening, Oriole had let out a strangled cry and clapped her hands over her mouth, trying to hold in her misery. Her body was shaking with sobs even though she wasn't making a sound. Jun-rui put his arms around her.

"Don't," he said gently, giving her a little shake. "There's no need to be so upset. You're forgetting all the reasons we've got for being happy—we'll be married before too long, and we'll spend the rest of our lives together." He smiled at her reassuringly, his eyes pleading with her to stop crying. "Surely we don't need to be so tragic, do we, about a brief period of time apart? Anyone would think I was never coming back!''

She dabbed at her tearstained cheeks with her handkerchief before replying.

''That's just it! That's why I'm crying. I'm crying because I...because...''

The words wouldn't come, and her face grew flushed with unspoken emotion. Jun-rui gave her another little shake. He wore an obstinate expression that seemed to be telling her, *I want to know what you were going to say, and I don't care if I have to wait all night for you to say it!*

She knew she'd have to tell him sooner or later—best to get it over with. She turned and looked at him earnestly. ''You *won't* come back. That's why I'm crying. I keep trying to pretend that you will, but deep down I know you won't.'' A fresh steam of tears gushed down her cheeks.

''What on earth makes you say that?'' Jun-rui asked, his voice trembling slightly.

''Because you'll forget me, that's why—as soon as you get to the city. There'll be all those pretty singsong girls flinging themselves at you and you won't be able to resist. You'll go—''

''Stop it!'' Jun-rui interrupted angrily, his eyes blazing. He moved a few steps away from her. It was the first time he'd ever spoken roughly to Oriole, and it drew her to a halt at once. Although his back was turned, she could sense his hurt. She waited quietly to hear what he had to say.

"You should know better than to talk like that," he said, coming to stand in front of her. His bearing was proud and upright; he looked like a man who knew what he wanted. "What do you think we've been doing together all this time? What do you think I've been trying to tell you? Do you still not realize how much I love you?"

He gazed at her fiercely, his eyes burning into hers. "Don't you understand? I don't *need* to look any farther. You're the only woman I want. There's no one else. There never has been, and I can't imagine there ever will be! What more can I say?"

He slid his arm around her slender waist and pulled her to him in one sweeping movement, then kissed her fervently, his lips melting hotly against hers. He was showing her, in this long passionate kiss, the depth of his love for her. She could *taste* his love, taste it so keenly that even when the kiss had ended, she could feel his ardor tingling on her lips.

He began whispering—almost chanting—in her ear. "You mustn't doubt me, I won't forget you. You must believe me, I will come back."

While he was whispering these words, he was reaching into his sleeve, and when he'd finished his chant, he said, "I want to give you something. Close your eyes. Hold out your hands."

She did as she was told and immediately felt him placing an object in her palms, something round and cold. She didn't need to open her eyes to know what it was; she could tell just by the feel of it. It was something she'd explored with her fingers many times before. It was Jun-rui's jade carving of the man and woman wrapped in their eternal embrace.

She would not have believed that Jun-rui would ever part with this little piece, because she knew how much it meant to him.

"It's to help you while I'm away," he explained. "Every time you look at it or touch it, you'll know for sure I'm coming back."

Oriole felt calm now and reconciled to their parting.

"I love you, Jun-rui," she said with all her heart. "I'll wait for you however long it takes. I know you'll be back."

She reached up to kiss him, her eyes brimming with love, her lips tender and trusting. They were in each other's arms, enjoying a slow kiss, when the door to the reception room creaked open and put a stop to further intimacy.

"Oops!" Scarlet exclaimed, blushing. "Sorry to burst in on you like this, but I've just been speaking with the abbot's boy, and I've got something to tell you."

They were both curious; one never knew what to expect with Scarlet.

Oriole smiled. "What have you been hatching this time?"

"Oh, nothing much," Scarlet answered in that noncommittal tone of hers that always implied the opposite of what she said. "The abbot and I thought it would be nice for you to see Mr. Zhang off tomorrow—the abbot's already spoken to your mother about it and they're both planning to come, too. As far as the Ten Mile Pavilion. It's all arranged."

Overjoyed, Oriole went rushing over to give Scarlet a big hug. Scarlet merely shrugged modestly and threw Oriole one of her more impish smiles.

"So you'll see him again tomorrow, Oriole. I thought you'd be pleased!"

THE NEXT DAY they were all up at the crack of dawn. The early hours of the morning—before the sun rose too high in the sky—were the most pleasant time of day, and everyone wanted to take advantage of the coolness.

Jun-rui would be traveling to the capital on horseback, with Lucky accompanying him on a horse from the abbot's own stables. If not for the abbot's generosity, Lucky would have been on foot. Jun-rui planned to set off for the Ten Mile Pavilion early so that he and Lucky could continue their journey before the heat really set in. Oriole's party was traveling to the pavilion by carriage—with Oriole, Scarlet and Di-di in one carriage, and Lady Cui, Constance, the abbot and his boy in the other. Lady Cui had arranged that the two groups would make their own way there and meet around eight o'clock, in time for breakfast.

Although the Ten Mile Pavilion was, in fact, ten miles from Puzhou, it was actually less than half this distance from the monastery. The road was a good one, being a major route to the capital and therefore quite well traveled. Oriole's party had been delayed in setting off, due to her mother's fastidiousness over the breakfast preparations, but once the carriages started out, they made good progress. They still, however, took longer to get to the pavilion than Jun-rui and Lucky.

There had been a lot of things for Jun-rui to sort out before leaving the monastery, but he'd managed to get them all done the previous night. The most time-consuming job had been his packing; he'd had to select the books he'd need, as well as enough clothes for a period of several months. He'd also cleared out the study and packed up the possessions he wasn't taking with him, which the abbot had agreed to put in storage. The study was only rented guest accommodation, and since Lady Cui had said nothing about continuing to pay for it during his absence, he'd decided he should probably clear it out.

Nothing remained to be done in the morning except to strap the bags of clothing and books to the horses' saddles. The only other piece of luggage was Jun-rui's precious zither, which he wouldn't hear of leaving behind; it was Lucky's job to carry this, in addition to his own small bundle of belongings.

Jun-rui was quite glad to have a little time alone at the pavilion to prepare himself for the parting that lay ahead. Once he'd tethered his horse, he sat down on the ground with his back against a tree a little distance from the pavilion. He glanced at its ornate carvings and the upturned curves of its green tiled roof, then looked up at the sky. As he gazed at the thick white clouds rolling steadily across the bright blue above, he resolved once again that he would do his utmost to make a success of things. He'd do well at the examinations, he'd get himself a good job—since it was so important to his prospective mother-in-law—and he'd be back as soon as he could to claim his bride. If Lady Cui thought she'd seen the last of him, he'd prove her wrong! And he'd make sure Oriole didn't have to wait for him a minute longer than necessary.

Jun-rui caught sight of the carriages when they were still some distance off, and he watched them slowly approaching until they'd drawn up nearby.

He saw Scarlet helping Oriole down from the carriage and escorting her along the little paved path that led to the pavilion. He watched Oriole looking around in every direction. She seemed to have spotted the horses and Lucky, but not him.

From where he sat, her face seemed pale. But her clothes were brighter and sunnier than the day before. She was wearing a lemon yellow gown embroidered with what looked like chrysanthemums, and it glowed cheerfully in the clear morning light.

When he went over to join them and had completed the formalities of greeting and bowing, he was able to see Oriole at close quarters. Her hair was done in yesterday's plain style, but her face was now free of makeup. It was her own skin color that made her so pale, not the powder. Despite her pallor, she seemed calm and collected—as though she'd come to terms with whatever had agitated her before. She even managed to smile at him with real warmth and conviction. He no longer felt that he would take his leave worrying about her and wondering if she'd survive his absence. Even though he could tell she was sad, she looked strong and determined.

There was little opportunity for intimacy that morning. Lady Cui soon had everyone seated inside the pavilion for an unnecessarily big breakfast, which no one really wanted. Since there wasn't a lot of eating going on, Lady Cui passed around the wine so they could all drink to Jun-rui's health and wish him well on his travels. She, the abbot and then Oriole each proposed a toast to him in turn. Although she'd said she didn't want to see Jun-rui's face again until he'd come back a success, the abbot had persuaded her to make an exception for the actual farewell. Lady Cui was being surprisingly good-humored about it.

Oriole had been very quiet throughout the meal, but when they'd finished drinking the wine, she suddenly began to speak rapidly, giving Jun-rui a whole string of advice. She told him to look after himself properly, to be careful what he ate and drank, to be sure to sleep well and not get soaking wet on the road or catch a chill, to take special care because soon it would be autumn and that was the time of year it was easy to succumb to illnesses.... There was no end to her concerns.

Not long afterward Jun-rui and Lucky went to untie their horses and they all walked to the road to say their goodbyes. Oriole handed Jun-rui the willow branch she'd brought with her from the Flower Garden; it was customary to give this to someone setting off on a journey, since it was said to offer protection to travelers. And, of course, there was also a special significance about the willow for her and Jun-rui—one she was pretty sure he hadn't forgotten!

In her final moments with him, Oriole also managed to furtively pass him the jade ring he'd given her. She only said a few words out loud, the meaning of which was lost on Lady Cui and the others.

"You look after this. It's of no use to me until you come back."

She then stood and watched him ride away, until he was no more than a speck on the far horizon.

CHAPTER THIRTEEN

ORIOLE PUT HER EMBROIDERY down on the sandal-wood tea table and smoothed it flat with her hand, admiring her work. She'd just finished the dragon's claws and had only the eyes to do—plus the beak of the phoenix—and then the whole thing would be ready. It was the undershirt she'd started making for Jun-rui months earlier, and it was definitely the finest and most intricate embroidery she'd ever done. She was proud of it; she'd also become very attached to it, since it had kept her occupied during the long period she and Jun-rui had already been apart.

The other project that had filled a lot of her time was the wedding quilt, but that was still a long way from being completed. Only yesterday she'd started stitching her twentieth butterfly; just doing one could take several days.

She gave an involuntary shiver and pulled her carved wooden stool closer to the brazier. It had been much colder that day, and all afternoon while she was working, she'd listened to the wind. It howled mournfully through the monastery buildings, tossing the fallen leaves and shaking the branches of the trees outside in the courtyard.

If anything, the wind was now blowing harder, and a bitter chill had descended with the falling light of late afternoon. The monastery felt bleak and deserted these days, and the howling of the wind only added to Oriole's sense of solitude and melancholy. She quickly got up and lit all the oil lamps and candles in her room, in the hope that this might dispel the cold and gloom of dusk and raise her spirits a little.

The past months had not been easy, and she'd had to struggle to throw off the despair that sometimes threatened to overwhelm her. When Jun-rui had first left, she'd been extremely concerned for his physical safety. The journey to Chang-an was not only long but could also be treacherous, since it involved crossing the Yellow River and then passing through some difficult steep and rocky terrain near Flowery Mountain—one of China's five sacred mountains, the one farthest to the west. In addition, there was always the danger of being attacked on the road. Even with Flying Tiger and his brigands disposed of, there were countless other robbers and bandits to menace travelers along the way. And the fact that Jun-rui was just an ordinary student and not at all wealthy-looking didn't help to reassure Oriole. There were plenty of people far worse off than he was, people who'd think nothing of doing someone in for a bit of cash or the bowl of noodles they could buy with it.

She also worried about not getting any news from one week to the next. Even when she'd calculated that he and Lucky must have reached the capital, there was never a letter to say they'd arrived safely. She just had to have faith that he was alive and well. She had no idea where he was living or what sort of life he was now leading, so it was hard to picture him there. But when she tried to imagine him at his books, she could almost see his look of fixed concentration, and she'd know he was doing what he'd said he would.

Later she'd watched the leaves on the maple trees putting on their autumn colors and becoming a warm rich red. She'd listened to the crickets and heard their autumn chorus reach a climax of loud chirruping, then gradually fade away. She'd seen the first flocks of geese flying overhead, making for warmer climes. And over the weeks, she'd noticed Scarlet and the other maids busily cleaning all the winter clothing on fulling blocks, getting it ready for wear.

It was soon past the date when the civil-service examinations would have been held, yet there was still no news. Oriole had been going to the Flower Garden every night after Jun-rui's departure to burn incense for him and pray for his good fortune. And when the exams drew closer, she'd devoted even more time to her prayers. The irony of it all was that she herself didn't care very much about wealth or material success. It was her mother who put such emphasis on money and career, and who held both of these in such high regard. Oriole was sufficiently practical to realize that his small inheritance couldn't keep them both; she understood that they could not survive on love and romantic sentiments alone. They'd need *some* way of supporting themselves. But apart from that, she had no exalted ambitions. She knew that the candidates who scored high in the examinations always secured the best jobs, but from her own point of view it didn't matter whether Jun-rui came first or last, just so long as he passed and got hold of some sort of job.

Of course, for his sake, she prayed he'd do well, because she knew it was what he wanted. But for her, the only important thing was that he come back to her safe and sound.

The actual waiting was a long lonely business, and not without its moments of despair. But on the whole she was surviving the separation better than she'd expected. She'd come to realize how crucial it was to keep busy and not allow herself to brood. Sometimes, when she was already missing him unbearably and letting her lonely thoughts get the better of her, she'd start doubting him; she'd end up convinced he'd forgotten her or been unfaithful to her and was never coming back. These troughs of despair were hard to pull herself out of, and at such times she was glad she had the jade carving to help her believe in him, to remind her of the things he'd said.

Fortunately, though, there must have been something strong inside her that *did* believe, because these periods of gloom were few and far between and were always conquered in the end—until gradually they ceased to plague her at all. With time, she became more confident of herself, as well as of him, and the more inner strength she had, the more she was able to reach out to others. Scarlet had been noticing that Oriole was actually doing things with Di-di these days, instead of just dismissing him as an annoying little brother; she regularly helped him with painting and calligraphy, and the two of them often went out together with Pug. Oriole hadn't realized until recently how fond Di-di had always been of her shaggy little dog.

Oriole had also managed of late to act in a surprisingly pleasant and cheerful way with her mother. Lady Cui's reserve—which dated back to the morning Oriole and Jun-rui's affair was discovered—had begun to wear down. It seemed to Oriole that she and her mother had come to the end of their deceptions. So why not put it all behind them and try to get on with the business of healing their shaky relationship? They couldn't go on resenting and punishing each other forever. Anyway, they'd be free of each other soon enough—when she and Jun-rui had their own residence in the capital—so they could at least make an effort to get along while they were still forced to live under the same roof. It could only make things easier in the long run, not just for themselves but for everyone else.

Lady Cui was slow to forgive and forget, but Oriole's persistence worked on her until she finally started to soften. She also wasn't in any hurry to outwardly excuse Scarlet's rude and confrontational behavior toward her that summer morning, when they'd argued about Oriole and Jun-rui. She wasn't accustomed to being told what to do—especially by a maid!—and she'd been quite shocked at the way Scarlet had spoken to her. It simply wasn't done! But what really stuck in her throat was that deep down she had a high opinion of Scarlet; she knew everything Scarlet had said that day was true. Even more infuriating, Scarlet never resorted to cringing or groveling. She had a pride and self-confidence about her that, despite herself, Lady Cui couldn't help admiring. So it was inevitable that she'd forgive the girl's insolence sooner rather than later. The hardest thing was not *showing* that she had!

None of this bothered Scarlet much. She always had plenty of work to do, and when she wasn't busy with chores, she kept Oriole company or helped her with her sewing. They often talked about Jun-rui and Lucky, and would try to imagine where they

were and what they were doing. If Oriole was looking wistful on a particular day, Scarlet would always think of something to buoy her spirits. One
evening when Oriole was at a pretty low ebb, Scarlet said to her cheerily, "I did the fortune sticks
again today, and the old woman says to look out
for the tenth of the tenth—it's a lucky day, and
something important might easily happen."

She stared at Oriole wide-eyed and excited.
"They'll be back soon, I'm sure of it—you see if
I'm not right!"

THE DAY THAT SCARLET'S old fortune-teller had
singled out—the tenth of the tenth—turned out to
be the same as any other day. Oriole had spent most
of the afternoon working on the quilt and had just
finished her twenty-third butterfly. Now she'd had
to stop because the light was fading. She couldn't
help feeling disappointed that the day had failed to
provide her with the good news she'd hoped for.
She sighed to herself as she lit the oil lamps and
candles—she should have known better than to take
any notice of what some foolish old woman had
said. After all, there was no end to the nonsense
these people invented.

She ate dinner with Di-di and her mother that
evening at Lady Cui's quarters and then went back
to her room thinking she might do a little reading
before getting ready for bed. She settled down next

to the brazier, with a heavy padded jacket thrown over her shoulders and a book of poetry open in her hand. The night was cold, and she was soon huddling even closer to the glowing coals. As she leafed through the book, a short piece by a woman poet caught her eye. She read it to herself, then started reading it out loud, ending with these lines:

It is easier to come by precious jewels
Than to find a man with a true heart.
Why wet your pillow with secret tears?
Why hide your heartbreak in the flowers?
Don't long for someone who will never come
back.

Considering that Oriole had spent the past few months waiting for the man she loved and persuading herself that he *would* come back to her, she found these lines especially discouraging. There was no hope in the poem, no hope at all. The words were so bleak. She wondered what sad experience the poet must have had to make her communicate such loneliness and despair. With tears running down her cheeks, Oriole read through the poem again. She felt herself falling into a void of hopelessness. She had almost reached the last lines when she became aware of heavy footsteps on the wooden walkway outside. She stopped reading to listen. It was someone running—fast.

Only a moment later Scarlet was standing in front of her, panting like she had just run ten miles. She looked wild and agitated, and her eyes were glowing like the coals in the brazier. But every time she opened her mouth to speak, she ended up producing strange breathless puffing sounds. Oriole could make no sense of them.

"Iss…isslah…lah…isslah…"

Oriole had to wait for Scarlet's gasps to subside before the message became intelligible. And when she finally realized that Scarlet had been trying to say, "It's Lucky!" she became every bit as excited as her maid. She was equally incapable of putting two words together for quite some time. Eventually, when she'd calmed down enough to converse properly, she learned that Lucky had just arrived at the monastery after five weeks on the road and was currently with her mother—being interrogated, no doubt.

Fortunately Scarlet had stayed at Lady Cui's quarters long enough to pick up the most important news. She was therefore able to give Oriole answers to the questions she'd been burning to ask. Much to Oriole's delight and amazement, it seemed that not only had Jun-rui passed the examinations, he'd done very well. He'd been paraded through the streets of Chang-an for three days in a row, with all the other candidates who'd placed at the top of the list. These young men had real cause for celebration; their examination results meant their future success was guaranteed. When Lucky left Changan, Jun-rui was still waiting for a government appointment, but it was just a matter of time. And he planned to come for Oriole the moment everything was settled; that was what Lucky had said to Lady Cui.

"Your mother looked like she'd seen a ghost when Lucky first turned up on her doorstep," Scarlet confided.

"Well, he's obviously had quite an effect on you, too!" Oriole retorted teasingly. "You were in a real state when you got here just now, and you haven't stopped blushing since! Every time you mention his name, your face goes all red!"

"Nonsense!" Scarlet exclaimed, blushing more than ever. "You're imagining things. He's much too young for me, anyway. I'm just pleased for you, that's all."

"Hmm…" Oriole said thoughtfully, giving Scarlet a suspicious glance.

"Well, shall I bring him over here?" Scarlet asked impatiently and much too eagerly.

Oriole laughed. Scarlet was clever at keeping other people's secrets, but pretty hopeless when it came to concealing her own!

"Yes, Scarlet," she said without hesitation. "Go

and fetch him. You know I'm dying to talk to him and hear all his news firsthand.''

ORIOLE HAD PLENTY of time to study Jun-rui's servant while he stood by the door taking off his dusty boots. The first thing that struck her about his appearance was how pale and worn-out he looked. He'd evidently had a hard journey and deserved a few days' rest. His clothes were dirty, and even from the other side of the room she could tell he was badly in need of a bath.

As soon as Scarlet had brought him, she went over to Oriole and asked in a whisper if she could go and get him something to eat. Oriole was horrified to learn that no one had thought of feeding the poor man sooner. It was late and he must have been famished, so she sent Scarlet off to the kitchens at once to see what she could scrape together.

While Scarlet was away, Lucky answered a whole stream of questions about his journey and the examinations and life in the capital, but mostly Oriole just wanted to hear about Jun-rui—anything and everything, as long as it was about him. Just hearing Lucky talk brought Jun-rui so much closer and made her feel so much happier than she'd been for months.

At one point Lucky asked her to wait a moment because he had something to give her. Without bothering to put on his boots, he popped outside for a second and came back carrying a cane box, which he put down near the brazier. This way Oriole would be able to inspect its contents in comfort and warmth. When she opened the box, the first thing she observed was that it had been very carefully lined with paper to protect what was inside. Lifting the top sheet, she took out a dozen lengths of silk, each neatly folded and individually wrapped in paper. As she examined the silks one at a time, it seemed to her that each was more beautiful than the last—the colors were so rich and the patterns so exquisite. It was many months since Oriole had been in the city and seen such exciting fabrics with such a wealth and variety of texture, color and design. These superbly chosen pieces left her feeling quite breathless.

She was also impressed by the care Jun-rui had taken with the wrapping. A piece of silk could snag very easily on a splinter of cane, and any amount of damage could be caused by dirt or bad weather after several weeks on the road. Thanks to Jun-rui's thoughtfulness, his gifts had reached her in perfect condition.

Beautiful though the silks were, perhaps the most wonderful gift of all was a sealed envelope lying at the bottom of the box. To judge by its thickness, it contained a very long letter. This was something she intended to save for later when she was alone.

Scarlet was back soon after with a meal for

Lucky—steaming hot rice, a plate of salted fish and a bowl of pickled vegetables, as well as a small jug of warmed rice wine. It was the best she could do at that late hour. Lucky immediately wolfed everything down. Soon afterward, he was practically falling asleep in his chair; Scarlet took him off to the monks' dormitory where there was bound to be an extra bed he could use for a few nights.

By the time Lucky had rested for a couple of days, he was ready to face the long journey back to the capital, where Jun-rui would now be waiting for news of Oriole. She'd had time to think of several gifts for Jun-rui, things that Lucky could take back with him in the same cane box. Some of these gifts were of no particular worth, but she knew he'd value them simply because they were hers. There was a pair of silk stockings, the sash she'd worn the first time she went to his room and a bamboo hairbrush, which was mottled as though stained with tears. There was also a beautiful jasper zither she wanted him to have. And, of course, she included the undershirt she'd embroidered for him— it was a labor of love and a source of pride. Last, she tucked in a letter and a poem she'd written in reply to his over the course of Lucky's visit. These things were the only way she had of telling him during this long separation how much she loved him and how much she longed for his return.

She gave Lucky plenty of money for the journey—ten ounces of silver altogether—to enable him to travel in more comfort, eating and sleeping at inns. She wept the day Lucky left, but at least there'd finally been some word from Jun-rui, and Oriole now felt that the red thread running between them had drawn tighter.

She was confident she would find the inner strength she needed to face this next lonely stretch without him.

CHAPTER FOURTEEN

AFTER THE FORTUNE-TELLER had been proved right in predicting something special for the tenth of the tenth, Scarlet made a point of going to see her at least once a week. The old woman lived in a village quite near the monastery and set herself up outside the main gate most days to tell fortunes for passersby or for visitors to the monastery—or even for monastery residents who wanted a change from what was available by way of fortune-telling inside the temple.

The old woman was proficient in her work. As well as the fortune sticks, she could turn her hand to fortune blocks, palm reading, physiognomy and divination by turtle shell. But what really clinched Scarlet's respect for her was the fact that—poor as she was—the old woman knew how to read.

Oriole, as usual, had less freedom of movement than Scarlet. As a cultivated young lady, she had to make do with the monastery's official fortune-tellers if she wanted any kind of divination. But she was always far more interested to hear what Scarlet's old woman had to say. Now that several weeks had passed since Lucky's visit and the excitement of it had worn off, both Oriole and Scarlet derived great comfort from the optimistic predictions of this strange woman.

One bitterly cold morning toward the end of the lunar year, Scarlet was hurrying through the monastery's First Courtyard on her way to the main gate, to see if her old fortune-teller was there. She saw very few people around—a couple of lay brothers carrying in supplies from a cart outside the gate and one of the abbot's novices, who'd just delivered a message to a guard in the gatehouse.

Ahead of her Scarlet suddenly noticed two men on horseback ride in through the gate, dismount and tether their horses inside the courtyard. One was obviously a servant. The other was wearing what looked like an expensive fur-lined traveling coat. From the style of his hat, Scarlet could tell he was someone fairly important—probably a middle-ranking government employee or something like that. The coat made him look big and beefy. The two men were ambling over to the gatehouse, and she heard one of the guards asking them who they wanted. The beefy man answered in a loud and condescending manner.

"Cui. Name ring a bell?"

Scarlet stopped dead in her tracks. The voice was very familiar, yet she couldn't quite place it. She'd gone only a couple of yards past the man and turned at once, trying to get a good look at his face. She was still peering at him when he discovered he was under scrutiny. His cheeks, which were already red, flushed crimson and he strode over to her angrily with his hands on his wide hips.

"What d'you think you're staring at? Rude little woman!"

His voice came in bursts like water spurting from a pump, and his long prickly-looking mustache jerked and twitched as he spoke. Now that his face was pressed close to hers, Scarlet had a good chance to study him.

He wasn't at all what you'd call handsome. He had a wide forehead, plump cheeks and rather small watery eyes. His mouth was mostly hidden by his mustache, but Scarlet could see the rolls of fat bulging under his chin.

Then her jaw dropped. She'd realized in a flash that she knew this person. The face was fatter, but it was definitely the same. There was no mistaking him. It was Heng.

Without stopping to think about what she was saying, Scarlet blurted out in horror, "Mr. Heng, what on earth are you doing here? We thought you were in the capital. You're not supposed to be here at all now that—"

Hearing himself addressed by name, Heng squinted in her direction. "Do I know you?" he interrupted coldly. "If so, give me your name. If not, mind your own business!"

Scarlet bristled. He hadn't changed a bit. He was as uncouth as ever. But she kept her thoughts to herself and bobbed him a token curtsy.

"I'm Scarlet. Miss Oriole's maid. I'm surprised you don't recognize me."

The transformation on Heng's face was instantaneous. Cold and irritable one moment, he was nothing but warmth and good humor the next. He flashed her a smile that was all whiskers and teeth, and looked her up and down with an admiring twinkle in his eye.

"Of course I recognize you—now that you've told me. How could I forget that pretty little face and that saucy little..."

He had taken a step or two toward her while he was talking, and suddenly—without any warning—he shot a hand up under her padded coat and grasped her buttock, giving it a hard squeeze.

"Always did like a bit of meat," he guffawed, as Scarlet stepped back from him in disgust.

Scarlet admitted to herself that she'd been wrong. He *had* changed. He was worse! She didn't care how important he was; she wasn't going to let that pass.

"You keep your hands to yourself!" she said, glaring at him. "It may be meat to you, but that doesn't mean it's yours for the taking!"

"Ooh!" he teased, raising his eyebrows. "So whose is it, then? Who's the lucky man, eh?"

Scarlet glared at him some more. "You're missing the point," she said disdainfully. "It's mine. It belongs to me."

"I thought so," he said in a pitying tone. "There wouldn't be a young man on the scene, now would there? Not when you're doing a life sentence with Auntie Cui and her merry clan!" He had a good chuckle at Scarlet's expense.

Scarlet stood there fuming. He really was the most insufferable man she'd ever met, and no one could have been happier than she was the day Lady Cui called off the engagement between Oriole and her pig of a cousin. Goodness knew how he'd managed to pull the wool over Lady Cui's eyes all these years—and even Oriole's. Scarlet had never been fooled, though. He might have appeared reasonably agreeable and well-mannered in company, but she'd seen a very different side to him in private, and if Oriole had ever had the misfortune of being forced to marry him, she would have seen it, too. In no time at all!

What worried Scarlet now was *why* Heng had turned up at the monastery. He couldn't have received Lady Cui's letter telling him the engagement was off, or he wouldn't have bothered to make the long journey. That could only mean he was still under the impression that his wedding to Oriole would be taking place. Naturally, if Lady Cui was a woman of her word, she could be trusted to break the bad news to him in person. But to Scarlet's way of thinking, it was far more likely that the moment Lady Cui learned her nephew was on the premises, she'd be changing her mind again and thinking of all the reasons the two cousins should marry, after all. Lady Cui's views had shifted this way and that often enough for Scarlet to look upon her inconstancy as second nature. Why should she believe it would suddenly stop? The situation was dangerous.

Just the thought of anyone or anything coming between Oriole and Jun-rui after all these long months of waiting made Scarlet feel sick to her stomach. If only she could think of something to safeguard Oriole's happiness. If only there was some way of preventing Heng from meeting up with his fickle aunt.

These worried thoughts all flashed through Scarlet's mind while Heng was still having his unkind chuckle at his joke about Scarlet's "life sentence" with the Cuis. The joke over, his face took on a hardened expression.

"How is the old bag?" he asked with a sneer. "Cold as ever? Or has she thawed a bit with age?"

Scarlet tossed him a look of dislike. He obviously wasn't interested in an answer, so she had no intention of giving him one.

"And what about my skinny cousin, the Stick

Insect?'' He laughed, putting great emphasis on the last two words.

Scarlet managed at first not to react, but when Heng started doing a poor impersonation of Oriole—sucking in his cheeks, fluttering his eyelashes and taking mincing little steps—Scarlet lost her temper and rose swiftly to Oriole's defense.

"What's she ever done to you that you're so nasty about her?'' she asked angrily. "The truth is, she's way too good for you—that's what you can't stand. In fact, she's everything you're not. She's got a trim figure for a start, unlike *some* people I could mention! And she's kind, and beauti—''

"Oh, spare me the long list, please!'' Heng protested, pretending to yawn with boredom. "I've heard it all so often from my tedious aunt—the Good Points, the Wifely Virtues and all that garbage. I really don't need to hear it again from you!''

Scarlet was still smarting from his insulting remarks about Oriole.

"Well, maybe it's about time you realized what a legible young lady she is!'' she retorted hotly.

Heng burst into loud laughter. "Legible? That's a good one! Eligible's the word you're looking for, my dear!'' he said condescendingly. Once he'd recovered from his merriment and dabbed at his watery eyes with a large handkerchief, he suddenly fell silent, then turned to Scarlet with a frown on his face.

"Look, don't get me wrong. I know what you're saying. She's a delightful creature. A good catch. She'll make a terrific wife for some lucky guy, no doubt about it." He paused a moment, but his frown only deepened. He continued speaking in a tone that was almost confidential.

"Trouble is, Scarlet, she's just not my type. Too pale and delicate for my tastes. Too serious about life. You know me, Scarlet. I'm a simple sort of man when it comes to the opposite sex. What I'm after is a bit of fun. Slap and tickle, that kind of thing!"

Scarlet looked at him in surprise. "You mean, you don't even *want* to marry Miss Oriole?"

Heng snorted impatiently. "God, no! What do you think I've been trying to tell you?"

He smacked his lips, and his little eyes glinted greedily. "Now, if you were to ask me about the luscious Miss Lily, that would be an entirely different matter."

"Who's she?" Scarlet asked curiously.

"Another cousin on my mother's side," Heng explained. "Good-looking girl. Lots of fun. Much more my cup of tea. She and I were getting on famously, had a very nice little thing going and then my damned aunt sends me a damned letter ordering me to come to this damned monastery in the middle of nowhere. Ruined everything!"

He looked cross and disappointed. Scarlet, however, was puzzled.

"But it was last spring she wrote to you saying that, wasn't it? Ages ago."

"Sure," Heng agreed. "That was her first letter. I'd already got mixed up with Lily then, so I decided to ignore it. Thought I could say I was delayed by official business or some such excuse. But then, damn it, she goes and writes again. Didn't see how I could ignore the second one, too. Not for much longer, anyway. That's why I'm here!"

Scarlet had just seen the light and was staring at Heng with an expression of horror. So Lady Cui had kept her promise by writing to Heng, all right— but she'd written telling him to *come*. As though Jun-rui didn't even exist!

"Damn her if she hasn't gone and lied to Oriole again, the lying bitch!" she cursed, more to herself than to Heng.

As for Heng, he just stood there, quite mystified as to why Scarlet had become so outspoken and so distraught—except that it apparently had something to do with his aunt.

"Tut, tut! Language!" he teased, pretending to chide her. But he was actually quite curious about what was going on, especially since he had a vague notion that it concerned him in some way. "So what's my naughty auntie been up to now?" he asked Scarlet.

"You wouldn't believe it!" she replied, shaking her head slowly. "She was supposed to write and tell you the engagement was off and you weren't to bother coming because Miss Oriole's engaged to someone else. But from what you've just told me, she didn't write any such thing."

"No, she didn't," Heng confirmed, raising his eyebrows in surprise. "She said I was to come without delay. It was urgent, she said. That's why I didn't think I could put her off a second time. But tell me," he said, looking at Scarlet closely. "Are you saying Oriole doesn't want to marry me, either? What's going on here? Since when was a girl engaged to two guys at once?"

Scarlet sighed. "I think I'd better explain."

It was hardly the weather for a lengthy outdoor storytelling session, but at least the stone arch of the gateway offered some protection from the cold. Scarlet tried to keep her explanation as brief as possible, but it still took awhile. Heng was very startled by what she had to say and for once didn't interrupt with too many clever or provocative remarks.

By the time Scarlet had finished, Heng, too, was shaking his head.

"Devious old bag, eh?" he commented wryly. "But one thing's quite clear—my cousin doesn't want to marry me any more than I want to marry her. So what do we do now? Any ideas? Do I just go and thrash it out with the old girl, or what?"

Scarlet's reaction was prompt. "No, that's definitely not a good idea. I think it would be a big mistake for you to see your aunt at all. If you do, you'll be trapped, you'll never get away, and she'll have you and Oriole married off before you can even blink."

"Well, what do you suggest, then?"

"I suggest you turn around and head straight back to the capital as quick as you can," Scarlet advised. "And don't tell anyone you've even been near this place. No one knows you're here except me and a couple of guards, and I can easily keep them quiet. It would be as if you'd never come."

"But what about my aunt and her damned letter?" Heng asked thoughtfully, fingering the rolls of fat under his chin.

"You can write her a reply now before you go," Scarlet told him in a self-assured tone. "Tell her you're forced to break off the engagement because another match has been made for you. Tell her about Luscious Lily and all that. I'll take the letter to her later today. I'll pretend it was delivered by a special messenger from Chang-an. She'll never be any the wiser."

"But she's hardly going to sit back and say it's fine if I go off and marry someone else, now is she?" Heng said, frowning.

"I don't see there's much she can do about it," Scarlet replied breezily. "She won't want this to come out in the open, not when it means admitting she cheated us all a second time.''

"But if her darling daughter's left on the shelf, an old maid, she's bound to do something about it!'' Heng said. "Suppose this Zhang—is that his name?—suppose he never shows up?''

Scarlet gazed at Heng long and steadily. "He will, don't you worry about that,'' she said in a solemn voice.

Scarlet soon had Heng installed in the gatehouse writing his reply to Lady Cui. In the end she more or less dictated the whole thing for him. Meanwhile, Heng and his servant were knocking back quite a few cupfuls of wine to warm them for the road.

Just as they were untethering their horses, Heng caught Scarlet off guard for a moment and grabbed hold of her buttock for another quick squeeze. Scarlet shook herself free of him in an instant and shot him a withering look.

Heng just threw back his head and laughed, then swung himself into the saddle.

"You're quite a girl,'' he called down to her with a look of genuine admiration. "A good head on your shoulders, as well as some first-class—''

"You'd better be careful, Mr. Heng,'' Scarlet blazed at him. "I'm warning you...''

Either he didn't hear her or he pretended not to. At any rate, he was laughing loudly and wobbling like bean curd on a plate all the way through the courtyard and out the gate.

BECAUSE OF HER extraordinary and most unexpected encounter with Heng, Scarlet never did get to see her old fortune-teller that day—but it hardly seemed to matter. There were evidently plenty of strange forces already at work without complicating things further.

That morning Scarlet debated with herself whether or not to tell Oriole about Heng's flying visit to the monastery. It wasn't an easy decision, and there were strong arguments both ways—but she finally decided against it. Not that lying to Oriole or keeping information from her was something Scarlet was particularly proud of. But once Oriole knew Heng had been there, it was only a matter of time before she found out about Lady Cui's second letter and its treacherous contents. And then all hell would break loose.

Of course, Scarlet felt perplexed by Lady Cui's letter to Heng. She tried to work out what could have induced the woman to write it in the first place. Lady Cui obviously didn't dislike Jun-rui, and she'd seemed won over by Scarlet's arguments in favor of his marriage to Oriole—so why would she go and do something calculated to make sure this marriage never took place? Why would she suddenly revert to the idea of Heng as a son-in-law? It didn't make sense.

The more Scarlet thought about it, the more she believed there was only one reason to explain Lady Cui's curious behavior. Lady Cui, she decided, must have been convinced that Jun-rui would go off to Chang-an and never come back. Handsome young students were always doing this kind of thing—having an affair with some girl on their way to the capital, then forgetting all about it. Why should Jun-rui be any different? And if there was one thing a woman like Lady Cui would never allow, it would be to have her daughter end up unmarried and disgraced. Yes, that had to be it.

No wonder she looked like she'd seen a ghost the day Lucky turned up on her doorstep bearing news and gifts! If Scarlet's interpretation was correct, he was obviously the last person she'd expected to see back at the monastery.

While Scarlet was weighing in her mind whether or not to tell Oriole about Heng, she also considered the depth of Oriole's feelings for Jun-rui and how terribly she'd missed him all these months. If Oriole was to find out that her mother had tried a second time to sabotage this precious relationship, she would be devastated. In fact, Scarlet felt sure that Oriole would never recover from the blow. No, this was one secret she would have to keep.

Scarlet knew she was taking matters too much

into her own hands, but her first concern had to be Oriole. And if Oriole was going to be married soon, surely she should at least be able to enjoy friendly relations with her own family. The truth about Lady Cui's duplicity would only destroy Oriole's happiness. So for this reason Scarlet said nothing about Heng or what had passed between them.

She did, however, do what she'd told Heng she would, which was to deliver his letter to Lady Cui that same day, in the afternoon.

She was quick-witted enough to appreciate all the complexities of the situation she now found herself in. To begin with, Lady Cui was supposed to have written a second letter to Heng, telling him that Oriole was marrying someone else and that the engagement between the cousins was therefore off. This was what Oriole, Scarlet and Jun-rui all thought she'd done, although Scarlet now knew otherwise. The letter Heng had *actually* received was one telling him to come at once and marry his cousin. He'd duly arrived, was intercepted by Scarlet, and together they'd devised a way of doing the opposite of what Lady Cui wanted.

When Scarlet put Heng's letter in Lady Cui's hand, Lady Cui would automatically assume that she—Scarlet—had no idea what it said. She'd never guess that Scarlet had virtually written the letter herself! Also, Lady Cui would think that Scarlet thought Heng's letter was a reply to the letter Lady

Cui was supposed to have written telling him *not* to come to the monastery.... It was all very complicated!

In view of all this, Scarlet was understandably fascinated to discover what Lady Cui's reaction would be on opening the letter. But in the event, Scarlet was disappointed. Lady Cui—being quite practiced in the art of deception—gave a brilliant performance. As she first glanced through the letter and learned that Heng was backing out of the engagement with Oriole and planning, instead, to marry a different cousin, her face flickered briefly with astonishment and irritation. But she quickly brought her expression under control and assumed a sort of auntlike smile.

"What does he say?" Scarlet asked, hoping she'd put Lady Cui on the spot.

"Oh, not a lot really," Lady Cui answered casually. "He just says to give his regards to Oriole and her new young man—because naturally I told him about Mr. Zhang. And he says to wish them all the best for the future. Reading between the lines, though, I'd say he's disappointed not to be marrying her himself. Says he doesn't think he'll be able to make it to the wedding—too much business in the capital. Asks how we all are. Talks about the shocking weather. That's about it, really."

While she spoke, Lady Cui had been skimming her eye down the piece of paper in her hand, as though actually reading bits from the letter. Her performance was so convincing, Scarlet felt utterly astounded. Did Lady Cui have an inexhaustible supply of deceit and artifice?

CHAPTER FIFTEEN

JUN-RUI CAME BACK shortly after the celebrations for seeing in the new year were over. It was the Year of the Dog, which was very appropriate in Oriole's opinion. All the good qualities that were said to characterize the dog—loyalty, devotion, honesty and simplicity—were qualities she believed were uppermost in what she and Jun-rui felt for each other. Of course, the dog's negative quality was its stubbornness. But hadn't she and Jun-rui been guilty of this, too? They'd stubbornly refused to accept defeat, remaining convinced that they were destined to be together in the end. And they'd been proved right. Long live the dog! Oriole smiled to herself happily.

Signs of spring were everywhere around her. The monastery's many gardens—bare and forlorn-looking during the long winter months—were now bursting with blossom. The willows in the Flower Garden were sending out their new leaves of healthy green. It was still cold during the day and even colder at night, but lately the skies had been a little brighter, as if to reassure those below that a kinder season was on its way.

The study had stood empty all winter, and Oriole had made a point of visiting it discreetly every day, accompanied by Scarlet. They never went inside; they just spent an hour or so in the garden, sometimes walking, sometimes sitting quietly in the little pavilion. For Oriole it was a time of meditation, when she could feel closer to Jun-rui in spirit, even though he was so far away.

One day in the study garden she'd noticed the old plum tree's first red buds, and she'd felt a strange mixture of delight and sadness. She was reminded of the second time she'd gone to see him in his study; he'd had the vase of plum blossom standing near the bed, fresh from this tree. Now she made sure she always had one of its sprigs in her room to constantly remind her of Jun-rui.

The day he came back, happiness swept through Oriole like a flood.

She found it a real struggle to exercise self-control. They weren't really able to express their love, and that was hard for both of them. They weren't officially engaged in the eyes of the world yet, which meant that they were expected to observe all the constraints. Still, despite the restrictions on their outward behavior, Oriole could read in his dark eyes how much he'd missed her and how he longed to make up for lost time.

As for her own feelings, she was positive she wouldn't have been able to hide them even if she'd wanted to. She felt as though she was shouting her love for him from the temple rooftop when she was actually only standing demurely in front of him, saying nothing. Her mouth wouldn't stop smiling and her cheeks couldn't help flushing. She was so full of love she felt she might burst with it.

It was so like him, she reflected when she was alone in her room, to make such a modest entrance. He hadn't drawn any attention to his success. Because he'd done so well in the examinations, he'd had his pick of top jobs in the civil service and had ended up with a good position in the same department as his father before him—the Ministry of Rites. As such, he was now permitted to wear the special costume—the colored robes and hat—that went with his high rank, and he was also expected to have a lifestyle with a certain extravagance. Oriole had already heard all the stories—from Scarlet, who'd been told by Lucky—about the way Jun-rui had been paraded through the streets of the capital for three days after the results were announced. And about all the young women in search of a husband who'd made such a fuss of him, each hoping to catch him for herself. The best story of all concerned his delight in telling more than one of them that he was already engaged!

Oriole hardly needed reminding that Jun-rui had

gone up in the world and was now someone to be reckoned with. It therefore made her all the happier that he seemed so unaffected by his newfound wealth and position. He and Lucky had made the long journey back to the monastery on horseback, without the fine carriage and groom they were entitled to. His behavior was as straightforward and considerate as ever. There was nothing pretentious or arrogant about him—he seemed exactly the same man she'd loved before.

She knew that once they were married, she, too, would be expected to dress in a more elaborate style, as befitted the wife of a high official. She would have a private carriage at her disposal and all the trappings of a woman of position. But the thought didn't excite her overmuch. What mattered infinitely more was the fact that they'd be united at last; she would bear his children and they would share every moment.

Naturally Jun-rui had presented himself to Lady Cui soon after his arrival. Oriole, who'd happened to be in the room at the time, was struck by the strangeness of her mother's reaction to him. Afterward, she'd discussed it at some length with Scarlet. Why should her mother—always so controlled and cool in her manner—suddenly become flustered and awkward upon setting eyes on her future son-in-law? What would account for her nervousness and

distant attitude toward him? Didn't she like him?
Was that the problem?

Her mother had actually gone quite pale when
Jun-rui entered the room, and at one point Oriole
could have sworn there were tears in her eyes. Now
that she thought about it, she remembered Scarlet
saying once that Lady Cui had looked like she'd
seen a ghost—that time Lucky came back. What
was it all about?

None of this made much sense to Oriole. She'd
assumed her mother would be pleased about Jun-
rui's good job and would welcome him, if not with
open arms, then at least with a smile on her face.
And yet here she was, behaving in a way that
wasn't only inexplicable but downright unfriendly.

Scarlet didn't really have much light to shed on
the situation, except to insist that she was sure Lady
Cui had a good opinion of Jun-rui and liked him
well enough. Then she put forward the idea that
maybe Lady Cui had never expected him to return.

This suggestion of Scarlet's had thrown Oriole
completely. Why shouldn't her mother have expected Jun-rui to come back and marry her? This
was what they'd planned. Why was it such a surprise? And why a cause for anxiety?

Scarlet apparently didn't have any answers, or if
she did, she was keeping them to herself.

Pretending not to know anything made Scarlet
feel more than a little guilty. She would've liked to

put Oriole's mind at ease, but she wasn't about to reveal Heng's appearance at the monastery or the contents of Lady Cui's second letter. All she could do was advise Oriole to wait for Lady Cui to calm down. Whatever was causing the upset probably wasn't as important as Oriole imagined, she said, and would undoubtedly sort itself out in due course. It was bound to be nothing more than a mother's realization that she was about to lose her only daughter. Or some such thing...

Oriole wasn't particularly convinced by any of Scarlet's comments, but didn't think there was much to be gained by discussing it further. She'd half decided to leave things be, but a second meeting between Jun-rui and her mother a day or two later—which proved every bit as awkward and uncomfortable as the first—made Oriole determined to take action. It didn't bode well for the future to have such strained relations between her mother and the man she loved. What was more, she was damned if she was going to allow the sweetness of this reunion to be soured by her mother's unaccountable hostility. It was time they had it out!

WHEN ORIOLE WENT to her mother's quarters later that same afternoon, she found only her brother and Constance. They were out in the small back courtyard cleaning out Di-di's canary cage. Constance told Oriole that Lady Cui had left for a walk in the

Flower Garden earlier and was still there, as far as she knew. So Oriole set off to find her.

The brightness had already gone out of the day as Oriole hurried along the path that wound around the west wing. She considered going back to her room for a jacket, but quickly decided against it. She didn't want to lose her momentum and risk missing her mother. On the other hand, there wasn't much daylight left and the chill of dusk would soon be descending; maybe she was being foolish and would only end up catching cold... But by the time she'd finished her inner debating and told herself to stop fussing, she'd already reached the outer wall of the garden. Turning back at that point would have been absurd. Instead, she pressed on with re-newed determination.

A gust of wind jangled the wind chimes hanging from the temple eaves as Oriole arrived at the Flower Garden's wooden gate and pushed it open. There were the usual noisy creakings and groanings of stiff old wood, and then silence.

Faced with three paths each leading in a different direction, Oriole had no idea which her mother had chosen. Somehow her feet seemed to lead her of their own accord along the middle path, and she made no attempt to resist. Then when she came to the smaller path branching off to the right and up the little hillock, she found herself following it without really knowing why.

Even before she'd reached the end of the path and stepped onto the paved area at the top of the hillock, she could see a figure in black crouched in front of the stone incense table. Several sticks of incense smoldered in the bronze pot. The huge ornamental rocks with the plantains sprouting among them towered behind, almost menacing in the fast-failing light.

Oriole stopped in her tracks and tried to stay quiet, but the rustling of her silk gown betrayed her. The crouched figure gave a start, then spun around accusingly.

"I should have known it would be you! Don't you know any better than to go creeping up on people from behind? It's enough to make me die of fright!"

Lady Cui had obviously received a scare. Not only had she failed to hear Oriole's footsteps until they were directly behind her, she'd also been crying and hadn't had time to hide the evidence. Her cheeks were streaked with watery trails. And teardrops mixed with face powder had left white splashes on the front of her black robe.

For a moment Oriole was at a loss for words. It had shocked her, seeing her mother in such obvious distress, and Lady Cui's sharp words had only added to her confusion. But what she instinctively felt was pity. A moment later she was stepping forward to offer words of comfort.

"What's wrong, Mother? Why are you crying?"

Lady Cui seemed almost surprised by the kindness and sympathy in her daughter's face and voice. Her bottom lip began to quiver, and she waved her hand frantically in front of her, as if telling Oriole to go away and leave her alone. She was shaking her head from side to side, looking more distraught than Oriole had ever seen her. Oriole knelt beside her, putting an arm protectively around her mother's shoulders.

She'd intended the gesture to be comforting. But the next thing she knew Lady Cui was sobbing loudly and clutching tightly onto one of Oriole's hands. She could think of nothing to say except, "Don't, Mother. Don't." This didn't seem to make the slightest difference, judging by the sobs that continued for some time and the tears that went on falling. With her free hand Oriole fumbled for the handkerchief in her sleeve and tried, not very successfully, to dry her mother's face. Gradually the sobbing subsided and Oriole felt Lady Cui's grip loosening. A feeling of calm and release descended on them, seemingly from out of nowhere.

She took her mother's hand in hers and stroked it thoughtfully, searching for the right words. "I was looking for you, Mother," she began. "I wanted to talk to you."

Lady Cui glanced up at her with a troubled expression. "What about?" she asked.

"About Jun-rui."

Immediately Lady Cui averted her face, and her lip trembled slightly, as though she might break into sobs again.

"What is it, Mother?" How can I help if you won't tell me what's wrong? I just don't understand...."

Lady Cui threw her a pleading look but said nothing. Oriole was confused and disappointed, and all of a sudden it was simply too much. She just couldn't restrain herself—the things she wanted to say wouldn't be held in any longer and the words came tumbling out.

"I thought you'd be so pleased, Mother. I thought you'd be really glad he did so well and got such a good job and made sure we'd have status and money and all the things you think are so important. But you've been unfriendly to him ever since he got back. You behave as if you don't even like him. Is that the problem, Mother? I have to know. I mean, I'm talking about the man I love—" Her cheeks had grown flushed with embarrassment and passion as she spoke.

"That's just it," Lady Cui interrupted quietly.

Oriole was puzzled. "What is?"

"You *love* him." Lady Cui spoke the words cautiously.

Oriole was still completely in the dark and wondered if her mother was well. It certainly wasn't like her to cry or display emotion; she'd never even *talked* about things like love before, not that Oriole could remember.

"What do you mean?" she asked her mother, frowning.

Lady Cui turned to Oriole, leaning her back against the incense table. She looked her daughter steadily in the eye and spoke softly and slowly.

"It wasn't like that for me. I never thought it was possible to be as happy as you are. Never. Not until now. And it's painful, you know—all those years gone by without happiness... Such a waste." In her mind, images of her husband, the other wives, the young maids, went racing by—all the bitterness and loneliness, the humiliation and despair of the past years. Even Scarlet's girlish face when she was still a virgin, waiting outside Lord Cui's bedroom door that first night... Why did it have to happen? Why had it been like that? She heaved a deep sigh and shook her head sadly before continuing.

"Do you remember that time you said you didn't want to marry your cousin because you didn't love him? I must admit I thought you were nothing but a foolish child who didn't know any better. And when Scarlet told me that you and Mr. Zhang were 'in love', as she put it, I refused to listen. I told myself the girl was talking nonsense. I was so sure there was no such thing. I thought love was just a word, some sort of romantic nonsense you only saw in books. But now that Jun-rui's here, everything's changed. I can see I was wrong. *I'm* the one who's been foolish. Foolish and...and so alone all these years."

While she was speaking, tears of remorse and self-pity ran down her cheeks.

Oriole was about to protest, but Lady Cui cut in quickly.

"When I think of all the harm I could've done, I feel so ashamed." Her head was cocked slightly to one side, and her eyes were wide and mournful. "You see, I was quite sure he was never coming back."

"But why?" Oriole asked. "Why shouldn't he come back?" She was confused about almost everything her mother had said, and this was no exception. Why should Lady Cui have had so little faith that Jun-rui would do what he'd promised? And even if she'd doubted him, why was she so upset about it *now,* after he was back? It didn't add up.

Lady Cui shivered a little and pulled her black outer robe more tightly around her matronly figure.

"Oh, I don't know," she began vaguely. "I suppose I thought it was one of those casual affairs young scholars often indulge in when they're on the loose. One hears so many stories about inexperienced young women being taken in by their promises, only to be abandoned and left to fend for themselves. I just didn't want to see my own daughter the victim of such a terrible fate.''

Lady Cui turned away to hide her emotion. She shuddered to think what might have happened if Heng had done her bidding and made his way to the monastery to claim Oriole as his bride. How would she have handled two prospective bridegrooms on the scene—and how would she have explained Heng's presence? Everyone would have found out about her devious behavior, and then they'd despise her. It was all so unfortunate. She'd only wanted the best for Oriole....

As if reading her mother's thoughts, Oriole gave her arm a gentle tug and said earnestly, ''I know you've always wanted the best for me, Mother, and things couldn't possibly have worked out any better—so there's no reason for you to punish yourself now. Couldn't we put it all behind us and get on with the present? After all, there's so much to be happy about...well, for me, anyway.''

Lady Cui gave Oriole an anxious glance. ''But suppose I'd succeeded in coming between you and Jun-rui. Suppose I'd destroyed your happiness...''

Oriole smiled at her fondly, but her voice was firm. ''No, let's not suppose! You didn't, and that's all that matters. It's all over now, and I don't want to hear any more about it.''

Lady Cui sighed and took Oriole's hands in hers.

It was the first time in many years that she'd shown such warm affection. They sat silently for a while, gazing down at the lake and the stone bridge and the willow trees in the distance. Oriole wondered whether to ask her mother what she'd meant when she'd talked about the past and not being happy and all those wasted years. Her mother's words made her wonder about her parents and their life together, and she was curious to know more. But it wasn't her place to ask, and she sensed that their conversation was over for the time being. Besides, it was pleasant just sitting here with her mother.

The silence was broken only by the occasional jangling of the wind chimes or the lonely calling of birds. Oriole recalled vividly that moonlit night when she'd come to the garden with Scarlet and the tall figure had stepped out from behind these same rocks. So much had happened since then. Such a great love had been born out of that first fumbling encounter.

As dusk fell and the light grew steadily dimmer, the water below them started to look quite black. The air had grown cold, too. Oriole shivered, which roused Lady Cui from her dreamlike state.

She smiled at Oriole and patted her hand. "You're a good girl," she said. "When you're married and gone away, I shall miss you."

Oriole felt a surge of warmth. "I love you, Mother," she said impulsively.

Lady Cui smiled again and nodded her head, but made no answer. She seemed to be lost in thought. Oriole was disappointed that her mother hadn't responded to her heartfelt words, but it was hardly surprising. She shouldn't expect too much at once.

A moment later Lady Cui drew a deep breath and pronounced briskly, "Well, this will never do! We'd better be getting back."

Oriole could tell that her mother had regained her composure. After heaving herself to her feet with a helping hand from her daughter, Lady Cui proceeded to smooth the folds of her black robe and pat her face with Oriole's handkerchief to even out the smudged powder. She also tried rubbing away the faint powder stains on her robe. When she was satisfied that she looked presentable, she made a last respectful bow in front of the incense table, where the incense had long since burned itself out. Then she and Oriole began to pick their way carefully along the little path leading down the hillock. They chatted amicably as they walked, and at one point Lady Cui paused to slap her sides heartily.

"Goodness, I'm hungry! I can't remember the last time I had such an appetite." It was hard to see clearly in the semidarkness, but Oriole was fairly certain her mother gave her a merry wink.

"We'll stop at the study on our way home, Oriole. You can ask that young man of yours to join us for dinner. It's about time he was more like one of the family, wouldn't you say?''

Accepting Jun-rui as a son was exactly what she'd promised, Lady Cui reminded herself. She felt a real sense of pleasure about finally keeping her word—to Oriole *and* her fiancé. After all, better late than never...

She hummed all the way back to the west wing.

CHAPTER SIXTEEN

CERTAIN THINGS never did come to light.

Oriole never worked up the courage to ask about her mother's married life and the so-called wasted years, and therefore never heard the sad facts about her mother and father and the wives and the maids—and Scarlet's fate, in particular. She also remained ignorant about the contents of Lady Cui's second letter and consequently never found out about her mother's second dramatic change of heart.

As for Lady Cui, she never heard about Heng's brief appearance at the monastery. Nor did she ever discover what had happened to the duck-and-lotus quilt Oriole was supposedly embroidering all those weeks.

The only person who knew all about everything was Scarlet, and she knew the answers to other important questions, as well. Such as how and when she and Lucky first became sweet on each other, and how Di-di had known about Oriole and Junrui's romantic attachment. *That* had occurred one night when he couldn't sleep. He'd heard Oriole's door open—and had followed his sister and Scarlet to Jun-rui's study. Scarlet had spotted him on her way back to the maids' quarters, hiding behind a maple tree. That was when she'd bribed him into silence with promises of cakes and crickets....

Di-di's secret had come out in the end, but Scarlet never breathed a word about any of the others.

One thing that *was* clear to everyone was the young couple's radiant happiness on their wedding day, which finally took place in the full bloom of spring. There'd been so many preliminaries—the long series of minor ceremonies, the exchanging of presents, formal wine drinking and so on. Just fixing a lucky date for the actual wedding had been a complex and serious business involving a sooth-sayer and the presentation of cards giving essential information about the young pair—such as the name of each person, date and time of birth, the wealth and property of each family and more. Pre-dictably Lady Cui preferred that things be done as much as possible according to custom.

A gift to the bride from her betrothed called ''the three golds'' was the sort of marriage custom Lady Cui approved of. This gift was given before the wedding and consisted of a bracelet, a small chain and a pendant, all of pure gold. Another such cus-tom was practiced on the eve of the wedding, when the bride's dowry was put on display for all to see. In Oriole's case, the dowry was an impressive one and much admired. Lady Cui had been extremely generous and put together a valuable collection of jewelry, porcelain and ornaments for her daughter, not to mention a large assortment of more practical items, such as pillows, silk sheets and pillowcases, bedspreads, hangings and quilts. In this display was the very handsome red silk wedding quilt Oriole had embroidered during Jun-rui's absence, complete with sixty bright and colorful butterflies and a large double-happiness symbol in the center. Oriole knew that making a wedding quilt with her own hand was something expected of every bride; to get hers finished on time she'd been forced to accept a little help from Constance and her mother at the last minute. Scarlet was too clumsy with a needle for such fine embroidery, but there were plenty of other jobs for her to do. With the wedding preparations in full swing, all the women had more than enough to keep them busy.

On the big day itself the bride was supposed to call on her parents-in-law, but this obviously wasn't possible, since both of Jun-rui's parents were dead. The abbot had very kindly offered to act in place of Jun-rui's father, and it had therefore been decided that the bridal procession—consisting of Oriole in a curtained sedan chair and various maids carrying torches and candles in the shape of lotus flowers—would make its way to the abbot's residence. As they went, the maids threw seeds, beans, coins or fruit to drive away evil spirits. When they reached the abbot's quarters, a carpet of green matting was laid out so that Oriole could walk right up to the abbot's door without having to set foot directly on the ground—which would have brought bad luck.

Later in the day the bridal couple entertained the family and a few guests in the study, where they would be staying for several weeks before setting off for the capital with Scarlet and Lucky. Jun-rui's friend General Du—without whose help Jun-rui and Oriole would never have been married in the first place—was as good as his word and made the fifteen-mile journey from Pu Pass especially for the wedding. Needless to say, there was a great deal of eating and drinking, and the merriment increased steadily with each passing hour. When there were particularly loud bursts of laughter, Pug joined in with excited yaps.

Everyone agreed Oriole had never looked as ravishing as she did that day in her vivid red wedding gown embroidered with bats and peaches and other symbols of good luck and married bliss. Her skin seemed to glow with some intense inner light, and her eyes were as dark and sparkling as the lake in moonlight. Her hair was piled in soft coils on the top of her head and held in place with dozens of gold hairpins. Lady Cui had actually praised Scarlet on her hairdressing skills earlier in the day.

As the evening wore on, Oriole found it harder and harder to keep her eyes off Jun-rui. Already the lotus-flower torches were burning outside in the garden, and the candles were flickering gently inside, casting soft shadows on the assembled guests—but no one showed any sign of leaving.

Oriole felt her impatience mounting. She was happy, of course, indescribably happy, and she didn't want to hurt her guests' feelings by driving them away prematurely. But she wanted Jun-rui to herself now. They'd waited so long, they'd missed each other so much when they were apart, and now they'd just endured several agonizing weeks of being close—both in the west wing again—but still unable to show their love for each other. They'd managed to sneak a kiss and a whispered endearment on those rare occasions they were lucky enough to find themselves alone, but it hadn't been nearly enough.

Oriole couldn't help herself. She could feel the pulse of desire beating strong inside her, and a tingling sensation creeping over her flesh. Her body was begging for his touch. She caught herself, in a sudden embarrassed moment, staring fixedly at Jun-rui with her lips parted and expectant, burning for his kisses. She quickly gulped and looked down at her hands, hoping no one had noticed.

Someone had. Lady Cui's eyes were as sharp as ever. But fortunately—as was often the case these days—she was in a generous frame of mind. She flashed Oriole the most knowing of smiles, then said loudly enough for everyone present to hear, "Dear me, how time flies! It'll be fourth watch before we know it! We'd better all be leaving, or the newlyweds will be too tired to eat any bean curd!"

This last remark of Lady Cui's sparked a considerable amount of spontaneous amusement, because everyone knew she was talking about the bridal couple and the physical joys that awaited them. Light titters came from the women, great guffaws from the men and embarrassed giggles from the monks. Oriole covered her face with her hands and groaned inwardly. She couldn't tell for the moment which was worse—having her mother ignore and censure her relationship with Jun-rui the way she had at first, or having her draw maximum attention to it as she'd done just now. But at any rate her comments had the desired effect. Within moments the laughter died down and all the guests took their leave with fond and drunken goodbyes.

A sudden quiet descended on the room, and Oriole found herself alone with Jun-rui. At last. But instead of the joy and excitement she'd expected to feel, she was oddly nervous, as though the man with her was a complete stranger. Who *was* this handsome distinguished figure she'd married today, in his smart official robes? Was this the same man who'd stepped out from behind the rocks in the

Flower Garden, reciting a poem in that smoothly seductive voice? The man she'd met in a dream, tied to her with red thread? The man she'd lain beside, here in this very room, night after night until they were discovered? Why did it all seem so far away, so long ago?

Without really knowing why, she went to the bed and sat down, pulling her red bridal veil over her face. This was what marriages were usually like for brides less fortunate than herself—two people, strangers, seeing each other's faces for the first time on their wedding night. What chance did couples like that have? What was the likelihood of these two strangers falling in love and finding happiness together? Was this what her own parents had experienced? She realized, not for the first time, how lucky she was, how lucky they both were.

Jun-rui had crept over to the bed so quietly she hadn't heard him, and before she knew what was happening he'd lifted the veil and planted his lips on hers, pushing her gently down onto the red quilt.

When he had kissed her long and hard, he drew away slightly and looked her up and down, as though sizing her up. He was joining in with her game—of the bride in her red veil—by pretending he'd never seen her before, and he began licking his lips with obvious anticipation.

"Yes," he said, pretending to talk to a third party. "An excellent match. She'll do very nicely.

I like her. I may even love her one day. Who knows?''

His eyes sparkled mischievously as he bent down and kissed her again. Then he was whispering tenderly in her ear. "It's hard to believe, but I love her already."

Oriole had no doubts whatsoever. "I love you, too, Jun-rui. More than ever, more than I can say."

"My darling..." Jun-rui began, loosening her gown and pulling her to him ardently. His tongue explored the soft warmth of her mouth, and his hands roamed impatiently over her willing body.

But a burst of barking put a stop to any further passion. Evidently Pug was feeling left out and wanted them to know it. But once he had their attention, he didn't bother barking again; he just disappeared around the bed and started dragging something out from underneath. It must have been fairly heavy, because he was puffing and wheezing noisily with the effort. All of a sudden there was a ripping sound, followed by an ominous silence.

Jun-rui leaned over the far side of the bed to investigate. Pug lay sheepishly beside a book. His eyes held a doleful expression that seemed an admission of wrongdoing. Part of a torn page hung from the corner of his mouth.

"Well, I never!" Jun-rui exclaimed. "It's the handbook! You clever little thing—imagine finding

that!'' He turned to Oriole with a puzzled smile.
''What was it doing under the bed, I wonder?''

As he reached down to pick up the book, he noticed that it was lying open. Furthermore, it was lying open at a vaguely familiar page. He sat up with the book on his knee to get a closer look at the picture, and as he looked, an amused grin spread quickly across his face. Oriole was intrigued.

''What is it?'' she asked him eagerly.

''You'll never believe it.'' Jun-rui laughed, poking her playfully in the ribs. ''It's the one we did by the lake, but I can't remember what it's called, and Pug's torn the top of the page. What was it now? Something about a willow tree. Willow in the—''

''No!'' Oriole cried, rolling over and laughing so much it hurt. ''No! Not that one! Not tonight! Anything but that!''

By the time they'd both finished laughing, they were ready to begin their loving in earnest.

AFTERWORD

The love story of Oriole and Zhang Jun-rui has been known to countless generations of Chinese readers ever since it was first told by the Tang dynasty poet Yuan Zhen (779-831). Yuan's story, *The Story of Oriole*, was also called *An Encounter with a Fairy*. It was only a few pages long, and was written in the concise but highly expressive classical Chinese used by the mandarin class in traditional China.

Some four hundred years after Yuan, in the early twelfth century, *The Story of Oriole* was greatly expanded into a more popular ballad form, with sung arias and spoken narration. The ballad was called *The Story of the Western Chamber in All Keys,* and was written by someone known as Master Dong.

Our story was then expanded yet again—during the brief Mongol dynasty which followed—into a full-blown lyric opera, *The Western Chamber.* This was the first golden age of the Chinese theater of music and mime, the beginning of the wonderful tradition that is represented today by the Peking Opera so well-known in the West.

The Western Chamber was actually a sequence of five musical plays in four acts each, twenty acts altogether. Most of it was written to be sung, and it is famous for its long love arias of great poetic beauty. The author is believed to have been a certain Wang Shifu, a native of Peking. His play has always been regarded as the classic version of the story, and later adaptations have all taken it as their starting point. Over the years, it has been adapted by storytellers of many kinds, by ballad-singers, by script-writers for all the many regional styles of

Chinese opera, by contemporary dramatists and screenplay writers for cinema and television. This new retelling of mine in the English language is the latest in a long line.

I recently had the good fortune to watch a performance in Hong Kong of scenes from a sixteenth-century version of *The Western Chamber*—it was a more elegant and refined style of opera from southern China. The cast was drawn from various companies in the Shanghai district, and included some of the most distinguished performers still alive. I was deeply moved by the lyrical and psychological intensity of the opera. By contrast, the more popular Peking and Shanghai opera versions, which I have also seen, tend to emphasize the comic antics of the maid Scarlet, or the disreputable behavior of some of the more worldly monks! Alternatively, they may give scope to the acrobatic possibilities of fighting scenes between Flying Tiger and General Du. The story has lent itself to a wide variety of treatments.

In my adaptation, I have kept to the play where essentials of plot are concerned, and have preserved the main characters intact—Oriole, Scarlet, Lady Cui and the young scholar Jun-rui. My story is set in the same period, and in the same place—a hundred and fifty miles or so to the east of the capital Chang-an. And the background of my story is still very much that of the Tang dynasty, when China was at its most confident and cosmopolitan, communicating via the Silk Road with Central and Southern Asia.

But while I have done my best to be authentic, I have not hesitated to follow in the footsteps of my predecessors, and to invent, adapt or expand certain details for the benefit of my new audience. Aspects of the old plot which might have offended or puzzled my reader have been removed: Jun-rui no longer makes a pass at Scarlet, or thinks to himself that he wouldn't mind having her as one of his concubines when he's married to Oriole!

Characters too have been invented or modified. Constance is a new creation. And so is Oriole's little dog, Pug—though such dogs were common in the Tang dynasty. Pug was introduced to provide comic relief and to add a "human dimension" to Oriole. He is also instrumental in the plot and partly responsible for exposing the lovers' secret, under rather odd circumstances!

Lucky is based on the "lute-boy" of the play. And Lily was dreamed up as a way of explaining Heng's lack of interest in Oriole as a marriage partner.

I have also developed certain themes that I felt might be of interest to my modern reader. In the case of Lady Cui, for instance. In all previous versions, she is portrayed as a deceitful and treacherous woman who conspires against her daughter's happiness for no apparent reason. In my version, I have tried to make her a more sympathetic character with some psychological depth. Her own unhappy experience of marriage is an attempt to account for her trickery. Her eventual remorse is a means of healing the rift between mother and daughter.

The Oriole of *Love in a Chinese Garden* is more purposeful, strong-minded and busy than in the play, and Jun-rui is less prone to fits of despair and weeping.

I have also taken the liberty of introducing certain elements of Tang dynasty Chinese culture which I thought would be of interest to my readers and which might help them to envisage the period and the setting in which this love story takes place. Readers will now find, for example, references to embroidery and painting, to books and poetry of the time. These would have been a part of the fabric of life for members of the upper class such as Oriole and Jun-rui.

Above all, in *Love in a Chinese Garden* the overall theme of the story remains the same: love triumphing over an overwhelmingly oppressive system. It would be hard in a few words to describe the sheer weight of the traditional Confucian ideology, and how it oppressed free-thinking spirits in feudal Chinese society. Confucius himself (551-479 B.C.) should not be blamed for the evil done in his name. What became known as Confucianism had very little to do with the Master himself.

It was nine hundred years before our story begins that Confucianism was adopted as the official state ideology of China. The social order was envisaged as a hierarchic pyramid with the Emperor—the Son of Heaven, the embodiment of Heaven's Will—sitting at the top. According to this model of the social order, all good subjects owed the Emperor total allegiance; all good families owed their ancestors unfailing remembrance; all good children owed their parents total obedience; and all good wives owed their husbands absolute subservience.

Public life for educated males was dominated by the monolithic civil service system, and by the grueling examinations young men had to pass in order to enter that system. The young Jun-rui is on his way to the capital to take one such examination.

Private life within this Confucian structure was

equally rigid. Marriages were arranged by parents, with the help of fortune-tellers and professional go-betweens. It was up to the fortune-teller to choose an auspicious day for the ceremony and to ensure that the horoscopes of the betrothed were in alignment.

To find a space for true love was difficult, to say the least. Men would more often than not resign themselves to a loveless marriage, and seek sexual pleasure and fleeting romance in the pleasure-quarters of the cities, or in the arms of one of their concubines. Women had much less choice. For a woman of good birth, occupying the often thankless position of First Wife (as Lady Cui did), such opportunities for escape were virtually nonexistent.

Side by side with Confucianism, there were two other religions—Buddhism (imported from India) and Taoism. These offered a spiritual dimension that Confucianism lacked. For a man, escape into a monastery, and the life of a recluse, was often seen as an alternative to a loveless marriage. For a woman of good family, the only options were to become a Taoist or Buddhist nun, or a high-class courtesan.

And yet, despite these obstacles, love somehow succeeded in finding a way into people's lives. Certainly sex did. From the very earliest times, the Chinese prided themselves on having perfected the Art of the Bedchamber. Sexual sophistication was imparted in the form of graphically illustrated handbooks. It is one such handbook that Jun-rui gives to Oriole in the novel. These handbooks developed a sexual terminology of their own, which was then adopted by all Chinese novelists when dealing with physical lovemaking. The masterpiece of Chinese erotic fiction, *Golden Lotus,* uses such language all the time. I have made use of this terminology in my version when quoting from the handbook, to give the reader a taste of this very important tradition. Sex was often referred to simply as "spring." Erotic pictures were "spring" pictures. Jade Stalk and Red Grotto were but two of the colorful terms for the male and female genitals. The Clouds and the Rain was a fancy way of describing the orgasm. Shedding tears at the sight of the gate was a veiled way of alluding to premature ejaculation. And so the list goes on. For our lovers, it was not that they were incapable of calling a spade a spade, it was simply a matter of tradition.

Figurative language and symbolism of all sorts pervades traditional Chinese culture. The lunar calendar, and the festivals associated with it, provides an important rhythmic progression through the year. Each month (or "moon") is divided into three ten-day sections, and the fifteenth day of any month was also the day of the full moon. The moon was the emblem of the Yin, or dark, feminine element. (The moon, incidentally, is very important in our story. Oriole is often in white, to Jun-rui, she seems like a moon goddess, their first meeting is in the moonlit garden, and so on.) By contrast, the sun was the emblem of the Yang, or bright, male element.

This Yin-Yang polarity is well represented in the famous Taoist symbol, which many westerners are familiar with. It runs through every aspect of Chinese life, including, of course, the relationship between the sexes, and the physical and psychological well-being of each individual. An imbalance of Yin and Yang within the human energy system (or *qi*) was seen as lying at the root of all disease. And this imbalance was treated by a vast array of traditional methods, including herbal remedies, acupuncture and moxibustion (the burning of moxa at certain sites on the body, as described in the novel)—all of these methods continue to be used today.

There is also a wealth of symbolic meaning invested in the natural world, even in objects and historical figures. Animals, birds, insects, plants, trees, flowers—all can denote good or bad fortune. In *Love in a Chinese Garden,* the reader will find references to bats, peaches, ducks, lotuses, dragons, phoenixes, butterflies and fish. There are thousands more to choose from.

Colors too have a very particular symbolism in Chinese culture. Red is the color of romance and marriage, of transient beauty (the falling petals of spring), of good luck and of wealth. "Red dust" is the Buddhist term for the mortal world of desire and craving—it indicates the empty illusion of the world. Red is also the color of life—Scarlet, as her name implies, is associated with this color, and it is no coincidence that she dresses in red. White on the other hand is the color of death, mourning and funerals. It is also the color of the moon.

It must be apparent by now that we are dealing with another world, one very different from our own, and that this brief Afterword can hope to do little more than scratch the surface or whet the appetite. The whole of Chinese culture can certainly not be covered in a few pages.

The China of the Tang dynasty is distant in time. And the China of today is distant culturally to many people in the west. Our story is a Tang story, far back in time. But many aspects of the Chinese culture and background mentioned in the story are as much a part of everyday life in some Chinese societies as they were then. A funeral party still wears white; red is still the color associated with marriage; lunar dates still dictate festivals, like the Chinese New Year; symbols and omens, astrology, geomancy, medicine, food—much remains the same.

It is often said that there are some stories that transcend time and place. I would like to think that this is one of them. I hope my reader will cope comfortably with the people in the story, without ever losing track of the fact that they are Chinese. And will read about them as Chinese, without ever losing track of the fact that they are people.

As an old Chinese proverb puts it:

"Humans share the same heart; and the heart shares the same reasons."

Rachel May

Dear Reader,

Thank you for reading *Love in a Chinese Garden*. Please take a few moments to tell us briefly about your thoughts on this book and about your reading preferences. Your answers will help us in selecting future stories with similar themes for your reading pleasure. When you return this survey, we will send you a copy of the collection "Outlaw Brides" as a token of our appreciation. Please remember to return your survey to the address listed below. Thanks!

1. Did you enjoy reading this book?

1.1 ❏ Yes—Why? _____

_____ 2,7

.2 ❏ No—Why not? _____

_____ 8,13

2. How interested are you in reading similar books with cultural story lines?

14.1 ❏ Very interested
.2 ❏ Somewhat interested
.3 ❏ Somewhat uninterested
.4 ❏ Very uninterested

Comments _____

_____ 15,20

3. Please indicate your age range:

21.1 ❏ Under 18 years   .4 ❏ 35 to 49 years
.2 ❏ 18 to 24 years   .5 ❏ 50 to 64 years
.3 ❏ 25 to 34 years   .6 ❏ 65 years or older

To receive your copy of "Outlaw Brides," please print your name and address clearly:

Name: _____

Address: _____ City: _____

State/Prov.: _____ ZIP/Postal Code: _____

Mail To: In U.S.: *Love in a Chinese Garden,* P.O. Box
1387, Buffalo, NY 14240-1387
In Canada: *Love in a Chinese Garden,* P.O. Box
609, Fort Erie, Ontario, L2A 5X3

PHCGSUR

Take 4 bestselling love stories FREE

Plus get a FREE surprise gift!

Special Limited-time Offer

Mail to Harlequin Reader Service®

3010 Walden Avenue
P.O. Box 1867
Buffalo, N.Y. 14240-1867

YES! Please send me 4 free Harlequin Historical™ novels and my free surprise gift. Then send me 4 brand-new novels every month, which I will receive before they appear in bookstores. Bill me at the low price of $3.69 each plus 25¢ delivery and applicable sales tax, if any.* That's the complete price and a savings of over 10% off the cover prices—quite a bargain! I understand that accepting the books and gift places me under no obligation ever to buy any books. I can always return a shipment and cancel at any time. Even if I never buy another book from Harlequin, the 4 free books and the surprise gift are mine to keep forever.

247 BPA A3UR

Name	(PLEASE PRINT)
Address	Apt. No.
City	State	Zip

This offer is limited to one order per household and not valid to present Harlequin Historical™ subscribers. *Terms and prices are subject to change without notice. Sales tax applicable in N.Y.

UHIS-696   ©1990 Harlequin Enterprises Limited

The Gentleman & The Hell Raiser

Don't miss these captivating stories
from two acclaimed authors
of historical romance.

THE GENTLEMAN by Kristin James
THE HELL RAISER by Dorothy Glenn

Two brothers on a collision course
with destiny and love.

Find out how the dust settles October 1997
wherever Harlequin and Silhouette
books are sold.

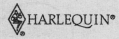 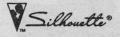

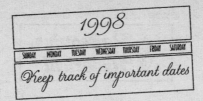

Three beautiful and colorful calendars that celebrate some of the most popular trends in America today.

Look for:

Just Babies—a 16 month calendar that features a full year of absolutely adorable babies!

1998 CALENDAR
Just Babies
16 months of adorable bundles of joy!

Hometown Quilts
1998 Calendar
A 16 month quilting extravaganza!

Hometown Quilts—a 16 month calendar featuring quilted art squares, plus a short history on twelve different quilt patterns.

Inspirations—a 16 month calendar with inspiring pictures and quotations.

Inspirations

A 16 month calendar that will lift your spirits and gladden your heart

Steeple Hill™

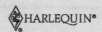 HARLEQUIN®

Value priced at $9.99 U.S./$11.99 CAN., these calendars make a perfect gift!

Available in retail outlets in August 1997.

Harlequin®
Historical

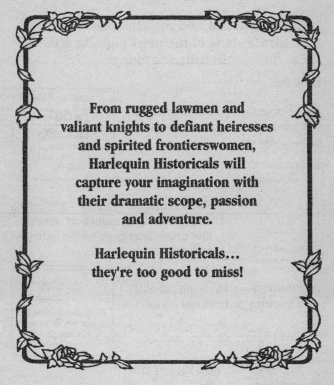

From rugged lawmen and
valiant knights to defiant heiresses
and spirited frontierswomen,
Harlequin Historicals will
capture your imagination with
their dramatic scope, passion
and adventure.

Harlequin Historicals...
they're too good to miss!

Indiscreet

Camilla Ferrand wants everyone, especially her dying grandfather, to stop worrying about her. So she tells them that she is engaged to be married. But with no future husband in sight, it's going to be difficult to keep up the pretense. Then she meets the very handsome and mysterious Benedict Ellsworth who generously offers to accompany Camilla to her family's estate—as her most devoted fiancé.

But at what cost does this *generosity* come?

From the bestselling author of *Impulse*

CANDACE CAMP

Available in November 1997
at your favorite retail outlet.

"Candace Camp also writes for Silhouette® as Kristen James

 The brightest star in women's fiction

Look us up on-line at: http://www.romance.net

MCCIND

Receive a second book absolutely FREE!

Love to read? Act now to receive a second
book absolutely **FREE** from Harlequin.

2 BOOKS FOR THE PRICE OF 1!

On the official proof of purchase coupon below, fill in
your name, address and zip or postal code, and send it,
plus $1.75 U.S./$2.75 CAN. for postage and handling
(check or money order—please do not send cash)
payable to *Love in a Chinese Garden* Offer, to: In the
U.S.: 3010 Walden Avenue, P.O. Box 9057, Buffalo, N.Y.
14269-9057; in Canada: P.O. Box 609, Fort Erie, Ontario
L2A 5X3. Please allow 4-6 weeks for delivery. Order your
FREE copy of OUTLAW BRIDES today—quantities are
limited. Offer for the FREE book expires June 30, 1998.

Love in a Chinese Garden
Special Offer!

Official Proof-of-Purchase

Please send me a FREE copy of *Outlaw Brides*

Name: _____

Address: _____

City: _____

State/Prov.: _____ Zip/Postal Code: _____

Reader Service Account: _____

090-KFU